DREAM FACTORY

DREAM FACTORY

A NOVEL

SUJATHA

TRANSLATED FROM THE TAMIL BY
MADHAVAN NARAYANAN

HARPERPERENNIAL
An Imprint of HarperCollins *Publishers*

First published in English in India by Harper Perennial 2022
An imprint of HarperCollins *Publishers*
4th Floor, Tower A, Building No. 10, Phase II, DLF Cyber City,
Gurugram – 122002
www.harpercollins.co.in

2 4 6 8 10 9 7 5 3 1

Originally published in Tamil as

P-ISBN: 978-93-5489-536-4
E-ISBN: 978-93-5489-564-7

Typeset in 11/15.2 Adobe Caslon Pro at
Manipal Technologies Limited, Manipal

Printed and bound at
Thomson Press (India) Ltd

MIX
Paper
FSC FSC® C010615

This book is produced from independently certified FSC® paper
to ensure responsible forest management.

I dedicate this work of translation to my parents, who between them taught and inspired me in different ways to appreciate languages in many forms—in grammar, style, meaning, slang, beauty, depth and rhythm.

1

THE GATE OF THE HOUSE on Burkit Road in Mambalam did not look very large from a distance. A large door and plenty of plants and creepers conspired to conceal the magnificence of the mansion inside. Next to this permanently closed gate with no gaps stood a fierce man wearing khaki, and beside him was a dog with the face of a gruff-looking politician. Across the house was a paan shop stocked with rows of local goli soda bottles, with a wooden bucket that had been filled with water the previous Thursday. Since dawn, four bums had been waiting in front of the shop to see if Arun Vijay was on his way out. A Fiat drew up and hooted gently. The dog wagged its tail. The door opened. The watchman offered a sprightly salute.

'Is this the man, boss?' asked one of the men. He had come all the way from Madurantakam for a glimpse of Arun Vijay.

'Chee, that's just his secretary,' an informed local corrected the visitor.

'Ah, I was wondering why he didn't look at all like Arun.'

'You do know about his complexion, don't you? Fair, glowing, like some white sahib...didn't you see *Vayasukku*

Vandha Ponnu? The way he twirled Sarita by the waist! Who could possibly do that but Arun? You've got to be a natural to do a thing like that!'

The fans resumed their banter as the Fiat drove in, and the gate closed again. The car stood behind three others parked in a row. One of them was being washed and polished by a servant carrying a diesel can filled with water.

Bhaskar got out of the car. 'You go straight to M,' he instructed the driver. 'Send it back to me at 8.30 a.m,' he said, shutting the door gently.

He walked on, crossing the portico and entering the office to the left. An intercom and two black phones were ringing non-stop. He picked one up and murmured, 'Just a minute,' and then said 'Hullo' into the other. Bhaskar looked about forty-five years old. He was showered and ready for the day, wearing a green shirt and bright white trousers. A small diary popped out of his shirt pocket. He cradled the phone between his neck and ears as he spoke into the receiver. On a closer look, one could spot a small dot of kumkum on his forehead.

'Tell me, Raju garu,' he said, pulling out the diary as he cradled the receiver between his shoulder and ears. 'Wait…hmm, let me see…November 1979? No chance, sir. He cannot give you a date until November '80—no matter what. No chance!'

His thin moustache and thin brows and lips made him look like a hurriedly drawn caricature. His was a face that did not reveal much emotion.

'Sorry, Raju garu,' he said again. 'There are so many new faces in the industry now. Why don't you cast one of them?'

He pressed the diary shut. 'So what if they can't speak Tamil? Who needs *that*? I am sorry, but there are absolutely no dates available for a year and a half,' he said, cutting off the call. He picked up the other phone.

'He is coming, man...he is coming for sure. It is only 8.30 a.m.!' he said into this phone. He looked at his watch and glanced, for the first time, at the people waiting in the office room. Two of them were completely unknown faces, and the third one was that public relations chap, Murthy. He had a scarlet bindi on his forehead and combed-back hair. He had played the lead role in a movie in the 1940s, but now earned a living with his PR skills.

'Bhaskar saar,' Murthy piped up. 'This is Mr Lakshmanan, SN Pictures.'

'I have heard of him,' Bhaskar said nonchalantly.

'He has a project. Ilayaraja has been booked, and the heroine is a first-timer.'

'Really?'

'We'll need dates from Arun in February.'

'Didn't you just hear me? No dates until the end of 1980.'

Lakshmanan looked like a cross between a wholesaler of perfumes and a musician who played the nadaswaram. He was a small man, five feet two inches tall, and had a lot of flab on his body. Sacred ash was smeared on his forehead beneath large brows that met each other above a pair of smiling eyes.

'You don't have to share the call sheet,' Lakshmanan said. 'All you have to do is agree to have the puja on the coming amavasai. All I want is a "yes" for the movie.'

'You mean you are going to buy off the dates from someone else?' Bhaskar inquired.

'Yes.'

'From whom? Venkat?'

'That's just one of the options. Do I have to tell you whom?'

'You know Arun doesn't like this trading in his dates.'

'Why don't we ask him?' Lakshmanan seemed persistent.

'He is asleep.'

'We can wait. He won't be first actor I am waiting on,' the producer said.

'Please, no, sir. Arun just won't agree. You'll launch a movie and take out an acre-sized ad in the *Dina Thanthi*. You know who sees that first? The income tax fellows! Whether you pay us a penny or not, they will add two and a half lakhs to his income.'

'Why only two and a half?' Lakshmanan said. 'We can go up to three and a half…'

'No, no. You've got me wrong,' Bhaskar said. 'I am not talking rates—I am talking dates.'

'I know…I know…'

'Why don't you ask Kamal or Rajini?'

'That's not for you to say, no?' the producer said. 'You should stick to speaking for Arun. You know distributors are now after Arun and want to finance his projects. The market is on your side now. If Arun doesn't sell tomorrow, there will come an Arumugham and we will chase him as well. You are the ones who change in life—I don't. Do you even know who all I have worked with so far? P.S. Govindan, K.R. Ramaswamy, SSR, Sivaji Ganesan, Gemini…'

'Come in, Mr Gnanasekaran!' Bhaskar shouted suddenly. He had already forgotten Lakshmanan and SN Pictures for now.

You could take a quick look at Gnanansekaran and immediately tell that he was a film journalist from Madras. A collarless, coloured shirt, a huge bag under his armpit, and a careless look on a face that sported a three-day stubble.

'Is Arun saar around?'

'He is asleep.'

'Is he? You must know he has given me an appointment for an interview.'

'Which publication is this for?'

'*Kungumam*. He is meeting college girls in a special meet-up.'

Bhaskar gently changed his focus. 'But why did you do such a thing, Gnanasekaran? You should not have written that about Arun in *Devi* like that.'

'Did Arun read it?' the journalist asked eagerly.

'He did and was quite upset,' Bhaskar said.

'Let him issue a denial. We can publish that as well, you know.'

'You won't get your interview today. He is already late for the studio.'

'How can you say that, man? I've brought these young women here so early in the day.'

'How many are there?'

'Eight. And they have come with their mothers. You know, the moms are the ones with crushes on Arun.'

'Take them all straight to AVM. We can do the interview between shots.'

'All right,' Gnanasekaran agreed. 'Well, see you then, Bhaskar. Thanks!' The journalist hurried off.

Lakshmanan was still there, waiting. 'So, his dates not possible in February?'

'I have already told you that.'

'You are acting so pricey,' the producer said. His vibhuti was smudged as sweat poured down his forehead.

Unperturbed, Bhaskar worked the phone with his deft fingers. 'BJ? This is Bhaskar. What happened to the air tickets?' As he waited for response from the other end, he asked Lakshmanan, 'What do you mean, *pricey*?'

He then put the phone down with a polite 'Thank you'.

'I am not leaving without seeing Arun.' The adamant producer stood firm.

'If that is what you wish, so be it, Lakshmanan,' Bhaskar said. 'Just wait. Let me see if he is up.' He pressed the intercom.

In an air-conditioned room a floor above, the intercom buzzed in melodic beeps. The room was still dark. Deep blue curtains hid the morning light. Arun was already up, and lay staring at the ceiling in a trance.

'Scene 67. Take 6!'

'Shekhar, I won't forget you!'

'Suguna, I won't forget you either!'

'Bloody shit!' he cried and sat up with a start. He then meditated for a while. The intercom buzzed again. 'Yes, Bhaskar,' he said, touching the button.

'Lovely morning, isn't it?' Bhaskar said.

'Lovely morning.'

'Should I come up?'

'Yes!'

Arun heard a voice call from beyond. 'Vanakkam.'

'Who is that? Sounds like a ghost...'

'Lakshmanan. SN Pictures.'

'Don't know who he is,' Arun said. 'Bhaskar, will you come up?' Arun got to his feet and opened the curtains. The morning sun assaulted his eyes. His eyes cringed as he walked back into the room.

Arun Vijay. Popularly known as AV. Age twenty-four. His face seemed to be everywhere. On the covers of magazines. On billboards. At road crossings. It was the kind of face that you wouldn't tire of wherever you saw it, irrespective of how many times you saw it. After two years of hard make-up, a strange kind of fairness had become frozen on his face. His olive black eyes had a clear tinge of sadness. A melancholy that deceived. The kind of eyes that made thousands of women lose sleep at night in yearning and agony. When his lips smiled, his hesitant eyes would take a while to join them. There was also a wee sign of a squint. Inside those rosy lips, one tooth looked a little out of place. There were those who said this was a significant feature of his good looks. Fans loved to discuss these quirks. And there were so many of them. So many.

Arun was still in the process of waking up. Standing at a height of five feet ten inches, he could look down at his female co-stars from where he could see the parting in their hair. Or peep into their brassieres.

He now wore a T-shirt with a lungi. Three hours of sleep deficit hung like a cloud over his droopy eyes. It was 1 a.m. when he'd hit his bed last night. Arun got up from the bed and peered into the mirror.

'When you peep into the mirror, do not look at yourself. Look at others.' He vaguely recalled a quote from Russian theatre guru Konstantin Stanislavski. 'Must finish *An Actor Prepares*,' Arun told himself. But when? He also had to read Jean-Luc Godard. But when? He needed to visit the National Film Archives in Pune to watch *Battleship Potemkin*. But when? And make that experimental film. But when? Visit Uttamarkovil. But when?

Bhaskar glided into the room quietly and eyed the bottle of pills on the bedside. 'So, you've started *this* again?' he asked.

'It's Valium, man. Won't do any harm.' Arun, unmindful of Bhaskar's presence, took off his T-shirt and lungi, and walked naked to the towel stand and wrapped himself in one. He brushed his teeth noisily in the washbasin and splashed his face with water. The cold water infused some life back in him. He hummed happily to himself.

'What's the day looking like, Bhaskar?'

'At 8.30 a.m., you're at AVM Studio B. It's a full day's call sheet. You catch a plane to Bangalore in the evening and shoot through the night. Balu is waiting for you there. By morning, SP will send you two reels for a dubbing session at Chamundeshwari. You come back home by car in the afternoon.'

'Eeeeeeeee! When am I going to get some sleep?'

'You have five hours in the car back from Bangalore, Arun.' Bhaskar offered him another towel, afraid he just might take off the one from his waist to wipe his face. 'Oh, I forgot to tell you. Gnanasekaran is waiting on the studio floor for you. To do an interview.'

'Gnanasekaran? Kick him! Bash him up!'

'The interview is with college girls.'

'I guess it's fine then,' Arun said.

'Apparently their mothers are tagging along.'

'Oh God, that is awful. Leave me alone,' Arun said, and then paused. 'But you never know. Sometimes, the moms are more attractive. Once, in Ooty, one of them took my hand, put it on her chest and said, "Look, how my heart beats for you."'

'There is also somebody called Lakshmanan waiting for you. He insists on meeting you. Been waiting for a while.'

'Let him wait, my dear machine!' he told the secretary. 'And do tell me when I am going to get some real rest.'

'Friday evening.'

Arun took a hard look at Bhaskar. 'I am finished. I am dead.' he said. 'I am going to hang as a portrait on the wall before I turn thirty!'

'Bhaskar, why aren't you married yet?'

'That's none of your business.'

'Tell me the truth—you've never slept with a woman before, have you?'

'Don't be silly!'

Arun combed his hair and then ruffled it with his fingers. He put on a black-and-blue shirt and trousers and zipped up in a hurry. An elderly lady walked in with idlis and filter coffee on a platter.

'Maami, how are you?'

She smiled in answer.

'Send me some boiled cabbage and cauliflower with salt and a bowl of curd for lunch,' he instructed. 'And just a spoonful of rice. Only this much,' he said, gesturing with his fingers.

'Okay, pa,' she nodded. She was about fifty years old, a widow fallen on hard days.

'And how about my wonderful relatives? Have they all woken up?' Arun asked.

'Hmm...'

'Have they all eaten their free meals?'

As the lady stood frozen in embarrassment, Bhaskar chided Arun. 'Don't you know what to speak and with whom?' And then he said, 'Maami, you please carry on.'

'Bastards!' Arun was not yet done. It was apparent he was fuming at someone not in the room. 'What movie are we shooting today?' he asked Bhaskar.

'*Annayin Thyaagam*,' he said. *Hmm. A movie on a mother's sacrifice.*

'My God! With that cow Premalatha! Bhaskar, she eats garlic and splashes *Charlie* on herself. Why does she use so much? I can smell it when I am crossing the Kodambakkam Bridge. Oh, these Andhra girls...'

They both walked downstairs. The phones were still ringing. Unmindful, Arun walked up to the car that was waiting for him in the portico.

'Glad you are back home, thambi,' Lakshmanan said, still hoping to get a word in. Arun walked on as if the man did not exist and got into the car. Bhaskar hopped into the front seat.

'Please, thambi,' the persistent producer dashed after him. 'I need those dates only in February. I can adjust the call sheets. You just have to sign and attend the puja on this amavasai.'

'Get lost!' Arun snapped harshly. The car sped off.

Lakshmanan stood stunned for a while as he watched the car leave and then muttered to himself, 'You creep! You call yourself a human being? I'll finish you off one day—you just watch.'

2

THE REAR WINDOWS OF THE car were tinted with a dark shade. A stereo rested easy in the front. As Bhaskar switched it alive, the vehicle was filled with some booming rock. *'Born…to be…wiiiiiiiild!'*

As the car crossed the gate, waiting fans suddenly sprang to life and pounced on it. Gripping the windows, they scampered along. A fan piped up.

'What's this, saar? Not saying a word…'

'Why should I talk whenever you want? Am I a transistor or something?'

'Don't be so angry, kanna.'

The car picked up speed. The man closed his shirt pocket to keep some money from falling off but still tried to catch up with the car. He ran a short distance in vain.

Bhaskar chided Arun softly. 'I think you can be a bit more polite with your fans.'

'What's the need? They are just primitives who wear terylene shirts.'

'But it is because of them that we ride in this car.'

'Awww. Come on, Bhaskar. Don't sound like Morarji Desai so early in the morning.'

He got into the car. Letters that had arrived the previous day were stuck on the inside of the backseat in a pouch. Bhaskar wanted Arun to read every letter that came from his fans, many from remote towns and villages. One of them read:

My dear elder brother Arun,

This is a loving message from G.N. Marimuthu in Gobichettipalayam...

'Bhaskar. Do I have to read *all* these letters?'

'Yes.'

As a loving gift from you, could you send me a hair from your head? I will cherish it all my life. Sincerely, G.N. Marimuthu, ninth standard.

Arun smirked. 'Maybe instead of a hair from the head...'

'Shut up, Arun. Will you please stop being so mean?

'All right,' Arun said as he picked up another one.

Arun! Did you read Desmond Morris's Watching*? I think it is an important book for actors like you. I don't have the seventy rupees to buy it. But I have secretly flipped through it in the book shop. When are you coming? S.S.*

As soon as he saw the handwriting, Arun's face lit up. The elegant, masculine calligraphy in which the letters leaned to the right. Black ink. S.S. Sundaram. His childhood pal.

Memories came pouring out. Uttamarkovil: the dark green streams, the railway line to Lalgudi, the Kollidam riverbed, the temple hidden inside the grove, the strains of *Thiruppugazh* on the local train...the literary meetings in the evenings...and Kalyani!

How was Kalyani now? It had been such a long time since he last saw her.

Where are you taking me? What's this, da?

You come, Kalyani. Will show you some magic.

Wait, let me bring Kamakshi and Lakshmi.

No, not them. You just come all by yourself. Come, na.

As his heart began to beat faster, he was moving up the stairs and calling out to her, 'Vaa di!'

The car got stuck in a traffic signal and voices cried out. 'Look! It's Arun!' In a jiffy, on all four windows of that car, there were many faces. Pressed faces. Palms that lacked blood. Flat noses. He felt a deep sense of discomfort bordering on fear. These faces had chased him in his dreams. Just faces. Empty faces.

'Durai! Durai,' a voice said as if he was some English sahib. 'Please sing a song, no?' a moustachioed face piped up.

'Arun, just an autograph,' cried out a ten-rupee note.

Through a small crack in the window, a hand thrust itself in and touched his cheeks. Then it pulled and twisted the flesh. A police whistle blew loudly. To the sound of many honking horns, his car started again.

Arun touched his aching cheek and wiped it. '*Bastard!* He pinched me, Bhaskar!'

AVM Studios. No. 38, Arcot Road, Chennai—600 026. Nine floors: editing, audio recording, re-recording, dubbing, bar projection, and rain-storm special effects.

On the fifth floor of the AVM building, a delicate-looking girl poured water into porcelain cutlery. Nearby, square-shaped reflectors flashed large beams of light. A small distance away, a thatched hut and coconut trees were moving on rubber wheels. A camera on wooden rails was being readied for a trolley shot. Some feet away, Premalatha sat on a chair placed on the grass. A little girl in a half-sari stood in attendance with a flask. Premalatha's mother, with an abundantly endowed bosom, was squatting on a dhurrie. Arun got out the car and went straight to his make-up room, and Premalatha's mother mumbled something in Telugu.

'Will you come now?' the director said to Premalatha. She sprang to her feet and ambled towards the director. The man holding her chair followed her.

Speakers fitted with playback gear away from the cameras blared out loud. *Shall I whisper a secret in your ears?/Will speak it only in your ears*—the lyrics rang out. It was a duet sung in male and female voices to match the movie's hero and heroine.

On the facade of the make-up room, a sticker read: 'If you find me unconscious inside this room, please send for a bottle of beer.'

How old would Kalyani be now? Eighteen?

'Make it light, man,' Arun told the make-up artist.

'Sir, did you go to Singapore?'

'Yes, and also to Hong Kong and Tokyo.'

'Who went to do your make-up?'

'Bhagwan Das.'

If she had got engaged by now, Sundaram would have sent an invitation. Must visit Uttamarkovil.

Premalatha was about five foot four inches tall. Three of those inches were the heels she wore. She still had some childhood left on her round face, and only that seemed her own now. Her coiffure seemed complicated, with many a trick having been played on her thick, lustrous hair. Her arched eyebrows were shaped carefully, like clearly drawn lines. Large eyes. And dimples that spoke when she smiled. Those were her trademark. In each one of the fifty movies she had appeared in, this smile would be there at least in one scene. In Coimbatore, they'd once held a public meeting one evening and presented her a silver plaque that conferred the title of 'Queen of the Dimpled Smile'.

Her neck and body fitted the needs of Tamil cinema perfectly. Exaggerated breasts, half of which was polyurethane. A piece of cloth gently wrapped over those seemed like a cross between a sari and a stole. A ghagra-skirt that stood barely below the knees. Silver anklets perched closed to her feet were such that if they jingled as she jumped, the censors would make a noise about her revealed thighs.

Arun stepped out, smelled the continuity outfit, and put it on.

'Hi Arun!' Premalatha greeted him.

'Hi!'

The girl in the half-sari gave Premalatha a glass of something.

'What's that? Amul spray?'

'No, it's whisky!' she replied.

'Shot ready, saar,' a voice called out.

The director approached Arun. Until recently, he had been a wholesaler of banians in Coimbatore, but now he was a celebrated filmmaker. His first film, *Ilamai Kaalangal,* had gone on to be a superhit. They said it was because of Ilayaraja's music and a double-meaning-laden song that caught the censors napping. Whatever the reason, this man who once sold vests now had four movies on the floors. He had a square face and sported a pair of recently acquired wide-rimmed glasses (a keen desire to resemble K. Balachander). He had graduated only a while ago from Berkeley cigarettes to the national brand of the film world in India, the 555 State Express.

'Arun, you have to walk behind Baby slowly. Then Baby turns and gestures like she is telling you a secret in your ears. Get it? *Should I whisper a secret in your ears?* followed by the line, *Will speak it only in your ears,* as if you are whispering something into her ears.'

'Brilliant!'

'Why are you laughing?'

'Aah, nothing. I am so joyous. Hey you, she of the dimpled smile! Are you ready?'

'Ready, saar.'

'Music...action.'

Arun suddenly forgot all the frivolous banter and switched to the actor he was. As Premalatha walked ahead with a smile, he serenaded her as if she had been his love from a previous birth.

'Shall I whisper a secret in your ears?'

Premalatha turned back and whispered into his ears. 'We shall see in Bangalore.'

'Your mom is not coming?'

She replied in the next rehearsal shot. 'No, I am coming alone.'

'If somebody sees us, we are dead.'

And in the second take, she said, 'I'll take care of all that.'

'All right then—tonight!'

'Okay, cut it!' shouted the wholesaler of vests.

Arun and Premalatha parted ways as if they had nothing to do with each other.

Have you booked the flight?' Arun asked Bhaskar.

'Done!'

'What's the movie?'

'It is a Kannada movie. The same Prema.'

'Really?' he said, and then cried out to the man approaching them. 'Come here, you ignoramus!'

Gnanasekaran came close and flashed a Bing Crosby smile. Some young women stood behind him. They all eyed Arun and stood with coy smiles on their faces.

'Look how many girls I have brought along for the interview!'

'Yup. But before that I need to take you away for a private thrashing session.'

'But that bit has appeared before in *Devi*!'

'Why are you guys so inhuman? Why do you lie so much in your columns? You will rot in hell!' Arun sounded angry.

'So what, brother?' Gnanasekaran reasoned. 'We can issue a denial!'

'You've already done the damage. Who is going to read your denial?

'Don't be angry, brother. I'll ask them to print it in large letters along with your photograph.'

'Okay, then take it down: I was amused by the news linking me up with Premalatha. Did your reporter hide under my veshti?'

'Please, no brother!' Gnanasekaran pleaded in uneasy tones.

'Okay. Whatever I discuss with Premalatha is on the sets, and all we talk is about the screenplay and our dialogues. Have you understood that?'

'I will do as you say. Are you happy now?'

'Who feeds you such stuff?'

'Don't ask! Earlier, there were just two or three of us on the ground writing those gossip columns. There are now twenty guys who feed us. They don't come anywhere near the studios and write the stuff from home. One guy said he had seen the two of you lying close to each other at the VGP Beach—with his own eyes.'

'Bring him here. I'll bloody...'

'Don't be angry, sir. Right now, let me bring those girls to meet you. Come on, girls!' Gnanasekaran cried out.

The girls came closer hesitantly.

Ah, the variety! Short, tall, plump, slim...Some had come of age only recently. Some had pimples. Some were overgrown. Some were skinny.

'Ask, na! Ask!' They were egging on one another.

'Arun, when was your first shot?'

'Oh, I was just one year old. I acted in a nude role and they clicked me.'

Giggles. 'Bad joke!'

'Let's talk about movies.'

One girl spoke in English. 'Who is your favourite actor?'

'James Dean. Have you heard of him?'

'Your favourite heroine?'

'T.P. Rajalakshmi.'

They looked at each other in disbelief. 'Come on, Arun! Cut out the comedy,' one girl said. She was nearly as tall as Arun.

'Do you play cricket?' he asked her.

'No! Volleyball!' Laughter rang out all around.

Arun muttered, 'I like all ball games.' There was more laughter.

He leaned towards Gnanasekaran and said, 'Don't publish all this, okay?'

'I can't put this stuff in *Kungumam*, brother.'

'Show me the article, okay?'

As the girls bantered on, there was just one who stood apart in a corner, mostly staring at the ground. She looked up at Arun only occasionally. At one such moment, their eyes met. He was confused for an instant and then he cried out. 'Oh my God! Kalyani! What the hell are *you* doing here?'

3

He had last seen Kalyani five years ago, and these five years had come with so many changes—dramatic ones! An ordinary student who had taken the 9 a.m. local passenger train to Trichy from a sleepy small town on the banks of the Kollidam river was now a phenomenon across southern India. 'Arun! Arun! Arun!' sounded everywhere like the final burst of Deepavali sparklers.

Kalyani, in those same five years, had grown beautiful in a gentle, quiet way. What magical chemistry was this? Her hair had grown thick, and her cheeks and bosom were filled out, with a special pout of the lips and a height that served her well. Wow! She was a delightful departure from the profusion of manufactured beauty he was used to. To bring that feminine shyness on screen, Premalatha may need a hundred re-takes.

Kalyani looked up gently and smiled with a dash of nervousness. 'You remember?' she asked.

'That's a question I should be asking! You know, on the way to the studio I was reading Sundaram's letter. Is he here as well?'

'No.'

'How is it that you are here?'

'This is my cousin Bhooma. She is crazy about you, Arun. She said she was going for a group interview with you, and I thought I would tag along for fun. Navaratri holidays, you know.' The Bhooma in question, sporting a white shirt and two long plaits, laughed loudly, the braces between her teeth showing.

'Navaratri holidays? Nah! Arun, her parents are here to have her meet a prospective groom,' Bhooma said. 'Hey Kalyani, won't you tell him that?'

'Aah, really? That's nice,' said Arun. He meant to say: 'Ah, really? I am so disappointed.'

'We see you in all the magazines, and virtually every movie.'

'Arun, is she really your childhood pal? I thought she was fibbing,' Bhooma said.

'No, really,' Arun confirmed. 'We are really friends.'

'It seems you played hopscotch as kids.'

'Yup, the grid shaped like an aeroplane.'

'With little girls?'

'Yes! And what was that song, Kalyani?' He lapsed into the village folk tune that went with the street game—something about a spider-like nose and coloured tongues.

'We used to keep scores with tamarind seeds,' Arun said. 'She was so young then. A crybaby she was!'

The girls roared with laughter.

'And what other games did you play?' an outspoken girl asked slyly.

Arun glared at her. Both of them remembered at once the game in question.

'Come! Come, na!'

'I am so scared.'

'So you played only with girls?'

'Yup! During Navaratri days, I would be dressed up as a gypsy, and Kalyani's elder sister would take me along.'

Gnanasekaran was taking notes furiously.

'Hey man! I'll break those pencils. Don't write all this, okay? Leave the personal stuff alone.'

'A photo, perhaps?' Gnanasekaran ventured.

'Nooooo!' Kalyani stepped aside, keen to avoid the spotlight. She looked scared.

'Don't you worry. This guy won't bite,' the journalist assured her.

'Arun…shot ready!' a voice called out.

'Just a moment,' he said. 'Kalyani, what are you studying now?'

'I'm at MSCR College,' she said without any elaboration.

'How long are you here?'

'I am going back tomorrow.'

'Why don't you stay back for a couple of days?'

'Aha!' said Bhooma.

The voice called out again: 'Arun, come on, please. The clouds are waiting for you.'

'See you later,' Kalyani said.

'Please give my regards to Sundaram. Tell him I'll drop everything one day and join him. How is he now?'

'He is still the same.'

Arun went back to the delicate mermaid. A female assistant was touching up Premalatha's face. The camera and the guys who pulled the trolley in crouching postures had changed places. The director was screaming at someone. A short distance away, a bear with its nose tied with a rope sat dejectedly.

For some reason, the director was furious. 'I'm telling you, this is horrible. One more time you let these guys in, and I'll blow my top. What's this farce between shots? I am telling you, man, I don't want any bear here.'

'Please don't say that, saar,' the bear tamer persisted. 'You just see what it can do once, no?' And then to the bear, he cried, 'Hey Rama!' He pulled the rope and the bear walked on its forelegs, legs up in the air.'

'Is there a man inside?' Arun asked.

'Illeenga!' the tamer protested. 'That's really a bear, I swear.'

Arun joked, 'Let's forget this script and do something with the bear.'

'No, sir,' the scriptwriter explained. 'This is a family subject, you know. Everything happens inside the house.'

'Sandow Chinnappa Thevar is done with his animal movies and all these street performers are now bugging us,' said the frustrated director.

'We haven't eaten for two days, saar,' the bear-tamer said.

'You or the bear?' Arun enquired as he moved close to Premalatha for the shot.

'The "*I'll whisper it only in your ears*" bit is over,' the director said. 'We have to move now to the next line: "*I'll bring the whole world to you.*"'

'Before that, may I have a glass of water?' asked Arun.

'Bring water!' The message spread on the sets like wildfire to help the lead actor.

'Who are those girls?' Premalatha asked.

'College kids.'

'You know, when I was in school, even I had gone to take Sivaji Ganesan's autograph.'

'Which school?' he asked. His eyes were still furtively looking for Kalyani. As the girls trooped over to watch the scene being shot, she was sitting in a far corner under a tree, reading a book. *Must ask her which one*, Arun thought. He felt uneasy pangs in his stomach as what Bhooma had said came back to haunt him. 'Her parents are here to have her meet a prospective groom.'

Meanwhile, the playback unit played a song whose lyrics dedicated the whole world to the leading lady. Arun summoned Bhaskar.

'You want the girl's address? I'll find out,' Bhaskar replied, without delay.

'Action!' the director's voice cried out.

Arun became a lover again and moved his lips to the blaring song. 'Cut, cut!' the director shouted. 'What's this Arun? What are you looking at?' To the assistant, he said, 'Come on, play that line again.'

'I'll bring the whole world to you,' the lyrics resumed.

About nine miles from the studios, in a double bedroom suite on the fifth floor of a five-star hotel, Lakshmanan sat shirtless. A glass of Scotch lay in front of him, and idlis and masala dosas were spread out on a plate nearby with no takers. Someone shaped a lot like Lakshmanan sat next to him. He wore a coarse khadi shirt whose pocket was bursting with large currency notes.

'I've been in this field for thirty-five years. No one has ever asked me to get out. I mean no one! And this little boy! What caste is he, Manikkam? A Brahmin?'

'There is no caste in our industry, no? It is all mixed. Guys marry twice, switch religions. All crooks!' Manikkam said.

A giant tape recorder was perched close by. 'Ilayaraja has set the music for our new film. Want to listen?'

'I have to finish this Arun off, Manikkam,' Lakshmanan said.

'Oh, leave him. He's a little boy! He will be famous for a couple of years and then vanish.'

'But I want to finish him off this year—right away!'

'So, who are you casting now? Rajini? Or one of those new boys? Sivachandran...our Sarathbabu, Sudhakar...any one of these?'

'No!' Lakshmanan was emphatic. 'I am going to bring a brand-new face to challenge this guy!'

'Wow! And who would that be?' Manikkam asked.

'My driver.'

'Who? That boy Kandasamy?'

'Indeed, yes!'

'We should cast him. He looks tough—looks like he can do a fight scene with sticks.'

'Nah, nothing of that sort is required,' Lakshmanan said. 'The director will take care of all that. Even speaking the language is not necessary. We can dub.'

'But can Kandasamy speak Tamil?'

'No. He just speaks the Madras bhashai,' Lakshmanan said. 'And don't pour me too much of this. The doctor says I am allowed only four—I keep getting burps later.'

As the Scotch flowed, Manikkam and Lakshmanan regressed into their past.

'The eyes that charm and a face like the moon,' Lakshmanan recalled the lyrics of an old hit song. 'No one sings like P.U. Chinnappa anymore. And those awesome tricks he played with the stick! Now that's what I call a stunt.'

'And five proper mini-concerts in one film—that *Jagadalaprathapan*!' Lakshmanan added, recalling the 1940s musical. 'And Manonmani in *Aryamala*!'

Manikkam spoke now as if on cue. 'Manonmani, can you come here, please?'

Manonmani, who was reading a weekly magazine in the adjoining room, appeared from across the curtain.

'I will take your leave, sir,' Manikkam said to Lakshmanan.

It was 8.30 p.m., and Arun was inside an outdated Avro headed to Bangalore. Two seats away sat Premalatha, her maid and her mother. The plane moved on the runway as the air hostess spoke her rehearsed lines in Hindi about not using transistors on the flight. Arun repeated the lines to himself, having gone through this so often. He stared vacantly through the window. An hour to spend, and there were three books to finish. Before he boarded the flight, Bhaskar had left him a note on a scrap of paper in his clear, elegant handwriting: 'She is staying with her uncle in Mylapore. 26, Angalamman Temple Street. The nearest phone is the butter shop nearby. The number is 743…'

Arun laughed to himself. 'Bhaskar the great! She says she will return home tomorrow. I must talk to her at least once before that.'

As the aircraft gained height, Arun felt a strange grip in the pit of his stomach. *Must be a bout of jealousy*, he thought.

'She is doing her MSc. She will finish this year. She sings well.'

'Why don't you ask her to sing? We'd be delighted to hear her.'

'Bring the Shruti box.'

'Don't sing, Kalyani,' Arun said.

'Beg your pardon!' said the old lady seated next to him.

'Sorry!' he said, sounding positively sheepish as he buried himself into one of his books. *We are here for no purpose. Unless we can invent one.* The lines in the book seemed blurred.

A chauffeur waited for him at Bangalore airport. He rushed straight to Chamundeshwari Studios. Sivanna was there, speaking his pidgin Tamil.

'We'll try to fix the climax scene today. Those big guys loved the stuff. What say, Arun?'

'Sivanna, please stick to Kannada. I think it is easier than trying to understand your Tamil.'

He tried dialling long-distance to call the butter shop number. No one answered.

'What's the time?' he asked a spot boy.

'9.30.'

'No one buys butter at 9.30 p.m. anymore?' Arun asked.

'What, saar?'

'Forget it!' Arun chuckled.

A van arrived, packed with large tiffin carriers, their containers stacked one atop the other and the spoon tucked in at the top to seal the containers. 'Bisi bele baath,' someone announced. The pungent smell of cloves filled the air.

It was 1.30 a.m. when Arun returned to his hotel. He fell into the bed without bothering to take off his shirt or trousers. He switched off the light. It was raining outside. The sound of a moving train could be heard in the distance.

The telephone rang. 'Arun, it's Premalatha! Can we just chat? I am in Room 510.'

He thought for a while. Some other dialogues were playing in his head. *'There's no need for silver cutlery or jewels, Maami. The boy likes the girl a lot.'*

'I am on my way,' Arun told Premalatha.

4

When Arun stepped out of his room, the waiter who seemed to have been waiting patiently stood up and smiled. 'I don't miss a single one of your movies, saar. I have seen *Vayasukku Vandha Ponnu* at least five times.'

Arun laughed gently and walked on. The man followed him, proffered a dirty currency note and asked for an autograph. 'I'll do it in the morning,' Arun said, as he got into the lift and pressed the lobby button.

'My name is Arumairajan, and I write poems,' the persistent waiter said, and as the lift descended, he flipped open a forty-page notebook from the jacket of his uniform. 'I read in a magazine you really like Tamil poetry. Here is some of mine: *To my heart that admired the distant sea divine/Came a woman who said all the world is mine.*'

'Look, Arumairajan, it's not exactly divine to catch a poem in a lift at 1 a.m. It jars!'

'Somehow please give me an intro to Ilayaraja.' The waiter seemed adamant.

Arun walked into the toilet on the ground floor, and the poet tagged along. Amid the smell of naphthalene balls, Arun said, 'You can do one thing. Write out your address on a piece of paper. Give it to my secretary in the morning.'

'Okay, sir. Is it true that you are a Christian? I read it in *Mookutthi*'

'The secretary will tell you that as well. I just have to do some work now,' Arun said, and stood before the cistern.

After the waiter left, he crossed the reception area and went to the fifth floor and opened the door to Premalatha's room.

'Why did you take so long?'

'I met a poet on the way.'

'At this time?'

Arun sniffed hard. 'What happened to your *Charlie*? Didn't bring it along?' he guffawed, sat casually on the bed and looked her in the eye. 'And what's that thing you are wearing, like Jatayu in Ramayana?'

'I think it is called a kaftan,' she said.

'You look so different without make-up.'

'I've shed that movie look.'

'Seems your mother is also here.'

'After she heard you were coming, she insisted.'

'I saw her on the flight. She had the hey-you-creep-out-to-rape-my-innocent-daughter look.'

'You see, these gossip rags write all sorts of things, no? That's why.'

'So you propose making some of that gossip come true?'

'Chee, no,' she said. 'Arun! All this while we were speaking lines others wrote for us. I thought I'll speak some lines of my own today.'

'Ah, just talking?'

'You can speak in so many ways. With your lips, your eyes...'

'Hold on! I think we have spoken these lines.'

'It was in that film, *Kanavu Kavithai*,' Premalatha said.

'And what was the story?'

'That was about a young girl who is dumb and has an elder sister. Arun, why did you call me a cow? Am I so fat?'

'So you got the news? Hmmm '

'I burst into tears, you know?'

'It's not because you are fat. It's just that you are always chewing something—like a cow.'

'It's only bubble gum. Do you know what we call you? Rangabhashyam.'

So, he thought, he sounded to them like an old Iyengar uncle from a village. Arun laughed. 'Call me whatever, but please don't eat garlic. Won't help me, you know.'

'You are poking fun at me just because I had it one day. By the way, did you see *Maro Charitra*?'

'I liked the part where Saritha asks for *Learn Tamil in 30 Days* and the book shop jerk says, "I have *Get Pregnant in 15 Days*."'

Premalatha giggled. 'Lovely movie,' she said, brushing her hair in front of the mirror and tying it up with a ribbon. She then came and sat next to him.

'Is Premalatha your real name?'

'Nah, it is Varalakshmi.'

'Vara...Lakshmi. So exciting. And what have you studied? Andhra Matric?' he said. She seemed like someone who had done an open school degree meant for dropouts.

'No, I was in a convent and dropped out after the ninth standard.'

'If your mother calls now, I am going to pick it up,' Arun joked, and mocked in Telugu, 'Evarura…?'

'Don't be silly!'

'Va—ra—lakshmi,' he said, poking fun at her somewhat rustic name.

'Rangabhashyam! Are you going back by the morning flight?'

'No, I am going to take a car later. I've got some dubbing to do.'

'Arun, what do you think of Sivanna?'she asked.

He flashed a charming smile. 'Look, what are we pretending to do now? It's 1 a.m. You have lied to your mother, and I have evaded a poet. We've conspired to get here…to talk about Sivanna? No way! It was you who said there are many ways to speak. With lips and eyes and body…'

'I did NOT say the last one!' Premalatha said.

'But I am saying it,' he said, pulling her by the shoulder towards himself.

He had touched her many times in front of the camera. Rubbed her cheeks on his. Hugged her by the waist. He had even thrown her up once like a ball and caught her as she came down. He had nuzzled her neck, chin, neck and lips with his nose, more or less kissing her all over. But now, without the usual instruction of 'Lights! Camera! Action!', the cautious studio code of conduct or garish make-up, this seemed totally different.

His conquest was now complete.

As the sounds of the morning announced themselves outside the window, Arun straightened his clothes and stepped out of the room to see a beaming Arumairajan right in front of him.

'You said you will sign an autograph in the morning, sir.'

Premalatha was audibly making affectionate noises from inside. 'Come on, Arun!' she moaned.

Arumairajan stood expressionless, clutching a currency note in his hand.

An angry, irritated Arun shouted: 'Come with me! What did you say your name was?'

'Arumairajan.'

He went down to the reception and burst out in English. 'Good morning. I want to register a complaint. This person follows me like a dog. I do not have a moment of peace in your hotel. He stalks me everywhere. I am not going to stay here for another second. Call the manager.'

'I'll call the bell captain, sir,' the nervous woman at the reception said.

A shaken Arumairajan pleaded. 'Please, saar. What is this?'

'Is it your job to follow me everywhere?'

'But, saar, it was you who asked me to come.'

'Bastard! If I asked you to come somewhere, was it to my room? Who told you to spy on me?'

'Forgive me, sir. I am just a temporary worker here. They give me two hundred and fifty rupees a month. If you complain, I'll lose my job. I have a wife and an infant to care for. I spend fifty rupees from my salary every month watching your movies, sir.'

The bell captain arrived. 'Yes, sir?'

'I want to lodge a complaint against this man,' Arun said.

The car was speeding on the Bangalore–Madras highway. Bhaskar was at the wheel, and Arun was half-asleep.

'You could have just let him off. They must have dismissed him by now. It is a private sector hotel. Poor chap,' Bhaskar said.

Arun woke up with a start. 'Who has pity on me? Don't I have any right to privacy? They chase me everywhere...the bathroom, lift, wherever.'

'That is the price of fame, Arun. But you are not angry because of that.'

'I know. You don't have to psychoanalyse me now.'

'What you did was foolish, and that too in a hotel, in her room. It's bound to come out in the gossip columns. Don't you remember the eleventh commandment? *Thou shalt not be found out.*'

'I don't care. Things like this have come out in the past anyway.'

'I thought that was all rubbish,' Bhaskar said. 'Now I know it is not. That's none of my business, of course. But I do worry about Premalatha.'

'Why?'

'She's not too busy, you know. Her projects are getting fewer. Does she have other plans?'

'Don't be ridiculous. It all happened by chance. Won't happen again.'

'If you really needed sex, we could have fixed it easily. There's no shortage of women.'

'Bhaskar, you won't understand. It just happened naturally. We are both very lonely, you know. In the middle of all this fame—like two islands. It's a goddamn golden cage. Bhaskar, I need some friendly affection, not a lecture. Believe me. I have a lot of doubts these days. What the hell am I giving back to the world while being an actor? What godforsaken contribution am I making to society chasing Jayamalini in a shiny jacket singing songs? A doctor can say "Hey, I saved the life of that Mannarsamy." An engineer can point to a bridge as his work. What the hell have I done myself? I just spread out like a shadow on a screen in the dark. What have I come to, Bhaskar? Why?'

'You have been reading way too many books,' Bhaskar said, his eyes firmly on the road. 'I have some good news for you though. Three of your call sheets are being cancelled next week. That's a small gift for you. You can go all by yourself to your hometown. What's the name? Uttamarkovil. I have arranged it. You deserve the rest.'

Arun jumped up. 'Bhaskar, shake hands with me, my friendly monster! This is great. For the first time, I feel like kissing a machine like you.'

Uttamarkovil!

The car was nearing Madras, passing through the nondescript suburb of Virugambakkam. The streets were barely dry after the recent rains. A man was sleeping atop a cycle rickshaw parked under a tree. Beyond it, Arun could see a tea shop, a grocery shop, International Steel Works, film box makers, and then a shanty joint that advertised: 'We supply paper flowers, costumes, bullets, guns and linoleum wigs at reasonable rates and minimum rentals. Typing of story and dialogues at affordable rates.' Then came a longish single-storey building. Six doors. Six families. It was 4.30 a.m. The radio was playing Vividh Bharati, blaring out a Malayalam song.

Manonmani entered one of those doors, shaking off her Hawaii chappals.

'Akka is here,' two kids shouted and hugged her.

Manonmani took a few hundred-rupee notes from inside her blouse, put them on the top shelf of an almirah and prayed to the portrait of Goddess Angalaparameswari, touching it and pressing her fingers on her eyes.

'Amma!'

Manonmani was twenty years old, but there were dark circles under her eyes already. Her lips were large and pronounced. A chain of plastic beads hung around her neck. Earrings that stood out prominently. She wore a simple voile sari and had a body that seemed to have been chiselled into an hourglass shape. Despite the grimy tiredness of her bus journey and her tousled hair, there was still something very attractive about her.

'Did you get the money?'

'Hmm.'

Her mother looked at the almirah. 'Three hundred rupees? Wow! Big part?'

She hesitated. 'Yes,' she said finally.

'Is your name Manonmani? Mine is Pandurangan. I distribute films. Uma Pictures. This is Lakshmanan.'

'We are investing two and a half lakh rupees into this film. Uma is my daughter's name. It is a lucky name. Come here.'

'I have to take a bath, Amma. Is there water?'

'I have filled a bucket. Did you have something to eat?'

'Drink that now. You'll get a kick. It is foreign stuff.'

'I have not eaten, Ma. Did anyone come from the association?'

'A guy called Marimuthu.'

She went to the bathroom, took off her clothes and splashed cold water over her body.'

'Look. I won't do anything to you. I have a daughter your age. You are my second heroine in the film.'

'What is the name of the movie?' her mother's voice travelled into the bathroom. The voice carried a tinge of worry.

'*Ilanthalaivan.*'

The cold water washed off her tears.

5

It was getting dark when they reached Chennai. The crows perched on three-pronged rooftop television antennas on the tops of the buildings were rushing home. In front of a movie hall at St Thomas Mount, Arun Vijay found himself smiling back from a forty-foot-long colour cut-out. He noticed there was not much of a crowd.

'So *Manam Nirambiya Malargal* is a flop?' he asked.

'Yes. They are taking it off in two weeks. Not much collection.'

'Good!'

'It's *not* good,' Bhaskar said. 'The director has even told a magazine that you did not cooperate properly.'

'That's a lie. The story had too many holes—no logic at all!'

'Who looks at logic these days, Arun?'

'The audience has started figuring it out, Bhaskar. They are now mature enough to appreciate camera work, editing and direction, and know the nuances. People are smart now. It is time to make art films.'

'I don't believe this—look!'

On the poster of a movie called *Gandharva Kanni*, a prince was crawling as half-a-tortoise in a mythological change of body. Jayamalini, the dance girl, was bathing in a waterfall, as she always did.

'What do you say to this?' Bhaskar asked.

'No, it has not done as well as *Jaganmohini*. But what do I care, Bhaskar? My dates are full until 1981.'

'You know that they can also be cancelled.'

'Has anything been cancelled so far?

'No.'

'Don't you worry then. One hit can offset ten shits.'

As the car entered Arun's home on Burkit Road, the fans waiting outside stood up. He walked straight into the building. As he entered the drawing room, his aunt's kids were playing carrom. They stopped all of a sudden.

'Arun! Good evening!'

'Evening.'

'You know, *Vayasukku Vandha Ponnu* has crossed seventy-five days. It's running full at Alankar even now. The balcony tickets are selling in black.'

They were evidently buttering him up. 'Is that so?' Arun asked, showing no expression. 'And who is this new face here?'

'Ramakrishnan. Ramu. Devaraj mama's son. Don't you remember?'

'Hello, Ramu!' he said.

'Hello, Arun Uncle,' the callow teenager replied in a voice that was still breaking.

'Don't call me uncle. Have you come here for your holidays?'

'No. I am going to study in Madras. Amma and Appa are here. They've gone to see a movie.'

'Where are you planning to stay?'

'Here, right here,' the boy replied.

'Okay, go play,' Arun said.

Bhaskar eyed Arun worriedly.

'Bhaskar, why don't you buy a few more carrom boards. And then, build an annexe at the back. Then, give me a typewritten statement on how each of these people is related to me and when they arrived here.'

'Are you serious, Arun? You know it is quite easy to ask them to go back to where they came from.'

'So many people staying here for so many days,' Arun said. 'They are all having fun. My mother and my father have not stayed here for even a single day. Someday, perhaps! Amma died before I became famous. And Appa just won't come!'

Arun stared at the ceiling as he recalled scenes from his home, and his rather unimpressed father.

'Your son is a famous actor.'

'What?'

'Your son is a big actor. He is earning in lakhs.'

'Happy to hear that.'

'Aren't you going to stay with him?'

'I am getting my pension. That should be enough.'

'Is there anything on the schedule tonight?' Arun asked Bhaskar.

'Yes, at Prasad Studios. You should be resting for an hour.'

Raji, his older sister's daughter, brought in something to drink. 'Maama, Boost.'

She was about twelve years old and had developed breasts. She went to a convent school and had two long plaits. She put the cup and saucer on the table and went back to her Mills & Boon novel. He felt like slapping her on the cheeks that were chewing gum. But he told himself that was not right.

He sent her and Bhaskar off, lay on his back and tried to figure out the roots of his anger. No, it was not the battery of relatives crowding his home. It was the movie hall at St Thomas Mount. And the warning the sight seemed to offer. This was the first time an Arun starrer was flopping at the box office like this. Though he could come up with excuses, it was clear that the you-can't-make-a-flop-if-Arun-is-in-it concept had now come apart at the seams.

The other reason was what happened in Bangalore. A pall of Premalatha's scent hung over his body. And he could not forget that eager grin on the waiter-poet's face at 1.a.m The whole experience made him uneasy. *It's all wrong*, he told himself. *It's all just wrong*.

He rummaged through a drawer, found the pill he was looking for and swallowed one with a glass of water. He put a handkerchief over his eyes, switched off the lights and tried to sleep.

'He sidelines the first wife, goes to another town, lies about being single and finds a new wife.'

The man was reciting the story, standing. Lakshmanan was reclining on the bed, biting into a piece of roast chicken. The food sent from home was lying uneaten nearby. On the shelf was a tube of Hadensa to treat his piles.

This was a story discussion in progress. In front of Lakshmanan sat the director, the director's nephew, an assistant director and the writer. On a sheaf of Sunlit Bond Paper that began with a dedication to Lord Shiva, the story was etched in a beautiful handwriting, all of one hundred pages.

The telephone rang and Lakshmanan barked 'Hullo!' into it. The writer carried on. 'The thing is, the new girl he has found is none other than his first wife's niece.'

'Hello? Coimbatore? Can you call VLS? *Hello! Hello? Hello?*'

Lakshmanan was on his call while the discussion went on. 'Is she his wife's own sister's daughter?'

'Yes, sir.'

'How is that even possible? Doesn't seem logical.'

'Let's make her a cousin's daughter,' the assistant director said helpfully.

Lakshmanan was still on the phone. 'Is that VLS? It's me, Lakshmanan. They have agreed for two and a half lakhs. What? Arun? Well, we are trying to get him, saar. Is that so? Okay, we'll do it. We will.'

He angrily threw the receiver down. 'Tcha!'

The director piped up. 'So, they are insisting on Arun?'

'Yes.'

'But *Manam Nirambiya Malargal* has flopped. The critic at *Kumudam* ripped it apart. The film got only 27 out of 100.'

'Shhhh! That is *Vikatan*!' Lakshmanan corrected the director for getting the magazine wrong.

The writer was droning on. 'You know, in that village they have a traditional belief. A grown-up girl is made to stand near a well and then her sari is taken off...'

Lakshmanan was still thinking of the money. 'After promising me two and a half lakhs, look what he is doing. Insists on Arun. Is that fair? And that guy is playing hard to get.'

'I hear Premalatha is his keep,' one of the hangers-on said.

'He won't last another six months. He is going nowhere,' piped up another groupie.

The writer persisted. 'Here, we have some powerful dialogues,' he said, and proceeded to open his bound script.

Lakshmanan fumed. 'Shut up! This story is horrible. Go change it.'

'How was the chicken, sir?' the director's nephew asked.

'Bland, just like this guy's storyline,' Lakshmanan said.

They all let out exaggerated laughter.

The writer, not giving up, changed his notebook. 'I have a hero subject, sir. I have a line treatment, a screenplay—the works,' he said, looking worried.

'Have you seen *Bensi*?' the director asked.

'It's not *Bensi*. It is *Benji*,' the producer corrected him.

'Yes, that. How about making it in Tamil?'

The topic shifted to a movie about a lion that died in a fight with a bull, torn apart by sharpened the bull's horns.

'If you need a lion to shoot with now, you have to go to Kerala,' the assistant said.

The writer stood near the door and asked, 'So when are you going tell me your decision?'

'There's nothing to decide,' Lakshmanan said. 'Bring me another story.'

'You said you would be using my story for your next project.'

The director replied now. 'Look, man, no one really wants a whole story now. We just need an outline. We write the stuff on the sets.'

'But I gave you five outlines,' said the writer.

'They are all rubbish!'

The writer watched helplessly as the topic shifted to a monkey available for shoots on Masjid Street.

The writer left, picking up his notebooks filled with stories, and tucking them all under his arms.

Lakshmanan was working the phone tirelessly, juggling his contacts for funds and stories. 'All engaged.'

The director was ruffled. 'We have a song recording tomorrow, and we need a story before that.'

Lakshmanan took a fifty-rupee note from his wallet and spoke to the director's nephew. 'Now, Raju, just go across the street and pick up a dozen or so monthly book magazines.'

The man left, and the cameraman asked, 'What's a book magazine?'

'You know, the novels they publish every month.'

'What do you think about Manonmani?' the director broached a new topic.

'Who is that?' asked Lakshmanan.

'Don't you remember, sir? Nice girl. Flawless face.'

'First, let us get a story,' Lakshmanan said.

Premalatha sang as she took a shower. Outside the plastic curtain, her mother was waiting with a huge towel.

'I heard Arun was also staying in the same hotel as you that day.'

'Yes, Ma. Even I heard about it.'

'But you never told me before.'

'I didn't know earlier, Ma.'

'Hmmm. Whatever. I am not hearing good things about him.'

'Don't believe all that, Ma.'

'You know, if male actors last fifteen years, it is just two or three for us,' her mother said as she towelled her daughter. 'Look now, your waist is already getting bigger.'

'I look fine to everyone else, Ma.'

'That won't do!' her mother said in a chiding tone. 'They now have those Punjabi girls with their slim, shapely bodies.'

Premalatha sprayed some talcum powder on her body and put on a top and a long skirt. She looked at herself in the mirror and smiled to herself, lost in her own world.

'Is this your first time?'

'Yup, that's right.'

'Swear!'

'Yes, I swear.'

'God promise?'

'You want me to swear upon my head or something?'

'You know, this is the first time for me as well.'

'I could make that out.'

'What's the matter? her mother asked. 'Why are you smiling to yourself in front of the mirror?'

'It's nothing, Ma—just remembering something funny that happened on the set.'

'You know, this is not like the touching we do in front of the camera.'

'Touch me, Arun. Touch me!'

'Lie down.'

Honey, the family Pomeranian stepped into the room, wagged its tail and barked. 'Don't say bow, my dear. Say love!' Premalatha picked up that puppy, hugged it tight and made the pet's fur caress her body. She felt something like electricity passing through her veins. She longed to be close to Arun again. *Amma does not know. No one else knows. It is a secret between me and Arun. Why does my mother stay here? Why doesn't she go away?*

Aloud, she said, 'I am going to rest awhile, Ma.'

'You know, Rathi, Saritha, Sridevi, Sripriya…even Jayasudha has now come to Tamil cinema.'

'Let them come.'

'They are getting more and more projects.'

'So what, Ma? I also have many.'

'Do you know they have dropped you and cast Sripriya in that god movie?'

'It was I who said no, Ma. The dates were not matching.'

'But they changed the dates for her.'

'So what if they did? What are you getting at?'

'I don't like the way things are headed. Look here, baby! You have to either act or you have to get married. Don't confuse one with the other.'

'What are you trying to say, Ma? I don't understand. Who is talking of marriage now?'

'A woman has to protect herself. It is easy to lose oneself. I am worried about you.'

'What's your worry?'

'What happened that day? Tell me now!'

'What?' Premalatha said. 'Nothing happened,' she replied, not looking at her mother.

'I hope and trust my daughter won't be doing any kind of stupid stuff.'

'Okay, Ma. Why don't you get some rest?'

After her mother left, she quickly dialled Arun's number. 'Get me Arun,' she told the man at the other end.

'Who is speaking?' Bhaskar asked.

'Tell him it is the cow.'

'Oh, Premalatha? Please wait a moment. What is this about?'

'Need to ask him about our schedule. Is it necessary to tell his secretary everything?'

'No, not like that,' Bhaskar said. 'Please wait. I'll get him.'

She waited. *What shall I tell him?* she wondered. She must surprise him. She must make him hit the ceiling.

Arun came on the line.

'Hello Rangabhashyam!'

'Oh, it is you? How are you?'

'Arun, what name shall we give it?'

'What name?'

'You know, the baby we are going to have.'

Silence. She smiled to herself. He must have jumped now in horror.

He sounded calm. 'What? Are you joking?'

'No, I am serious.'

'Look,' he said, 'This is not a Tamil movie scene for some congratulations-you-are-going-to-be-a-father line. Stop fibbing. Even if something awkward has happened by chance, go see Dr Savitri. Her consulting time is 3 to 4 p.m. Good night!'

The phone went dead as he cut off the call abruptly. Premalatha dialled that number all over again, with no luck.

6

IT WAS TO BE THREE days of much-anticipated freedom from the strange glints of movie cameras, the heat of thousand-watt bulbs, from the manufactured display of affections in front of a dozen people, and from the glycerine sorrows of the tinsel world. Arun neared Uttamarkovil in the searing heat, his trip a closely guarded secret. He'd had to tell several lies to shape this visit. He asked the driver to get out of the car as it neared his destination and asked him to relax for two full days in Trichy, the nearest city. He drove into the suburban temple town all by himself.

This was the place he'd been born in. Wild plants sprouted out of the stone mandapams of the temple town. In the shadow of the Ayyanar temples with their fierce, moustachioed village deities, lazy men were enjoying their siestas. The canal was, with its dark green sheen, in full flow in the glory of August after the monsoon rains. A small rail bridge connected two banks of the canal. Arun used to walk across them as a child, anxious that a train may arrive before he crossed over. Yonder, on the west side, buffaloes were being washed not far from a coconut tree that bent over, trying to kiss the canal. One urchin from a group plunged every five seconds into the green-hued waters, making a splashing sound that filled the serene rural air.

Beyond the railway gate, away from the regular tar road, he entered the kuccha Sannidhi Street, and his childhood memories burst forth as if it was today. There they were, the triple-lined walls that were his cricket stumps. The corners where he crouched when he played hide-and-seek. His ears were buzzing with the sounds of friends calling out as they played, looking for the den. There was the landlord Namsivayam's iron-gated house. The revolving gate served as a bus when they played out their imagined journeys. The bus used to go to Trichy, Madurai and Rameswaram, and if you paid a hundred tamarind seeds, even London was accessible.

They played chillakku, a hopscotch of sorts with a circle marked out on the ground. Here, in earning one hundred tamarind seeds scattered outside the circle, Arun had felt an enjoyment as yet unmatched by the millions he earned now as a movie star. And there was the forever locked house of Pattappa, where mysterious sounds of anklets could be heard in the dead of the night. Krishniah's home now had a functional board that announced: 'Japanese watches, gramophones etc. can be repaired here with a guarantee.'

Arun's own home was locked. No father. No mother. The low, thatched-roof house that had recently acquired some fame was securely locked, and just across the street stood Sundaram's house.

He parked the car carefully and shut the door gently. It seemed to him that if he shut it a little harder, the entire town would feel some pain.

Sundaram, who had just gotten up and was picking up that day's *Dinamani* from his veranda and biting into a bark of neem, clutching a brass pot full of water, stood shocked. 'Hey!' he said. 'What kind of a surprise is this?'

'Your sister did not tell you?'

'She did, but I never believed you would come. Wow, you actually made it!' Sundaram had a beard now, and his cropped hair and square jaw reminded Arun of B.V. Karanth. But the eyes were less intense, more ready to smile.

'How many hours are you planning to stay?' Sundaram asked.

'Two days.'

'Two days? Some film shooting here?'

'No.' *Should I tell him I have come to see his sister?*

'Can you stay put for that long? Will they let you?'

'No one knows I have come here.'

Sundaram gave him a piercing look, as if trying comb out all the falsehoods in him.

Must tell him everything in these two days, Arun told himself.

'Appa, look who has come?' Sundaram shouted.

'Who is that, da?' Sundaram's father stood up, revealing the teeth that still remained firm after seventy years on the planet. 'Oh, Viju! Our Viju!'

'He is not your Viju, Appa. He is Arun. The *famous* Arun.'

'For all of you, I am still the same old Viju,' Arun said.

'Adeiii, the whole country is talking about you. When I go to buy my fertilizers, I meet one chap who actually worships your photograph. But I don't watch films. Aeyy Kalyani! You sleepyhead! Get up! Look who is here!'

As the old man pulled off the bedsheet spread over Kalyani, she got up with a start, eyed Arun and sat up confused. Then she understood, showed a fearful wonderment in her eyes and adjusted her half-sari and hair. She flashed him a quick smile and vanished inside in a jiffy.

'I'm told she is doing her MSc,' Arun said.

'Chemistry. But all of this will go waste.'

'Why?'

'She is going to get married, no? Should I ask for your house to be opened?'

'No. If you don't have any objections, I can stay over at your place.'

'Tchai! What's to object? We would be delighted! I'll take leave for the day. I'm sure the parcel office at Ponmalai can survive for two days without me. Aeyy Kalyani, why don't you clean the first floor? And get a table fan from next door.'

'No need for the fan, Sundaram,' Arun said. 'I want to stay here among you for a couple of days.'

'Is that even possible? You said your visit was a secret, but look what is happening outside.'

A group of about four or five people had assembled already at the gate. 'Mama, isn't that Arun?'

'Really?'

'Yeah, the guy we've seen in those colour photos.'

One voice called out, 'You know *Vayasukku Vandha Ponnu* running in Wellington? This is the hero from that movie.'

Someone, verifying this information, asked him, 'You come in the movies, no?'

As Arun walked in, he bumped his head on the short Chettinad-style door with ornamental brass handles. He rubbed his forehead. A dark front hall stretched inside. Beyond that lay a well-lit square hall with four round pillars. He went in and sat on a chair with oil stains.

'Off with you all!' Sundaram was driving away the curious gang of youngsters as his mother welcomed Arun.

'Come, Viju. Are you well? You know, we had visited the city last week to check out a groom for Kalyani.'

'Is she engaged?' Arun asked.

'More or less. We expect to get a detailed letter today. You saw Kalyani, no?'

'She is so shy!'

'Hey, come here, di! Look, this is Viju, di. What's there to be shy about? The two of you used to fight so much. Do you recall that, Viju?'

'I haven't forgotten.'

'It seems you are earning a lot. Stay blessed like a maharaja. What a pity your mother and father are not enjoying your riches. What happened to your sister in Jamshedpur?'

'Everybody is now in Madras,' Arun explained.

'Your father, poor man, was paralysed for a year and could not even speak. He suffered a lot. Who has he made the house over to?'

'It's all in my name. Do you need the house?' he asked.

'It would be convenient for the groom to stay during the wedding,' she said.

'Amma, he has already been here so long. Is there no coffee for him?' Sundaram asked.

'Of course there is. Look who is bringing it!'

Kalyani arrived with the filter coffee She had washed her face, combed her hair and made a quick bindi on her forehead.'

'She was talking a lot about meeting you in Madras.'

'But she was hardly saying anything when we met,' Arun said.

'She is like that only. We haven't spent a penny to educate either of the kids—all from scholarships!'

Kalyani put the coffee tumbler on a stool and disappeared quickly. Her long hair flipped for a wee second as she breezed out. Wearing a half-sari at the age of nineteen, she was unusually attractive. Her fair skin was glowing. There was a red mark where she had tied her pavadai string around her waist. The elegant swell of her bosom flashed when she turned about. She was wearing a long-sleeved blouse, and beneath her anklets was the deep orange hue of mehndi.

'Must ask her before dusk,' Arun said to himself.

They had made some spicy pongal for breakfast, and a sour chutney-like something with it. The curd was thick. Arun had to resist the impulse of going for a dip in the Kollidam river. The crowds would give him hell. Besides, the waters were muddy. He bathed in the backyard well, drawing the water himself with an iron bucket attached to a rope. In place of his usual toilet soap, he used an aromatic herbal powder mixed with gram flour.

Another coffee followed. He borrowed a veshti from Sundaram and dried his shirt and trousers that he had washed with his own hands. He clambered up to the first floor, clutching a rope that connected the makeshift stairway. On the door above, a blackboard announced in chalk: 'Tamil Centre, Twice A Month.'

The apparent teacher at this Tamil school, Kalyani, was presently sweeping the floor. 'If I send a story, will you consider it for publication?' he asked.

Startled, she started sweeping the floor in a hurry.

'Here, let me see the magazine,' he asked

She hesitantly proffered a copy of the handwritten magazine. On the cover was a picture of Goddess Saraswathi's veena (artwork by Kalyani). The first page was dedicated to her loving mother and father. The page that followed had a landscape sketch. He flipped the pages and paused at the page that said: 'Meeting with an Actor.' There was a photograph of Arun and a byline that read: 'Our Cinema Reporter.'

'For all of you, Arun is a famous actor, the shining star of the south, and possibly the leading actor of Asia. But for us, he is Viju,' the article began.

He looked up at her. 'So, you wrote this?' he asked. She nodded. Her cheeks were flushed pink. 'Do you remember what happened in this room when we were in the tenth standard?' he asked.

'Hmm. No,' she said.

'Shall I remind you? I was playing a tailor who took measurements. And also a doctor…'

'Kalyaneee!' a stern voice called out from below.

She disappeared at once.

Arun read on. 'Viju, just like in the movies, is strikingly tall. His sandalwood complexion glows. You have, of course, heard his voice. There is no way that Premalatha seems suited to him. She will need really high heels to match up to him.'

'What's going on?' Sundaram's voice sounded from behind.

'Your sister's Tamil magazine.'

'Yes, she publishes that kind of stuff,' Sundaram said. 'She stages plays with little girls on the first floor. Story, dialogues and music by Kalyani. All this, of course, within the four walls of this house. Outside, she is quiet as a mouse—and positively scared when she attends college.'

There was a short story up next. 'A city called Avanthipuram was once ruled by a king called Arunadittan.' After that, there was a short story by K titled 'The Palace Garden'.

'She is still a child,' Sundaram said.

'Sundaram,' he said. 'I have to discuss something important with you.'

About two hundred and fifty miles away in Bangalore, at a church near Coles Park in the cantonment area, an eight-day-old child closed its eyes and cuddled in the warm embrace of his mother as he waited for his name.

The old church stood tall and proud with its majestic arches. The morning sun made magical patterns through its many-hued tinted glass windows. At the far-right corner stood a church organ and at the centre was the Son of God on a cross. There were some more statues: Mother Mary, the birth of the Messiah in a cattle-shed. The priest, a red shawl slung over his long robe, watched Sagaya Mary intensely as the infant boy perched in his mother's arm, awaiting God's blessings and a baptism that would liberate him from the sins of men that stretched down its lineage from Adam and Eve.

The child's father, Arumairajan, stood wearing his only terylene shirt. Though he smiled often at Sagaya Mary, deep down he felt pangs of pain about his recent job loss. He'd had to borrow some money to make his contribution to the church. After deducting the advance that had been given to him to buy a bicycle, the hotel had given him all of 139 rupees as they cashiered him out. Thanks to that, the child now had a silk shirt and his wife a voile sari. He'd had to incur some expenses buying snacks for the occasion. He eyed the infant who was half asleep, unmindful of the circumstances in which he was born.

The priest put a white cloth on the infant's head, rubbed holy oil, looked down at his registration book, dipped the little one's head in water and announced: 'Louis Dominic Arumairajan, I bathe you in holy water. Join me, Sagaya Mary!'

'What should I say, Father?'

'The child can't speak, no? You have to take this place now. Say with me: "I have left Satan and his ways."'

She repeated after him.

They stepped out of the church to resume their life full of uncertainties.

Arumairajan did not have a single paisa in his pocket. Anthony and Philomena, who walked with him, were chattering non-stop. Sagaya Mary was playing with her eight-day-old boy. 'Hey Louis Dominic, will you take care of me?' The child looked back, without blinking.

'Louis after his father, and Dominic after mine. Arumairajan is the general family name,' she said to no one in particular and asked her husband, 'Why don't we take an auto? The child looks a bit tired.'

'What? You're taking off in an auto? No chicken curry for me, sister?' asked Anthony, who operated the projector at the nearby Adarsha Cinema.

'Ah, the little boy's father works in a hotel. He will bring some chicken roast.'

'Let's all eat and watch a matinee show. Everything is on Rajan today, right?'

'Anthony, will you come here?' Arumairajan summoned him to the side.

In the distance, the waters of the Ulsoor Lake gleamed. As cars waited in the shades of huge trees, soldiers of the Madras Engineer Group were jogging in a row.

'Anthony, I have lost my job.'

'Oh, no! Does sister know this?' Anthony asked, and lit a cigarette. Arumairajan already owed him one hundred and fifty rupees.

'No, not yet. If I tell her, she will start crying. I am trying to avoid telling her today. Anthony, will you manage two hundred rupees somehow for me?'

'Why?'

'I have to go to Madras. You know Arun? Our Arun? He has promised to introduce me to Ilayaraja. I am going to write lyrics for movies. Anthony, they give one thousand rupees for each song. My dark days are going to be over.'

7

By the time Arun could tell Sundaram what was on his mind, there was a sound of the wooden stairway creaking under a heavy weight. All of Sannidhi Street was now upstairs. 'This is an auspicious day for all of us. Our town's lad has returned after conquering the world. We are really happy. I came to get an autograph for my granddaughter, and I have informed my son-in-law in Lalgudi. He is trying to get here by the next train,' announced a Brahmin who looked like a temple priest.

The man did not stop talking. Arun was a bit dazed, taking it all in. Everyone stared at him with sheepish grins, as if he was a double-headed goat being paraded during the winter festival at the local temple. Faces were pressed to windows to whispers of 'Hey, look! This is the man.'

He stared helplessly at Sundaram. 'And I came here to stay in peace for a couple of days.'

Sundaram laughed and told the crowd, 'Everybody! Please go home now and come back in the evening. He has only just arrived.'

'Just one autograph, Sundaram,' someone pleaded.

'All in the evening. See you then?'

'The God agrees but the priest blocks the way,' someone said, taunting Sundaram.

'No, he won't sign an autograph now.'

'Hey, Ambi,' someone called him by the common village honorific for local boys. 'Won't you say anything, da?'

Arun was giving them an empty stare. 'Tamil Nadu, Andhra, Kerala, Karnataka—whichever corner of these states I go to, I have no escape,' he told himself.

'Ah, is he so conceited?' said a voice.

'These movie people are like this only.'

'Come guys! He is acting too pricey.'

'All because of this Sundaram.'

'Hey, let us see. We want to hear him talk.'

Someone piped up, 'Hey Arun, why don't you sing?' as he asked for a song from one of Arun's films.

'All that is dubbing,' announced a local know-it-all. 'It was SPB who sang it.'

Sundaram whispered, 'Viju, open the back door and go to the top floor. There is a staircase that leads down to the backyard from there.'

Arun opened the door and crossed mildewed walls, beyond which he could see several coconut trees. Further afar, he could see the towering temple and the canal. Generous mounds of sand in the coconut grove told tales of the river Kollidam flowing nearby.

As he descended the precarious stairs, a brass pot was boiling with water over a wood stove near the well. Not far, in the bathroom, Kalyani could be heard humming. She stepped out presently and stood looking at him, shocked.

She had bound up her hair in a bun. Her barely dry face had some droplets of water around her brows and forehead. The smell of her soap wafted to his nostrils. There she stood, with a towel across her breasts with a pavadai below, like some rustic beauty from Kerala.

'Why are you here?' she asked.

'There is a big crowd outside…'

'My college friends won't believe this. Should I bring them?'

'You have not answered my question,' he said.

'What question?'

'Do you remember…'

'I do,' she said somewhat hesitantly. She looked at him straight in the eye for a moment. It seemed like in that second, the two were married and had already spent their wedding night together.

She stepped on a patch of moss and slipped all of a sudden. He lunged to take her in his grip and in that intimate moment, kissed her hard on the cheek…

There was no moss, and no Kalyani either. She had suddenly disappeared inside. He stood stunned. Here was a heroine who would not fit into his screenplay. She was an elusive deer amid the shadows. And he, King Arunaditthan of her handwritten story.

I must certainly ask for her hand today. Maybe right now.

But whom should he ask? Her mother? Her father? Maybe Sundaram? He had, in countless films and in several languages, loved so many women. But here he was, utterly helpless, not knowing what to do.

'Sundaram, I want to marry your sister and...' *Nah, I cannot do that*, he told himself.

'You want something, boy?' Sundaram's mother came in. He did feel like telling her what was in his heart, but...

'May I have some hot water to bathe with?' he asked instead.

'But you have already had a bath. Hey Kalyani, you said he had already bathed?'

'He has!' Kalyani's voice came from somewhere.

'Oh, I forgot!' he said sheepishly.

Her mother changed the topic. 'We are going to make a special meal for you today. Tell me what's your favourite food.'

'Does Kalyani cook?' he asked.

'Ah, she can cook enough to serve eight villages,' the mother beamed proudly.

'You please cook like any other day,' Arun said. 'Treat me as if I was just one of your household.'

'You earn in lakhs, and you show us so much respect. I must make at least a payasam.'

From behind the doors, he could hear the gentle sound of bangles. Kalyani was draping her sari.

'Have you visited your house yet?' the mother asked.

'Not yet, ma.'

He could hear the sound of anklets now. She was walking, the gentle sound of her anklets accompanying her.

'The house is exactly as it was the day your father passed away,' the mother announced. 'We have not even moved his glasses, and all your childhood photos are intact. There is one in which you wear earrings, looking like a girl, with hair covering your forehead. You know, your mother used to force a full cup of castor oil on you and pull off your drawers to clean your stomach.'

Sundaram appeared presently, having driven off all the unwanted visitors. He sighed in relief.

'Sorry, I have given you folks so much trouble,' Arun said.

'That's all right. Let one day in a year be a little different,' Sundaram said. 'Can't bear this if it happens every day. I'll go mad. You know, there are rows of people already coming in from other streets. And that Pichumani has even informed Lalgudi. Viju, how do you put up with all this?'

'I am just used to it, that's all,' Arun said. 'I can just switch off. You can't be in the movies if you fear public attention. I could be speaking strange lines like: "What solitude! What splendour!" as one crore people stand outside the sets.'

He heard a giggle. Ah, she was listening. Knowing now that she was paying attention, he thought up some funny anecdotes for Sundaram. He could talk about the female horse that had done strange things when they were shooting for a king and queen movie. But that would be a bit risqué. This could wait until after the wedding. He instead gathered his wits and said, 'Sundaram, I want to talk to you in private for a while...'

'Let's do something,' Sundaram said. 'You have a good meal and take a nap. Then we'll play dice for a while. Kalyani is an expert at this. After the evening coffee, we can drive in your car for about five miles to a riverside grove. We can talk there.'

At the riverbank, Sundaram had brought along a volume of Santayana and another tome called *Worldly Thoughts.* The Kollidam flowed gently, and the sunset on the horizon was a riot of colours with a ruddy, angry edge to the distant sky. The sky had shades of dark blue and light blue and cyan, as if the clouds had daubed on some make-up.

'It's so beautiful!' Arun said.

'There will be wonderments every moment, A dream anew every moment,' Sundaram was quoting romantic lines from the nationalist poet. 'We are forgetting the lines of Bharati within a generation,' he said wistfully.

'This generation is like that.'

'Shhhhhh,' Sundaram quietened him. 'Listen carefully.'

'Trr…trrr…' Arun could hear soft, sharp chirps, like someone had crafted the sweet sound of a flute into little pieces. 'Look there!'

A green-hued sparrow-like bird flew past, with its neck shining a dusty red.

'We call it panchittan. Look at its needle feathers and black beak. You can spot a dark line around its neck. It looks for food in the fields. It sits on telegraph poles and grabs the flies that buzz around.'

The bird sounded somewhat shrill now.

'I think it has forgotten its tune' Arun said.

'This one has a cousin,' Sundaram said. 'A blue-tailed variety, a little larger than this. You know, you could write your fortune off to that blue tail. Try reading about the migration of birds. Wonderful stuff!'

'Sundaram!' Arun announced. 'I positively envy you.'

'And I am not jealous of you at all,' his friend grinned. 'After seeing all those people tearing you apart this morning...'

'Hey, look! What's that diving bird?'

'A kingfisher.'

'I only know of Kingfisher beer,' Arun said.

'What was it that you wanted to talk about?' Sundaram reminded him.

Arun hesitated for a moment. Where should one start? 'Hmm. Is Kalyani engaged now?' he asked.

'Yes, we have even paid our counter,' he said.

'What's that?'

'You know, like a dowry. I took a loan from my provident fund and sold a bit of our land, raised four thousand rupees. Why do you ask now?'

'I want you to cancel the engagement.'

'Why?' Sundaram looked him in the eye.

'Tell him. Tell him now,' a voice inside told Arun. 'Let me marry Kalyani. I am saying this with all my heart. There is not a bigger fortune that I could have.'

'Wait a minute!' Sundaram said. 'What is this, Viju? You are talking as if you are in one of your movies.'

'This is not cinema, dammit!' Arun sounded a bit aggressive.

He went on. 'Sundaram, I have pretended enough in my life—in front of the camera and away from it. I know I pretend a lot. But what I am telling you here by this river is the truth. This moment is true. My words are all genuine.

Like that sparrow, like that kingfisher…Sundaram, I love your sister with my body, heart and soul. Tell me what you think, Sundaram.'

'But we have given the money!'

'So what? What's four thousand rupees? It is what I earn in a day.'

'That's a lifetime's earning for me,' Sundaram said.

Arun felt a pinprick of pain. 'I should not have spoken to him like that,' he told himself.

Sundaram said, 'To work hard in life, to borrow money, to worry about your next meal, to pawn or sell some jewels…you know there is some joy even in such a struggle…such a life.'

'I did not mean it in that sense, Sundaram. I just said that it is so easy to reverse what you've done.'

'You know, it is going to take a while merely to digest what you've sprung on me like this. Give me some time. I need to talk to Amma and Appa about this. We also have to ask Kalyani.'

'I think she will say yes. You just have to convince your parents. You have to talk them into this. That's your job. Right?'

'Kalyani is still a child. You have burst in like a storm trooper. I am stunned! I need to ask Appa anyway. Are you in a hurry? I'll let you know by tonight.'

'No problem. I am prepared to wait. Do whatever but please get them to say yes. And please don't mind my saying that about the four thousand rupees,' Arun said.

'I won't. But after a point, isn't money a big pain?'

'I don't keep any money with me. Look at my pockets. Empty!' Arun said. 'I am a pauper!'

'Tell that to those income tax officers,' Sundaram smiled.

'Look, Sundaram. Read out something to me. It won't make sense to me but still, I feel a joy in merely listening to the voice of an intellectual like you.'

'Ah, you are buttering me up now. Are you trying to tell me, "Give me your sister's hand and I will listen to your stuff?"'

'Tchai, no! What is this *Wordly Thoughts*?' He opened the book.

'When you see a pot, you can conclude that there was a potter behind it. However, by looking at the world, we cannot conclude that there is a god behind it. Because the first thing can be verified by experience. The second one is beyond experience. It is not bound by proof.'

They returned home well after it was dark.

While Arun was waiting for a reply to his question, on that very night, Manonmani was waiting at Prasad Studios. A spot boy was looking at her from a height. She covered her breasts. Everybody was waiting for someone or the other. In the asbestos shed, there was a pall of smoke and the nebulous dust scattered by dry paint triggered by the heat of powerful bulbs that oozed kilowatts of brightness.

'Ah, you are sitting?' She heard a voice whose face she had seen before. About thirty years old, the woman was wearing a half-sari and had a long plait with an ornamental kunjam. 'Gopalu, my love, can you get me some coffee?' she hollered to someone who promptly responded, 'Will do, Akka.'

'We are all a little short here. You are tall. All those Telugu girls who come, you know I have danced with them. All of them are so tall. Like some heavy wooden planks…'

'Is your dance over?' Manonmani asked enthusiastically.

'Nah. The big man has not come. He will be late.'

Manonmani remained quiet.

'These are the kings of the industry,' she said. Turning, the woman told the helper boy, 'Thanks for the kaapi, raja. You'll be a hero someday. You have such a lovely hairstyle.'

And she turned to her, 'What did you say your name was?'

'Manonmani.'

'Here, have some kaapi.'

'No, ma'am, You go on.'

'Don't be shy. If you are shy, there is no place for you here. There was an outdoor shoot near Madhuranthakam in the afternoon. We had to change our clothes behind a single palm tree. There were forty of us women. The whole damn village was watching us.

'Have you acted in any films? Your face looks familiar.'

'I have danced in *Latchathil Oruvan*,' she said. 'And then there was a wedding scene in which I was escorting the bride. I even spoke one line: "They have all arrived." They shot us as we climbed the stairs. I have climbed the stairs in a hundred and fifty movies,' the woman said. 'I wish someone celebrated such milestones.'

'What's your name?' Manonmani asked.

'Paappa,' she said, the Tamil endearment for a baby.

'You are addressed like that?' Manonmani asked.

'Yes. So many people have done things with me calling me just that.'

Manonmani was startled.

'I am a bit crude, no?' Paappa said. 'I am sure you are new to these parts.'

'I am thinking of going home,' Manonmani said. 'I don't think I'll get my chance today.'

'Wait, my dear. Look now, the big man is coming. Elder brother. Lover. Warrior!'

Vijayaraja, popularly known as Rasigar Mannan, was walking in briskly with a swagger matching his epithet as the king of fans. He wore a thin terylene shirt, and no vest. His hairy chest reminded one of a bear, and his trousers clung to a slight paunch. He wore a loose gold chain and was grinning from ear to ear.

'He thinks he is very handsome,' Paappa joked. 'Look at him grinning. Don't you absolutely feel disgusted?'

'I have been promised a part in *Ilanthalaivan* by a man called Pandurangan,' Manonmani told her. 'Second heroine, in fact.'

'Look there!' Paappa said. Manonmani saw a group of twenty young women seated in a row.

'They are all the second heroines of *Ilanthalaivan*.'

8

Sitting in the room on the terrace at night, Arun flipped through the books in Sundaram's collection. His mind, however, was not focused on the poet Vannadasan. His attention was downstairs, where the family was talking. He could hear them clearly in the quiet of the night hours.

'He is an officer in a bank, has a good future. We have exchanged betel leaves and fruits. They've even presented a sari. We've paid for the watch and the suit. You can't be changing things at this hour.'

'But all that means nothing to him, pa.'

'What does that mean?'

'Appa, the problem now is not money. Money has become a very small issue. The important issue is whether we agree to his wishes or not.'

'What has he studied?'

'Appa, Appa!' Sundaram laughed. 'You can't seem to make up your mind. That's why you are evading the point.'

'What can I say conclusively? What do you have to say about this?' Sundaram's father asked his wife.

'You are the one who decides,' she said. 'Sundaram, what is his salary?'

'Look here, ma. What our family earns in a generation, he earns in a month.'

'Does he have any debts to clear?'

'Ayyo, Appa! What the hell are you talking about?'

'What are you trying to say, anyway?' his father asked Sundaram.

'Listen, you are passing the buck to me again and again.'

'Will he stop acting in the movies after he gets married?'

'How can I ask him that?'

'Why not? Ask him, no?'

'But that's his profession. How can he give that up?' Sundaram asked. 'And why should he give it up anyway?'

The father raised his voice a little. 'Why, you ask me? Look at this!' he said.

Arun was taken aback. What was he talking about?

'How can I look at a picture like this and give my daughter's hand to someone like that? Tell me. Tell me! Why don't you call him and show this and ask him?'

'Please don't shout, Appa!'

Arun, who could not bear all this anymore, descended to the ground floor. 'May I come in?' he said.

The three of them sat there like a scene from a Rajam Iyer novel set in the 1920s. There was an ancientness about their demeanour. The father sat in a chair, fanning himself. The mother stood nearby, her hands in an L-shaped gesture with one palm joined at the elbow of the other hand, in the ever-attentive pose of devoted wives. Sundaram, bare-chested, sat at his father's feet. A little beyond, standing near sacks of paddy, was Kalyani. It was 1929 all over again!

'Come, son!' the father beckoned. 'Sundaram told us. We were talking about you, in fact.'

'I did hear that, maama,' he said.

The father's hand clutched a copy of *Filmalaya* magazine. In the Tamil remake of a Malayalam movie, Arun was lying without clothes on. Lying him on top of him was a woman. Arun had even forgotten her name. Some actress who could not make a career in Hindi films and had tried her luck in Kerala. Her name was some-la he could not remember. Arun was biting his lips in the picture, with his eyes closed and his fingers were pressing her back ad his other hand was looking for the hook of her bra...this was a picture that left no room for doubt.

'Tell me, how do you think we feel when we look at something like this?' Sundaram's father asked.

Arun could not say anything immediately. He just felt angry. His hands were shaking. His lips craved for a cigarette.

'What are you trying to say, sir?' he asked.

'Even if we say bygones are bygones, what if you keep on acting in such roles?'

'What do you want me to do? Stop acting in films? You want me to give that in writing?'

'No, not like that. What I mean is, there are all sorts of forces at work in cinema. It doesn't suit people like us. To give your daughter's hand to film folks means...'

'Maama, you say "film folks" as if it was some dirty word. I don't like that.'

'What do you expect after we see this?' he brandished the picture again.

'How do I tell you, sir? All this is some kind of acting.'

The lady spoke up. 'You know, they wear thin clothes inside. All this is trick photography, you know.'

'You stay put, you idiot,' the old man chided her.

Arun, losing his patience, said, 'Look here, sir. You were a schoolteacher. What a blackboard or a piece of chalk is to you, this girl and this stuff is to us—just a professional prop.'

'How can the two be equal? She is lying on top of you. How can that be equal to a piece of chalk?'

'Can't these wretched folks publish good pictures?' Kalyani's mother asked.

Amidst that tension, Arun felt ready to laugh.

The father spoke on. 'You are laughing at this. But for us, this is no laughing matter. We have fixed a marriage, finished the engagement and given the token money in front of the community. To cross all that, and give my daughter's hand to a cinema…to you, what happens to my word given in the first place? Won't people spit at me?'

'Saar, all that can be managed amicably without anyone being disrespected. First, tell me if you are in favour of this or not. You can also say no in a clear manner.'

He stared silently into the old man's eyes. The old man's brows were knit, and the veins moved. He looked at his wife. Then he looked at Sundaram. He let out a big sigh. 'How can I say yes? I don't want to go back on my word,' he said.

'Why are you going on and on like this? I have assured you there will be no issues,' Arun raised his voice. 'All right. Kalyani, you tell me. You can say it freely. You are an educated girl. What do you say? Yes or no?'

From behind the sacks of paddy, after a few moments of silence, Kalyani spoke up. 'I'll do whatever my father and mother say.'

'Bloody heck! Sundaram, I am off,' Arun said.

'Where are you off to?'

'Towards my city. The movie man is going towards movie folks.'

'Don't be angry, pa. You should look at our side of the story also, no?'

'Surely, saar. Why should you be insulted before your community?'

Sundaram stared at him. 'You said you would stay two days, Viju.'

'No, pa. I am leaving.'

'Why don't you eat?' Sundaram's mother said. 'I've cooked a feast for you.'

Without a word, Arun left and got into his car parked outside. He slammed the door shut and started his car up.

It must have been around 9 p.m. when he left. Where was the driver? He didn't have a clue. He was ready to go to Chennai. He could reach by morning. He looked at the petrol tank. It was at 'E'. He was on the concrete road that connected Trichy with Chennai. On the 'T' point beyond the river, he stopped at a petrol pump.

'How much?' asked an old man with a grey moustache in a khakhi shirt.

'Make it forty litres.'

As the man moved the pump, Arun felt his pocket and realized he did not have a penny on his person. The tank was filling up. Twenty-four...twenty-five...twenty-six.

'Will you call the owner?' he asked the old man, as the tank stopped at forty.

'He has gone to Manachanallur. Shall I make the bill? With oil and air check?'

'Who is there in place of your owner?'

'Me. Why do you ask?'

'Do you recognize me?'

'No, sir. I don't. Who?'

'I am Arun.'

'Arul?'

'Not Arul. Arun. I am a cinema actor. Don't you know?'

'No sir, I have no idea. The last movie I saw was *Rambhayin Kaadhal.*

'Don't you read magazines?'

'Who has the time for all that?'

'You know why I am saying all this? I don't have any money to pay now.'

'What? If you didn't have the cash, why did you buy that petrol?'

'Look here, sir. What's your name?'

'How does that matter, whatever my name is? Hey, you better pay the money and move on. Else you don't get the keys. Get that clear.'

Arun thought for a while. The old man was thin, emaciated, sporting a khakhi shirt with a veshti around his waist. It seemed he would lose half his weight if his large moustache was shaved off. He could easily grab the key from him. But no!

'Listen boss, you temporary boss. Look at this. It is a watch from Singapore. It is worth nine hundred rupees. You can keep this. Leave me alone.'

'I don't want the watch. The forty litres cost you a hundred and sixty rupees or so. You just give that and be off. Cinema man? I have seen movies too. M.K. Thyagaraja Bhagavathar films. I stood on a temple car at Kanchipuram and watched him in real life once. With his red earrings and long silk jubba and fair skin.'

'When is your owner coming?'

'He will come by the 6 a.m. bus.'

'May I stay here till then?'

'Sure,' the old man relented. 'What did you say your name was?'

'Arul.'

'Arulsamy?'

'Yes.'

'Christian?'

'Yes.'

'Will you have some?' The topic shifted to booze as the man at the petrol pump offered Arun a drink.

'Sure…'

'Don't tell the owner, okay?'

'Nah, no way!'

The potion the old man offered smelt of wet paddy. Arun felt as if he was swallowing a hot stove.

'What is this? Ginger?'

'Not Kamala, it is Kalyani.' He was talking about country-brew brands.

At 1 a.m., as the old man listened in on the backseat of the Fiat, Arun, with a turban around his head, was looking for an audience. 'Old sir, will you listen to a new-age poem?'

'Tell me, dear Thyagaraja Bhagavathar,' said his drunk partner.

On that same night, in a hell called an unreserved railway compartment of the Bangalore–Chennai Mail, in a passage that connected the passenger seats to the lavatories, on a tin trunk that measured two feet by one and a half, Arumairajan and his wife Sagaya Mary squatted uneasily. The infant in her lap was sniffling frequently.

'Why do you worry now?' the poet said. 'We'll try our luck and if we don't succeed, there are enough hotels in Chennai. Right, Mary?'

'I can even get a job somewhere,' she replied

'What about the child?'

'Oh, I forgot about the child. Look at him smiling in his sleep. He looks so much like you.'

'I don't see that at all,' Arumairajan said, and spoke to the baby. 'Daai…' After a pause he said, 'I feel like writing a poem about him.'

'Now?' she asked. They were quiet for a while. 'And what are you going to do about the money?' she asked.

'I have no idea how long hundred rupees will last.'

'It will last ten days. Just the milk for our child will cost one rupee or a quarter more per day. Then we have to pay the hotel rent and for the food.'

'You said your cousin was here…your periyappa's son.'

'Let's avoid them, please,' Mary said.

'Why are you worried? I am just going to see Arun straightaway. I am going to tell him, "Look, it is because of your complaint that I lost my job. You have to put in a word for me and introduce me to Raja sir." All he needs to do is to give me a letter…I am just thinking of which song to show him first. You remember, when we were in Cox Town, I wrote that poem, "Oh, black cloud/my lover's hair, my shroud"? I think that would really fit into a song.'

'You've written hundreds of poems. Only one of them has to click.'

'I believe they just give four or five hundred rupees for a song in the early stages. But Kannadasan rakes in thousands—even Vaali.'

'Cluck!' The child was making some noise. Mary casually touched her and then felt its forehead.

'Doesn't it seem like he is warm?'

Arumairajan felt the infant's forehead and then his own neck and said, 'Slightly. Must be the heat in the train.'

'No,' said Mary. 'He has a fever.'

9

THE EARLY MORNING SUN HIT him along with the smell of rubber tyres. His dream was interrupted.

A strange kind of girl had taken his autograph and had kissed him on the cheek unexpectedly, and before he could react, his dream had been shattered. The potion called Kamala from the previous night was making Arun's head feel heavy. He rubbed his eyes and looked up.

'Hey! Is this him?' The owner from Manachanallur had arrived early in the morning, as expected. He was freshly bathed with sacred vibhuti smeared on his forehead and was appropriately dressed from head to toe in homespun khadi.

'Yes, sir,' the old man Friday was telling the owner. 'He tanked up last night and offered his watch instead of the cash. I could not let him go like that, could I?'

'You stupid cretin! You old bitch! You know who this man is?'

Arun stepped in. 'Please don't scold him. He really took good care of me last night,' he said, and suitably winked at the old man, who gestured back. 'Don't give me away,' his eyes said.

'Now, off you go quickly,' the owner told the old man. 'Run and get a cup of coffee and hot idlis. Take the bicycle and get it from Meenachi. Don't go as far as Srirangam.'

After he left, the man in khadi lamented. 'Ufff, adadaaa. I didn't know you were coming.'

'I didn't have the money. I just could not pay for the petrol immediately.'

'Ayyo! Does that even matter? You can send the money at leisure, no? I have two daughters. If they know you are here, they'll drop everything and rush to see you.'

'What are they studying?'

'One is in the eighth and the other in the fourth standard,' he said. 'Are you here for some shooting?'

'No. I came on personal work. Everything got over early and I started out. But I usually don't keep money in my pocket.'

'Forget about it, sir. Don't even talk about it. You've already told me, no? Where are you headed next?'

'Back to Madras.'

'Should I make a trunk call to inform someone? You are going alone, after all.'

'No. I don't want that.'

'Do you want to have a wash? You want to go by the fields, perhaps? Do you want a mug or something?'

'Yes, please,' Arun said.

As red-hued gulmohur trees whizzed past on the highway, the car sped at eighty kilometres per hour and the cassette player was blaring Boney M's 'Rasputin'. The events of the day before were still playing on Arun's mind. The eager expectations with which he had arrived at Uttamarkovil had been dashed to pieces.

'To marry a film chap…'

'Ah, to hell with you!' Arun was fuming mentally. 'I don't want your daughter. For every finger I wiggle, a woman will line up, okay?' he shouted out aloud. 'Keep her in your lap and marry her off. Let the wedding drums sound!' He spoke out the wedding mantras in a fit of frustration: '*Maangalyam dhantunanena mama jeevana hetuna!*'

Oh God! The number of times I have tied a thaali around a woman's neck in those movies. And here I am, can't tie one according to my wishes. Shooo, go away! Marry her off as you please. That damn guy is a bank clerk. Will he get four-hundred-odd rupees a month? What's the annual increment? Fifteen damn rupees? He will inspect the ledgers every day and reach home at 9.30 p.m. Will he get paid for overtime? He'll spread out the bed on reaching home. Will she get pregnant in the third month of the wedding? Her body will be swollen, she will lose some hair, she will have dark rings under her eyes, and her breasts will sag…

Outside the windshield, Kalyani was now an out-of-shape hologram. He sang out loud in English:

'One thing is sure and nothing is surer,

The rich get richer and the poor get…children.'

At 1 p.m., he reached his home in Chennai and blew the horn out loud. No one arrived fast enough. As he got off to open the door, a voice called out from behind him. 'Sir, sir! I have come.'

Arun turned around. Where had he seen him before?

'Who are you?'

'I am Arumairajan, saar. You know, I lost my job after you complained that day. I have struggled hard to…'

'To reach here? Okay, so what now?'

'You said you will introduce me to Raja sir.'

Arun glared at Arumairajan, who was grinning.

'Look here. Go straight and you'll find a water tank with iron stairs. Climb and go right on top…' But before he could come to the go jump part, Arun called out someone else's name. 'Hey Kittu, come on in!'

Kittu, who had just arrived, came close as if to hug Arun. 'Viju, my dear…'

'Kittu, I am not in any shape to be hugged now. Come later, okay? Now, this guy here wants something. Just find out what he wants and send him off. He has been chasing me all the way from Bangalore.'

'You go right in, sweetheart. I'll take care of him.'

'Look, Arumairajan,' Arun said. 'Go with Kittu. He will make all arrangements.'

'Okay, sir,' the poet said happily. Arun got back into the car and asked Kittu to shut the door.

'So you are just shooing me off?'

'Get rid of him!'

The portico was now empty. 'Everything falls into place when I am not here,' Arun thought to himself. As he got in, his relatives were taking their siestas. The ceiling fan was running at full speed like a monster. He went quietly up to his room on the first floor and heard soft laughter. He tiptoed quietly and swung open the handle swiftly.

Raji and Thyagu got up with a start, straightened their clothes and stood up in embarrassment.

'What's going on, Raji? Are you playing "You show me yours and I will show you mine"?'

As the girl stood with a sheepish expression, her head bowed down, he said, 'Tchaaai, run off!' Both of them vanished and he looked at the safety pin left behind on the bed.

'Nooooo. I won't do that. I certainly won't do that.'

'Kalyani…look here! Marbles.'

'No. No.'

She had rejected other offerings as well, a lot of stuff. In the end, he had to bribe her with a lot: a real clock that had a functioning hand, one hundred tamarind seeds, a new top and a black something he had found on the riverbed.

He laid down on the bed, staring up at the ceiling. A tear flowed in self-pity. He picked up the phone and pondered what to do next.

'Here, come with me,' Kittu said, and eyed Arumairajan for a while. Kittu was about fifty years old. He had long, grey sideburns that sprouted like flowers from his ears. There was not much hair left otherwise near the head, which presently reflected the afternoon sun shining over Mambalam. He had a carefully parked kumkum mark on his forehead. He wore a safari suit, and carried a bagful of papers with a bus pass for easy local transport.

'What did you say your name was?'

'Arumairajan.'

'Oh, that's you?'

'You've heard of me?'

'Arun was telling me yesterday that there would be this guy coming from Bangalore.'

Ah, I must tell Mary, Arumairajan thought.

'Come, let's have coffee.'

As they walked towards the bus stop, Kittu spoke. 'Tell me, Rajan, what help can I be?'

Arumairajan perked up. 'I write poems, sir. Arun told me in Bangalore that he would introduce me to Ilayaraja.'

'That's all?'

'I mean, after the intro, if there was somehow a chance to get my song in a movie.'

'Is that all? Sure, we can do that.'

They crossed the Muralikrishna Cinema and had coffee at the corner eatery. On the radio, some woman was singing the Bilahari ragam in an odd hour. Autorickshaw drivers were piling up mounds of rice on their plates, filling up the holes in the middle with sambar and pouring oil on them.

'Have you brought your poems along?'

'Of course, sir.' Arumairajan fished out a notebook.

'You can't hide your talent like this in your banian. But you know, it still won't go waste. Hey, what's hot on the menu?'

'The rava dosa is hot, maama. The rest is just okay.'

'I'll have two roasts,' Kittu said, and turned to Arumairajan. 'And you?'

'Just coffee for me, sir.'

Kittu flipped through the pages of the notebook and read,

'The moon-woman wore moonshine on her eyes

They spread like silk on her self—those blue skies.'

The sound of dosas being made on the griddle filled the air.

'Shaabaash! Wonderful,' Kittu said.

Arumairajan beamed.

'Like the vermillion peaks of a mountain girl's bosoms...'

'No,' said Kittu. 'The bosom part won't get past the censors.'

'We can change that, sir,' Arumairajan said. 'I can change the poems according to the situation. This was just a natural description.'

Kittu patted the notebook with the back of his hand. 'You know, if Kannadasan had written the same stuff today, he would get five thousand rupees.'

'How much would I get?'

'You won't get anything. In the beginning, you are the one who has to pay. That's the sad part. Just wait a minute. Let me check if Raja is free or not. I don't have the change for the phone call. I just have a big note.'

'I'll give you that, sir.'

Kittu went to the cashier's counter and dialled a number on the phone. He laughed as he spoke on the phone and returned after a while.

'He is in the composing session. We can meet him in the evening,' Kittu said.

Arumairajan paid the bill, and the two stepped out of the eatery. Kittu then took him to a lodging house near the corner of Motilal Nehru Road.

'Have you come here alone?' he asked.

'No, sir. With my family. My baby boy has fever.'

They crossed some carpenters at work on the outside, and then a typewriting institute, climbed a narrow staircase and entered a room that said: 'GK International (Prop. G. Krishnamurthy).' Kittu took away an old typewriter and made space for Arumairajan to sit.

'This is our branch office,' he announced. 'The main office is in Mount Road. We also have a branch in Singapore.'

'Is that so?'

'Look here, Arumairajan. You know how may lyricists are there today? About one hundred twenty. In such a place, whatever the level of your talent, if you want to make it, it is not easy. You may have to spend a thousand bucks.'

'Who should I give that money to?'

'To many parties.'

'I was told they pay us…'

'That is after you become famous. You see. all professions involve some investment. The thousand rupees is like that. After that, when you get a thousand bucks a day, if you remember this Kittu, that would be very nice. Right, Rajan?' Kittu said and poked him with a finger on the hip.

'But I don't have a thousand bucks, sir.'

'How much do you have?'

'I have about forty.'

Kittu's face changed suddenly. 'Ah, all right. I think you should return to Bangalore then. You have just enough money for two return tickets.' He paused. 'I was just thinking that a good chance was going to waste...'

'You see, we can meet him this evening itself for an intro and for all you know, a recording may happen tomorrow. You know, Rajan, this has nothing to do with the music director. He just plays with whichever lyricist the producer points to. To meet the producer, you have to see the production manager. And that guy has half-a-dozen sidekicks. It's okay, then. Doesn't matter. If not this month, maybe we can do something next month, or the month after that. You are not going away, and I'm not either.'

Sagaya Mary's bangles now flashed in front of Arumairajan's eyes.

'Can you wait two or three hours?'

'What's the time now?' Kittu shook his watch and checked the time. 'It's 2.30 p.m. now. At 4 p.m., I have another meeting in the industry chamber.'

'I'll be back by then, sir.' Arumairajan rushed out. He actually ran.

The director was correcting the heroine's diction.

'We can fix that in the dubbing,' she told him. 'You know I studied in a convent. I can't get all those Tamil letters. May I go home now?'

'Just one more shot?'

Premalatha made a sad face in mock annoyance and sat on a chair in the corner of the set.

A make-up girl arrived with an elaborate kit and pressed her face with powder puffs. Premalatha picked up a comic book.

'Tarzan, is that you?'

'Jane! What happened?'

Jane pressed her face on Tarzan's chest and said, 'I saw a monstrous man. He had large eyes and was wearing a black hood.'

'Premalatha! There is a phone call for you. It is Arun on the line.'

She dropped everything and ran into the audio studio on the sets where the phone was.

'Hullo!'

'Prem? This is Arun. Uff, catching you on the line is so difficult. Prem…I have a question…'

'What?'

'Will you marry me?'

10

Premalatha's home was on 9th Cross Street in Indira Nagar. The high compound wall and the surrounding bushes properly hid the happenings on the grass lawns inside. Through the only crack from which one could peep in, Chellayee, the beggar girl, was eyeing the hundreds of porcelain plates with pieces of chocolate cakes on them, arranged neatly on white tables. What she fancied, of course, was the soft, dark base of the cakes and the sugary cream that rested above. About a hundred people stood near the table. Electronic flashlights were clicking unobtrusively. Arun, with his arm around Premalatha, practically hugging her, escorted her from inside the house to the lawns, setting the waiting cameras in motion.

Lots of smiles, lots of flashes, gentle rounds of applause and congratulations all round. There were many kisses on the cheeks and bear hugs to match.

'Gentlemen, let us eat,' announced Arun. Everyone rushed to the tables and grabbed a piece of cake each and opened their mouths for big bites. Chellayee watched their jaws move intently, even as waiters attired in maharaja turbans moved with trays of coffee cups. Bhaskar, who stood alone in a corner, watched reporters, friends, cine world crocodiles, directors, co-stars, lyricists and composers in a pan shot. Finally, his eyes rested on Chellayee, peering through the crack, her hands separating the bushes for her to have a better view. He walked up to the table, grabbed a large piece of cake and offered it to her with a signal to eat. The little girl took the piece, her eyes showing amazement, fear, mistrust and happiness all at once. She then rushed off to 10th Cross Street so that she could share it with her younger sister Letchumi, who was busy begging.

'Arun, when is the wedding?' someone asked as the conversations began to flow inside.

'Oh, we actually wanted it yesterday.'

'Some say the wedding is over.'

'No, brother. Do you think we'd do anything without informing you?'

'Has the date been fixed?'

'January,' said Premalatha.

'And where will you be honeymooning?'

'Switzerland.'

'But it's horribly cold there.'

'Will you both continue your acting after the marriage?'

'You know, after marriage, everybody has to act a bit,' said Arun, and added a wink to good effect. He then hugged and smelt his fiancé. The bulbs flashed again. 'Prem has been in my heart for a long while now. I really love her,' he said.

'What do you have to say that, Prema?' asked a reporter

'All of this seems like a dream to me.'

As Arun pinched her bottom, she screeched and said 'Haaa!'

'This is not a dream. This is real,' he said.

'I have four Telugu films, two in Malayalam and four in Tamil. After I finish them all, I am going to stop acting,' she said. 'He can go on acting. I have no objections.'

'And after giving up a career in acting, you'll stay at home?'

'I am going to be his wife and help him,' she said. 'I am also going to have babies. What better fortune could an Indian girl ask for?'

Bhaskar moved off from the scene gently. He went inside the house and dialled a number on the phone inside.

'Ravi! This is Bhaskar. I have to book Rajeswari for January and also arrange a party at the Coromandel.'

As Bhaskar fixed venues for the wedding ceremonies on the phone, the puppy hovering near the table growled and barked a little.

At about the same time, at the AVM recording theatre, another celebration was on. LP (Lakshmanan-Pandurangan) Pictures was launching *Ilanthalaivan.* Strange-looking musical instruments arrived in taxis. A tuft-sporting Iyer priest was offering flowers to a plethora of deities. In the asbestos-covered veranda, filter coffee was flowing like a river through neatly washed steel tumblers, besides '77' and Gold Spot—the recently arrived replacement for Coca Cola and Fanta, now kicked out of the country. The musicians were tuning up their instruments. As someone touched the bass button of the synthesiser, the hall boomed with a rich sound.

Lakshmanan, for a change, was actually wearing a shirt. They were all waiting for the arrival of several industry stalwarts and ministers from the government. Conversation flowed on the planned movie.

'What's the story?' someone asked.

'Oh, it is a bit offbeat.'

'The title sounds like a historical—*Ilanthalaivan*. The story is about a young warrior?'

'No, no, it is a family subject.'

'*Ilanthalaivan*,' said someone, twirling the title on their tongue. 'It seems numerologically sound. But if you add two more letters, it would be ideal.'

'We can't be doing all that now. Let us first find a story.'

'But how can you go to a recording without the story in the first place?'

'Ah, it is only a song. You don't need a story for it. It is a general composition.'

'You know, if we know the lines of the song, it would look good in the press,' said Gnanasekaran.

'Why not? Can be done. Let's have that paper, Pandurangan.'

Gnanasekaran opened the folded paper, which read:

'*He'll do good to all,*

Won't harm anyone by far,

Our Young Warrior,

Our Young Warrior!'

'The first two lines look familiar.'

'What? You are fooling us, right? You know, those read like Subramania Bharati's lines.'

'Oh my God, I hope he doesn't sue us.'

'But he is dead, sir,' someone piped up helpfully

The topic changed. 'Hey,' Lakshmanan asked the reporter. 'You didn't go to Arun's party?'

'Oh, I have not been invited.'

'What? Not invited? You are such a big journalist! They kept even you out?'

'Well,' Gnanasekaran shrugged. 'I have no idea.'

'Filthy snob, that guy.'

Presently, the women arrived, clad in silk saris. Arun continued to be a keen topic of conversation.

'Is it true that he was keeping a mistress in his hometown?'

'True, sir. It's true. I even have a photo of that woman. Her name is Kalyani.'

'Bring it here,' Lakshmanan said. 'Bring it along.'

No one really cared about Manonmani, who was standing in a corner. She had been nursing a migraine since the morning and her head was splitting. Those were familiar signs.

As she wiped the sweat off her brow, she could see Pandurangan at a distance. He was standing under a tree, making grand gestures with his hands and feet. He saw her for a fleeting moment and quickly turned his head away. She was not sure who she was waiting for. Or why. She needed to meet Pandurangan privately and find out.

'This shirt is not good. Let us take it off.'

'We can take this off as well.'

'And this one too.'

'My dear, shall I count? One, two.' Manonmani's body was being touched. Slowly, the forefinger was roaming in slight touches all over.

Manonmani walked slowly and entered the hall. She passed the musicians busy tuning up, sat on a bench beneath a tree and closed her eyes. All sorts of psychedelic colours flashed before her shut eyes: the irresponsible father she had seen as a child, and the way he had brought strange women home. When she'd heard soft laughter in the other room, Manonmani had spent confused nights not knowing what was going on. When her mother packed her off to her uncle's house for her studies, Uncle Gopal said he would show her some tricks and pushed her to the ground and hugged her, and she recalled biting him. Then there were memories of Meera, who she watched through a window as she practised dancing and sensed the lust in her voice that said, 'You want to learn how to dance? Why don't you come home?'

As she was finishing school, one day her father arrived with loads of good things to eat, jasmine flowers and paavadais and half-saris and announced: 'Mano dear, you are getting married. I have brought you a king from Pondicherry. Enough of your studies now.' Her father fought with her uncle and dragged her off to another town and made her sit in front of strange faces. 'You look at this girl? She looks like an apsara. She does all the work at home. She can make upma and chicken curry. Sir, you are lucky. Please come. Manonmani, salute these elders. And this is your groom.'

When she lifted her eyes, she was stunned. A rickety car had stopped outside and from that stepped out an elderly man with grey hair, a diamond ring on his finger. This was the groom her dear father had chosen! The temple was a little far away, waiting for them to arrive for the wedding. The priest had been told to turn up promptly at dawn. 'We need to finish this off fast. Don't blabber and stretch the ceremonies.'

New currency notes were being counted at night. 'Everybody has to be happy tonight!' was an order dipped in whisky.

As her drunk father slept fitfully that night, currency notes popped out of his silk jubba. She ripped off a few from the bundle, quietly opened the back door, crossed the sewer, walked through ghostly coconut palms looming in the night, hid in the stinking ladies' lavatory in the railway station, and as she saw a train ambling through an opening in the red brick wall, she moved out stealthily and got into the ladies' compartment. As the train crawled out slowly, she felt a hand on her shoulder, startling her.

'Amma!'

'Yes, di,' her mother said. 'I am also joining you.'

Manonmani opened her eyes as the sound of clapping hands filled the air. Vijayaraja was walking in from the next set, his make-up still on. They were honouring him with a garland that matched his huge build. Pandurangan and Lakshmanan posed next to him and Manonmani approached them.

'Who is the second heroine?' she heard someone ask.

'There is a college girl called Usha. She looks like Hema Malini from an angle, and she dances well. Doesn't know

Tamil too well, but she speaks well. We can write the script in English and make her read that.'

Manonmani stepped even closer now.

'Mr Pandurangan, will you come here? What did you tell me that day? You told me you'd give me that role—and you made me do so many things in that room. Should I tell all the folks here? Shall I?' There were many things she felt like saying aloud but did not. She quietly left the studio and walked on.

'Shall we go by taxi?' the familiar cabbie asked her.

'No, Chinnaraju!'

'Should I come near your place at 9 p.m.?'

'No, Chinnaraju. Not today.'

'You're not well, my daughter? Take care of your health. You don't have to pay me the fare. I'll just drop you home.'

As Manonmani returned home in a taxi, on the other side of town, Arun and Bhaskar were returning home in their car.

'What, Bhaskar? You are not saying much. You're not happy?'

'Chee, chee, no. Nothing like that.'

'I had to get married someday, no?'

'Arun, let me be frank. You've done this in great haste. Why this hurry? What for? I just don't understand. You are at the peak of your career now. No one has the kind of movies you have on hand now. You've actually just begun acting. All these days you were merely sporting nice outfits and dancing. To talk of marriage at this stage…'

'Can't I act after getting married? What nonsense are you speaking? Your worries are unwarranted. You are a pessimist by birth. Relax, Bhaskar.'

Bhaskar laughed gently.

'Aah, you are smiling. So rare, like the moon on Eid,' Arun joked.

'I think I am going to lose my job,' Bhaskar said. 'Your future wife is already announcing that she is going to look after your affairs.'

'Chee! You know that won't happen. She is a lazy bum. I know her well.'

'That's what you think, Arun. I remember what I read once about Clark Gable.'

'What was that?'

'Clark Gable never really married anyone. A number of women married him. He just went along with the gag.'

11

ON THE REAR SIDE OF that ramshackle 'hotel' on the road connecting the Madras Central railway station to Egmore, rooms were available for five rupees a day. The common toilet that served ten rooms was filled with the stench of ammonia. If you walked past a wall that had not seen a whitewash, after passing through a wet passage (beware of the moss!), and opened a tin door corroded by salty winds, you would come to the room where they were staying. Inside, Sagaya Mary, Arumairajan's wife, squatted on the floor and tried to pacify her wailing child, patting its back and humming, hoping that would put the infant to rest. The jewellery around her neck was gone, given to her husband. At this point, she had no interest in the jewels or her husband's grand plan to earn big money by writing song lyrics. She was ranting: 'Look at this child. Can his body take such a high fever? Can a baby weep so much? Can it be in spasms like this? Where the hell is this man? Why has he not returned after leaving with the doctor? Why did the doctor not speak to me? Why did he take him along like that? Oh, Lord, if the baby gets cured, I will make a pilgrimage to Velankanni. I must offer gold at the shrine.'

At the doorstep of the hotel, shady men with beedis on their lips were getting ready for sinful acts. The doctor solemnly told Arumairajan: 'The baby has really severe jaundice. It's too late.'

'Shall we take him to General Hospital right away?' Arumairajan asked.

'It is of no use,' the doctor said.

'Will the child die?' Arumairajan asked, almost in tears.

'Looks like that,' the doctor said. 'Please don't cry. Are you here on your own? Are you new to Madras?'

Arumairajan, in tears, nodded. 'My wife's cousin is in Perambur. Doctor, is there no hope?'

'Sorry. I don't want to lie to you.'

Arumairajan cried copiously. A woman with a big bindi, chewing betel leaves and sporting a flowered voile sari, stared at him for a while and then moved inside.

'Can I help you in anyway?' the doctor asked.

'Is there a Catholic church nearby, doctor?'

'Go straight from here, and there is a church opposite the Government Arts College. May I take your leave now?'

Mary was startled as she saw the priest arrive with Arumairajan. She burst into tears. 'His breath is ebbing,' she said. 'And his head is sagging.'

'You've brought him this far. You didn't even take him to a hospital for treatment,' the worried priest said.

'We have no one, Father.'

'Louis! Dominic Louis!' Mary was sobbing uncontrollably. The child was steadily giving up on its battle to survive.

'My son, Father, my son! He's not even twenty days old.'

'Please don't cry, my dear. This child is like an angel of the supreme God. What sin did it commit? None at all. Do you know that the kingdom of God awaits him? When this little baby gives up its ghost and rises, angels in heaven shall receive him at a golden door. What did you say his name was?'

'Louis Dominic Arumairajan.'

'Louis Dominic Arumairajan, go in peace unto Jesus. Let your soul rest with the supreme God.'

As the priest rubbed holy oil on the infant, the little breeze called life's breath left him for its journey into the infinite.

As Arumairajan banged his head on the wall, from the next room, he heard a harsh voice. 'You, you better pay the amount you had agreed for.'

Louis Dominic Arumairajan, born in Bangalore and having lived for all of eighteen days, was interred in a cemetery on the outskirts of Madras in a very small coffin.

'From earth you came, to earth you go. Rest in peace with God!' the priest murmured. Sagaya Mary sat in a corner of the street outside the cemetery. Her breasts were oozing mother's milk, drenching her blouse.

The invitation from Arun Vijay was terse.

Dear Friend,

As you know, I am marrying Premalatha. Please come for the wedding and the cultural programme thereafter.

– Arun Vijay

Place: Rajeshwari

Day: Sunday, 7-10-1979

Muhurtham: 10.30 a.m. to 11.30 a.m.

Reception: 6.30 p.m.

RSVP: 441978

The invitation was being printed in golden letters at RJ Press. At the same time, at Srirangam's Sri Vani Vilas Printers, a clunky machine was gently pressing rose-and-yellow invites in Tamil letters one at a time

'In the coming month of Purattasi, on Sunday the 21st, on an auspicious day with Scorpio in the ascendant, my sister Sowbhagyawathi Kalyani, the elder daughter of Uttamarkovil Sivasankaran, shall be given away in marriage to Chiranjeevi Viswanathan, the second son of Mannargudi Rangaswamy Iyer (retired tehsildar), as decided by our elders…'

In order to enjoy his twenty-day honeymoon, Arun shuffled his call sheets, packing in two or three shifts a day, until his unslept eyes burned and his weary legs ached.

Premalatha, with the intent of fulfilling her commitments, was also slogging to complete the films she had on hand. From Hyderabad, she phoned Arun regularly, making a trunk call every 30 minutes. 'Arun! Guess what I am doing now?'

'How am I supposed to know?'

'I am in the shower! I am dripping, and calling you from the bathroom.'

'Oh, I can hear the glug-glug,' Arun said. 'Prema, dear, do me a favour. Why don't you call ten minutes later? I have eight people with me. We are all serious and want to finish off what we are doing tonight.'

'So the story discussion is more important than me?'

'I didn't say that, darling. Look here, just tell me what number you are calling from and I shall call back.'

'No, I won't tell you. No way! I am upset with you.'

'Shall I put the phone down?'

'So soon?'

'Talk then.'

And Premalatha talked on. Arun held on to the call with his 'Hmms' and covered the mouth of the receiver and told the men to go on.

The screenplay-dialogue-director man said, 'Then both of them leave for Ooty. He becomes the gardener in her house.'

'Who?'

'This man.'

'Okay.'

'The girl is rich. How shall it work out? You see, they are so apart in social status and cultural habits.'

'Indeed, how will they accept this in society?' Arun said, but was lost in his own personal world on the phone.

'And you know, I have bought eight new saris already. Arun, my dear, my lollipop! Sweetie pie. Tch, tch.' Prema's affections were overflowing.

'Are you eating the phone or something?' Arun asked.

'No, sir. Why do you ask?'—the lines were crossed as the director replied from his own universe.

'Oh, not you, sir. You go on. You were on about culture.'

'As you know, they don't match in traditions. At this time, you know what happens? The villain, our Vijayan, turns up in Ooty on a business trip.'

Arun's mind was neither on the story nor on the phone call. It was wandering around Uttarmarkovil.

They were polishing old kitchenware in Uttarmarkovil, making them all shine anew. Kalyani's grandmother's jewels had been melted and made into new designs, with the jeweller sitting on the front veranda, blowing his pipe through husks of bran. Kaveri Ammal had been informed about the milk. They picked leaves from the temple garden and applied mehndi on each one of Kalyani's fingers and toes. Her father went to Lalgudi and brought home utensils for the wedding feast from his elder brother's home. A hundred coconuts had been ordered. They were all building up to the wedding, like sparrows building nests. The bride and her friends were busy chatting.

'Kalyani, is it true that the first night is on the day of the wedding?'

'Go away!'

'What do they do on that night?'

'Who?'

'Aaah, look at the way she pretends!'

'Don't you know? You've seen a lot of movies, no?'

'But Chitra told me it is not like in the movies, you know?'

'Chee! Don't you have anything else to talk about?'

'They have decided to marry me off in the coming Chittirai. My akka has promised to teach me everything.'

'What's that? Filmalaya? New issue?'

'Yup. Look at this! Arun—the man from our town.'

Arun was filling up a page against a red velvet backdrop. The picture was printed to perfection, as if he was emerging out of the page in three dimensions.

'Kalyani. you tell me. You are an educated girl. What do you say? Tell me if you like this or not.'

She tried to alter the face in that picture and tried to visualise Viswanathan in Arun's place. It was difficult. She had seen Viswanathan for all of five minutes. She could not recall his face exactly. She had mostly had her head bent down and had looked up at him just once. He had large eyes peering in from behind his glasses. His hair was oiled and combed down as if stuck with glue. The very clean all-soaped-up Viswanathan.

My mother and father will only do good to me. They have enquired about the family and the gotra and chosen an appropriate groom for me. Chee! It is wrong to desire him. Forget him now!

'Let's go to the temple, di,' someone said.

'When is the wedding, man?'

'The seventh. You didn't get the invitation?'

'Why should he send me an invite, man? You know I don't get along with him. He has snubbed me, remember? Hmm. Even if he invites me and sends me an Ambassador Mark IV to bring to the function, do you think I am going? Tell me, Gnanasekaran, did you get an invite?'

'I have not been invited either, saar. But maybe he has sent one. I haven't looked at the post today.'

'You won't get one. After all, you wrote that stuff about him in *Devi.*'

'Yes, seems like it.'

'But what you wrote has come true, no? The two of them are getting married. The whole outrage has fizzled out.'

Lakshmanan opened a paan-beeda from a packet and pushed it into his mouth. As the tobacco inside stirred a river of spit, he kept quiet for a while.

'What happened to your film, sir?'

'Hmm.'

'Will it make it for a Pongal release?'

'Hmm.'

'I heard you have not selected a heroine yet.'

'Hmm.'

Lakshmanan pushed his neck out of the room's window and spat out the stuff. 'Hey, forget about my movie. That is going to drag on. You said you wanted to show me some photo.'

Gnanansekaran plucked out a palm-sized photograph from his backpack and gave it to Lakshmanan. It was taken from a distance at the AVM Studios by a sharp camera with a telephoto lens. It was crystal clear.

Kalyani stood in a side profile and Arun was looking at her. The lensman had smartly captured that moment.

'Is this the girl?'

'Yes sir.'

'Real stuff this is. This is the one he is doing it with in his town?'

'That's what they say.'

'Aah, he is quite a playboy. You have to be lucky for this kind of stuff. Gnanam, you leave this picture with me. Pay off the photographer—whatever is needed.'

'What are you going to do with it?'

'I am going to use it, what else? I have to get it out in the right magazine at the right time. When did you say the wedding was? Sunday the seventh?'

'Let's not do it, sir. Something might go awry.'

'I'll take care of all that.'

'Please keep my name out of this.'

'Tchai! Nothing of that sort. What did you say the girl's name was?'

'Kalyani.'

'Will she act in our movie? Why don't you find out? You have the address?'

'She is an Iyer girl studying in a college, Trichy district. That kind won't act in the movies. Let me take your leave now.'

After he left, Lakshmanan kept staring at the photo for a while. The light green telephone in the room buzzed ever so softly.

'This is Bhagyam. Are you coming home for dinner?'

'No, dear. I have some important work. Why don't you send it over?'

'Will you be home at night at least?'

'Let's see. Has Babu gone to sleep?'

The way she hung up without replying told him how angry she was.

Lakshmanan put the phone down and reclined on the bed. There was a knock at the door.

'Who is it?'

'It is me, Manonmani, sir.'

The girl more or less forced herself into the room.

12

LAKSHMANAN DID NOT LOOK AT Manonmani entering the room hesitantly and said, 'What?'

Her hair was tousled. She was sweating. Her nail polish looked scraped. 'You said you'd give me a part in *Ilanthalaivan*.'

Lakshmanan felt aroused by the patches of sweat on her blouse. 'We can do it. We certainly can. Venu is the one looking after the casting. Have you seen him?'

'I did.'

'What did he say?'

'He did not say anything, but…'

Lakshmanan hurriedly took an envelope out of his khadi shirt hanging in the coat stand and asked, 'Have you got any money for your expenses?' When she did not reply, he said, 'Keep one hundred rupees. Go home now and wash your face and wear a nice sari. We can take a screen test.'

'But they've already done that. He made me stand and walk, the director.'

'I have changed the director, no?' Lakshmanan's face turned a little stern. 'I'll have nothing to do with that arrogant guy. He fights with everyone. He says he will cast his brother-in-law as the hero, or he wants Naseeruddin Shah from Bombay. He wants no make-up for the artistes. I am thinking of casting my driver as the hero. But these distributors insist on Arun. And I don't even have a story. I just have the titles. So much hassle. Hmm. Come here now. Why don't you massage my fingers a bit?'

Manonmani, without moving, said, 'What do you have to say to me?'

'I have considered it. I have changed the director. This is a new guy who has worked with Bhagyaraj, from Madurai. You meet him once.'

Manonmani started off, looking weary.

'You don't want the money?'

She turned around, looked at him and said, 'The money? What for? To act?'

'Of course, what else? Keep it. You are like my daughter.'

'Even Venugopal said that. He called me daughter all the time. He did not even send an invite for the poojai.'

'You didn't get it? How can that be? I'll ask that chap, Ganapathi.'

She saw his eyes roam all over her body. She knew he was not going to commit to anything. He wrote an address on a piece of paper. 'This is the address for L.V. Pictures. You go there and...'

Before he could finish, Manonmani walked away, not caring about the paper. She had now understood the rules of this game. Nobody really said no. Lakshmanan would pack her off to see Venugopal, who would send her to a production manager, and that man would not be at home at all. No one would know when the shoot would take place. Suddenly they'd say, 'Outdoor!' and then do the shooting inside a house in Mylapore. Whenever they got a chance, they would offer some money, ask her to change her sari and show up somewhere.

She walked slowly. The taxi driver's grin showed she had sized her up as a streetwalker. 'This one is on the take,' he seemed to say.

As cars whizzed above the flyover at Gemini Square, under it a woman with scattered hair was lighting a makeshift stove with wood. She had an aluminium pan, two bricks, a mat, a husband, and around her waist, a little baby sucking her breasts like a province breaking away from a country. As she looked up and eyed Manonmani for a fleeting second, Manonmani felt a kind of happiness. She stood at the bus stop, not sure of her purpose. In front of her, twenty-foot cut-outs of actors towered above gleaming letters that advertised flopped movies. The bus wouldn't come. She started to walk again. Her slippers snapped again. She took a safety pin from the chain around her neck to fix the break.

A middle-aged man approached the taxi driver who had grinned at her. The man was sporting a muslin jubba through which shone a gold chain. He had talcum powder on his face and some moisturiser. His hair was well combed. He smelt of some cologne.

'Are you coming?' he asked the taxi driver, who looked about thirty years old.

'Where, sir?'

'Wherever you say,' he said.

'I don't get it.'

The man in the silk jubba got into the taxi and flipped open a gold-plated cigarette case he'd taken out of his pocket. He picked a long-stemmed cigarette, tapped it and put it on his lips. He patiently lit the cigarette and asked, 'What's the going rate?'

'For whom? What are you talking about, sir?'

'Don't pretend you don't know,' the man said and pressed a fifty-rupee note in the driver's hand, crumpling it a little.

'Oh, that!' the taxi driver said, shifting gears, and revved up the car. 'I just saw one going past,' he told the passenger. 'Virugampakkam. Shall we check her out?'

'Oh, sure.'

'You know, one night, I dropped off a white man at Palm Grove. I have to tell you what happened then…' the taxi driver said, opening up. 'You smell really good, durai.'

Manonmani, wanting to enter G.N. Chetty Road, clutching one of her slippers in her hands, turned into a lane, walking in the dark.

'You know, the white man says, "Gopalu, I see London, I see Paris but Madras women very good."'

'Really?'

'You've got to admit their style. They light cigarettes with hundred-rupee notes. Where is durai from? Coimbatore?'

'No. I am a local, Egmore side.'

'Aah. That's why you looked familiar. Look, the one entering the lane, she is the one.'

Manonmani walked close to the walls of the lane. Her feet were aching without the slippers she was used to. She felt needle-like pricks under her feet. The taxi pulled up and a voice said: 'Hey Kamala, where are you off to?'

'Home,' she said hesitantly.

'The car's going that side. Hop in.'

The taxi driver looked familiar. She did not see the face of the man sitting in a corner in the dark. Uncomfortable without her slippers, she opened the door and looked startled.

'He is our man, get in,' the driver said.

Manonmani huddled in a corner of the seat. The smell of cologne assaulted her nose. The car started off.

'Tell me, dear. Where do we go? To my place or some hotel?'

'What are you talking about?' Manonmani asked.

'I'll tell you where to go,' the man in the muslin jubba said. 'Drive to the police station.'

'What? Are you kidding me?'

'I am telling you now—go!' the man snapped at the driver.

'What's this mess? You get out of the cab now.'

'I am telling you to drive on. You know who I am? The superintendent of police.'

The next day, in a corner of a match-box flat in the Integral Coach Factory housing colony at Perambur, Arumairajan sat with his hands on his head. Sagaya Mary sat next to him, staring into emptiness. Her cousin, her uncle's son who worked in the factory canteen, was scolding Arumairajan.

'How could you do something ridiculous like that? You should not have brought the baby here in the first place. Just an infant! All right, you brought it here, so? Could you not have come here? Are we not family? Did you have to stay in a hotel? I wouldn't let my sister down, would I? It's true we fought over some four thousand rupees in the past. But this is something else, my son-in-law. Am I not right, Mary?'

Mary did not respond. 'My child!' she said.

'You've wailed so much for eight days, sister. You'll spoil your health like this.'

'So what?' she said.

'Peter, you know that man had taken my money and asked me to come over for the recording. In that situation, I could not go,' Arumairajan said.

'Yes...right,' Mary spoke up now in a numb tone. 'That's all that matters to you.'

'No, Mary. I had sold off your jewels, no? Is it not my responsibility to get it back somehow?'

Mary said nothing. Another wave of sorrow assaulted her. 'Louis Dominic!' she cried and broke into a new spasm of sobbing.

'You carry on and take care of your work,' Peter said. 'I'll take care of my sister. She has not eaten anything. Look here, Mary, it was an infant and it has gone to heaven.'

'They will hold a prayer for the baby in November, the priest said. They have an empire waiting for my prince there. They even have a golden cradle there for him, it seems. And I can't rock it! Why did they need MY little one? He had not even started smiling. He had large eyes and kept looking at the light and us. Oh God, the fever, it was so horrible!' Mary, engulfed in an ocean of grief, cried, tears flowing down her cheeks, her nose puffed up.

'You go, please,' Peter told Arumairajan. 'When she looks at you, my sister cries even more.'

Arumairajan got out of the house and waited for a bus to arrive. Across the road, they were opening the shutters at Karuna Bakery. The dust swept off near a paan shop glittered like gold in the morning light. Words flowed inside him.

'He bloomed to give much joy,
Oh, my lovely little boy.'

A bus came along, and he got in. Arumairajan really had no clue where to look for that Kittu. He hung around Arun's house for a day or two, but the gates did not open. Coloured bulbs glowed inside, and they seemed to be celebrating something. Where would Ilayaraja be now? He wished he could meet him without middlemen and tell him, 'I'm sorry I could not make it the other day. There was a tragedy in my family. My child, my little boy, left me—God took him back. And that's why I could not make it.' *Kittu must have arranged it all that day*, Arumairajan thought. To think, artistes of the calibre of Raja had been made to wait because of him! 'I must explain everything to him,' Arumairajan said to himself. 'But where on earth can I find him?' He did not quite know where the studios would be. Kodambakkam? Well, probably. He must be there.

'Kodambakkam?' the bus conductor laughed out loud and tore of a ticket. 'Get off at Parry's!' He grabbed a one-rupee note from him and fished out the change from the leather bag he shook.

Arumairajan was looking at the hoardings that whizzed past him. 'Learn English in One Month,' and such. Nothing really registered in his mind, but the words inside were flowing out well.

He bloomed to give much joy.
Oh, my lovely little boy.
He couldn't rest in his mother's lap,
He died, the impatient boy.

'Louis!' he said to himself.

The bus had reached Parry's Corner. The driver, the conductor and all the passengers had moved out. Arumairajan sat still inside the empty bus.

Pop! The cork broke off and the liquor fizzed out. 'Bottoms up!' they said a while later.

Arun and Bhaskar were in an air-conditioned room amid the city's heat, celebrating Arun's last day as a bachelor somewhat quietly. Bhaskar always went for a non-alcoholic ale. As a grand exception to mark the wedding, he was sipping a beer today. Arun, as ever, was sipping Scotch.

'My friend! You know, there was once a guy in a play. He could talk aloud only when he was drunk. When he was sober, he would start blabbering. I am like him. When I am one drink down, everything looks crystal clear to me, Bhaskar.'

'Well, you can't drink anymore.'

'Why? We will drink together.'

'You don't know Premalatha.'

'Bhaskar! Let me tell you one thing. Nothing is going to change in this house because I am getting married. Understand?'

'Let's hope so.'

'What do you mean? Is this not MY house?'

'Of course it is.'

'I am the king in this house, okay?' Arun poured himself another Scotch, dropped an ice cube into the glass and gulped it down. The potion hit him and he was quiet for a while.

'You are drinking as if it was your last day. Easy, baby, easy.'

Arun squatted on the bed. 'Bhaskar! I haven't asked for a single thing until today. I asked for something only once and I didn't get it.'

'And what was that?'

'I asked Kalyani, "Will you marry me? Marry me?"' He slurred as the Scotch slowed him down.

'Okay, so you asked, and she said no?'

'She did not say no. You know, she has those parents. She says she follows her mother and father. I mean, I said, "Aren't you an educated girl? Don't you have an opinion of your own? Will you go to the toilet only after asking your parents?"'

'All that is over now, Arun. What's the point in repeating it now?'

Glug! Another gulp of Scotch. 'Bhaskar, I want her. Get her, Bhaskar!'

'Look, Arun. You are getting married tomorrow—to someone else. This is not the kind of stuff you should be talking about now. In any case, it is not you talking—it is the Scotch.'

'Get her, Bhaskar. Bring her to me!'

'All right. You want her? Okay, we'll talk about it in the morning.'

'It's wedding time in the morning. Cheers! Let's have one more, Bhaskar!'

'The bottle's over.'

'Get a new one.'

'Okay, I will. You lie down now.'

'Kalyani is getting married in the morning,' Arun announced.

The telephone rang and Bhaskar answered. 'Arun, this is Prema,' the voice at the other end said.

'This is not Arun—it's Bhaskar.'

'Bhaskar! What are you doing in his bedroom?' Premalatha screeched.

'Arun is asleep.'

'Wake him up, Bhaskar.'

'I don't think I can right now.'

'Bhaskar, are you going to wake him up now or not?'

'I didn't say I can't wake him up now, did I? It's rather late, Prema. He is tired.'

Premalatha slammed the phone down. 'Ma, I have to get rid of this Bhaskar first,' she said.

13

Arumairajan stood outside Prasad Studios, watching cars go in and out. There were those on foot who managed to get in, and it seemed that he was the only one the watchman would not let in. Mustering up some courage, he went up to the guard. 'I have to see this gentleman called Kittu…'

'Who is Kittu?'

'He is a fair-skinned man, bald, wearing a new shirt.'

'I don't know him. Clear off. This is the time the boss arrives.'

'Where are the other studios?'

A taxi-load of giggling girls, all wearing make-up, went inside.

'There is Prakash nearby. Most of the studios are on Arcot Road. Vijaya, Vauhini, AVM, Vasu, Bharani…'

He asked around in each one of them, and until the midday heat assaulted his head, there was no news of Kittu. Pangs of hunger clawed him inside. If he ate a masala dosa with the change left in his pocket, he would not be able to make it to Perambur again. He bought himself salted peanuts for four annas from a street vendor. Suddenly, he spotted

Kittu, reclining on the backseat of a rickety taxi at the petrol pump. He ran to catch him.

'Kittu saar, Kittu saar.'

Kittu turned around. 'Who are you?'

'Don't you recognize me, sir? Arumairajan. I write songs.'

'Oh, Rajan! Hey, what happened to you that day? Why didn't you come? You know the orchestra was waiting, all set for you.'

'My baby died, sir.'

'We were waiting for you, and I had given them my word. I was really hassled. Krishnamurthy, one has to keep one's word, no?' Kittu asked the man seated next to him.

The said Krishnamurthy sat quiet, reading a comic book.

'When should I come again, sir?' Arumairajan asked. He was a little scared about asking for the thousand rupees back, fearing it might botch up matters.

'What day is it today, Rajan?'

'Thursday.'

'Come at 6.30 p.m. sharp on Saturday, okay?'

'Okay, sir.'

It was only after the taxi had left that Arumairajan realized he had not asked where he was supposed to turn up. He ran after the taxi but could not spot it in a group of yellow-topped ones. He stood in the shade of the bus stand across the road and munched his peanuts. 'Chee! What kind of a fool am I? In this fast-paced world, Kittu is such a busy man. I should have got the details from him,' he told himself. 'I have already blown one chance. The second one seems to be slipping away as well.'

Inside a glass case nearby, a wood board mannequin with a picture of Hema Malini stuck on its face stood wearing a green sari. It would look good on Sagaya Mary, but the price tag said one hundred and fifty rupees. Oh, he thought, there were once times when songwriters were honoured with silk shawls by kings. Arumairajan saw buses he did not recognize come and go. He walked in the general direction in which Kittu's taxi had gone slowly, and a little further, there was a severe traffic jam. All sorts of vehicles were blowing their horns. Kittu's taxi was stranded in the middle of the road, and its driver had his head under the bonnet, trying to fix something in the engine. Kittu and Krishnamurthy stood nearby, hands on their hips.

'Kittu saar, Kittu saar!' Arumairajan cried, nearing him.

Kittu turned around and said, 'Oh, it's you. Finally here.'

'You forgot to say where to meet you on Saturday.'

'I told you, AVM complex. RR Studio.'

'And then, sir…'

'Are you talking of the money? Don't worry, it is safe. They usually ask for a thousand bucks. But I told them you were new, and we need to encourage new poets and fixed it at seven hundred fifty rupees.' He patted his packet. 'The balance is safe. If you can muster up another five hundred, we can do two songs. A single song won't have that large an impact.'

'I simply have no money, sir,' Arumairajan pleaded. 'I am now struggling for my next meal—I am also staying with distant relatives. If something does not work out in the next week, I am in deep trouble. In fact, if you could return that two hundred fifty rupees, it would be a great help. If the lyrics and meaning are strong, even one song can take us far, no?' he said, addressing Krishnamurthy, hoping for some kind of support.

'Why don't you check the carburettor?' Krishnamurthy said to the driver, seeming to avoid Arumairajan.

'No, the pump has heated up,' the driver announced. 'It is also guzzling loads of oil. I've told the owner a month ago.' The driver took off his vest, went to a nearby eatery, drenched it in water and came back to wrap it around the faulty pump.

Kittu continued, 'It's not just the two hundred fifty rupees, I can refund you all one thousand. I have no intention of playing with your money, but if you count the trips I made to Ilayaraja's house and the cash I spent on taxis, the rent I paid for that Yamaha and the advance I paid the orchestra guys, you owe me a hundred and fifty rupees. We've begun all this and paid the advance, right? Why don't you show up on Saturday?'

The engine, by now cooled down, sprang into life in a cloud of smoke. 'It's fixed now,' the driver announced.

'You want to join me now for a recording, Arumairajan?'

'Sure, sir!'

'Hop in, then.'

Seated inside the cab, Arumairajan felt a surge of pride. As the taxi entered the studio compound, the guard saluted them. Cine world! he thought, *here I come!*

Some fifteen people from the groom's family turned up on the Trichy–Lalgudi passenger train. Sundaram had welcomed them at the railway station and had chaperoned them all the way back home. All the single-bullock carts in Uttamarkovil were ready for the event. At the railway station, the musician tuned up the nadaswaram and played Kalyani ragam. 'Do you recognize it?' Sundaram asked the groom.

'I don't know anything about Carnatic music,' Viswanathan replied.

The marquee for the wedding more or less blocked the whole street. The much-welcomed groom's party had been parked in a neighbour's home. Pots of kaapi were sent to the gang. In the open space in the backyard, sambar was boiling in large pans perched on makeshift stoves. The town's widows chatted non-stop as they chopped vegetables. Kids from the city swung back and forth in home swings that they had never seen before.

They made Kalyani sit in the large storeroom and braided her hair with fragrant yellow thalampoo flowers. They clucked their tongues to ward off evil eyes and made small dark spots on her cheek and forehead. The groom's uncle was keen to know where in the Trichy area he could get his flavoured tobacco. Little Ambi wanted to know which cinema hall in Trichy was showing *Kali Kovil Kabali* so that he could catch the movie. As Sundaram returned after arranging supplies of milk, he stopped at Achuthan's shop to enquire about the betel leaves.

'Sister's photo has appeared in a magazine,' Achuthan announced.

'You have a sister?'

'Not my sister, your sister. Kalyani.'

'What's this, man? What are you talking about?'

'Look at this!' Achuthan flipped open a copy of *Cinemalaya.* The page was filled with images of Arun and Kalyani. This was a photo shot with a telephoto lens when Kalyani had visited the AVM Studios to watch some movie being filmed. As Kalyani and Arun eyed each other with affection in the picture, the elaborate description below left little to the imagination: 'They say this girl was among those who have been close to Arun Vijay. Her name is Kalyani, and she is a college student from Trichy. What is she trying to say? "Is it fair to reject me and marry someone else?" Rumours that the two had been married earlier are false. But it is true that Arun made a special trip to see her before his wedding.'

Sundaram's blood boiled. 'Rascal!' he said. 'Achu, how many copies of this magazine do you have?'

'About fifteen, they're selling well.'

'How many have you sold?'

'Oh, it just arrived. Sampath took one copy with him.'

'Give me all the remaining copies. Is there any other shop selling this stuff?'

'Not in our town.'

'Wretched guys. How can they do this?'

'Who are you swearing at, sir?'

'The guys who printed this. Bloody liars! Okay, put all the copies on my account.'

Achuthan took all the issues of *Cinemalaya* off the clips they were hanging from. 'Should I pack them?'

With the bundle under his arm, Sundaram returned home. 'By this time, Sampath would have gone to Trichy,' he told himself. 'I must catch him when he returns.'

Sundaram felt furious at Arun. He must have done it on purpose! What a cheap thing to do! Chee! He never thought Arun would sink so low—not in his wildest dreams! He rushed off to the telegraph office and filled up a form.

'For heaven's sake, stop further publication of photo and drivel appearing in recent Cinemalaya. Don't take undue revenge and create mental agony—Sundaram.' the telegram read.

He felt at ease after sending the telegram, but his hands were still shaking. The monster! Vicious man!

'Hey Sundaram! Where did you vanish? Everybody is looking for you. The groom's party wants warm water.'

'Wait! I am coming.'

'What's that bundle under your arm? Why don't you put that aside?'

I just won't do that, he said to himself. *The wedding muhurtham is in the morning and here is this photo. He has done this on purpose!*

He went to where the groom's party was staying and asked the groom, 'Which magazines do you read?'

'Who has the time for all that?' Viswanathan said, and added: 'I do read *Sunday* and *New Delhi*.'

'And in Tamil?'

'*Kalaimagal*. But only rarely.'

Sundaram heaved a sigh of relief. 'What about film magazines?'

'I don't read them at all,' the groom said. 'But I do watch movies. It seems Arun is from your town.'

'Yes, Uncle,' a voice explained to the groom. 'Look there, the house across the street. That's supposed to be his place.'

'You know him?'

'Yes, I do.'

'He is so famous! To think that he came from such a small place…amazing! He is a good actor. Did you watch *Vayasukku Vandha Ponnu*?'

'No.'

'Does he ever visit?'

'He does.'

Sundaram thought for a moment. *Should I tell him? Is this the right moment? Hmm, no. It's too big a risk. Let the wedding get over first. If he clears the air after that and separates rumour from fact, the groom will be satisfied. After all, he looks like a simple guy—a nice guy, in fact. Good family and all that. But there's no point in hiding the truth for long. One can tell the truth right away, but his parents may not be able to stomach it. It is better to inform them that the two knew each other as kids rather than let them discover the truth. But when should I tell them?*

Sundaram felt miserable.

'Why are you looking so upset?' someone asked.

'No, it's nothing really.'

'Where is the groom? We need him to begin the sankalpams.'

After that, until the beginning of the wedding procession that night, Sundaram forgot about the magazine and the feelings it had stirred. He felt elated when his sister, all decked up in a new sari, came out of her room, greeted the people around her and sat next to Viswanathan who was wearing a new suit. Kalyani looked beautiful. Suddenly, Sundaram felt a pang in his stomach.

She had the good features of both her parents. Her nose was chiselled, and there was a glow of youth in the corner of her lips, the curves of her fleshy cheeks and the shape of her forehead. Sundaram was worried about his sister who was standing at the threshold of a blissful married life.

Viswanathan, the groom, was eyeing the bride seated next to him in various mental visuals. 'Aah, I am so lucky. Is she really going to be mine?' he said to himself. 'I shall guard her as if she was a delicate flower. I'll get her everything she wants. I'll work night and day and build us a house. I'll decorate it so well and will take care of her as if she was a pearl. I am so lucky! She is a gift that God has given me.'

As Ambi returned from Trichy, where he had gone to watch the matinee show, he picked up a copy of *Cinemalaya* at the railway station. On the train, he slowly flipped through its pages.

After he crossed the page where the dancer Gracie was holding forth about how her life resembled a cabaret girl's, there was one where Sripriya and Sumitra were striking glamorous poses.

They say this girl was among those who have been close to Arun Vijay. Her name is Kalyani, and she...

Kalyani? The name sounded familiar.

At roughly the same time as Ambi was reading that issue of *Cinemalaya*, Sundaram's telegram was delivered to Arun's home. It lay piled up in a bunch of greeting telegrams and awaited the arrival of Bhaskar, who was busy on the phone.

'This is different,' he was saying. 'Call it a mini honeymoon. Switzerland. And register the names as Mr and Mrs Shekhar. We want to keep it private.'

Bhaskar flipped through identical greeting telegrams with their lotus designs as he spoke. 'I thought they'd wait till January. But then they insisted on October. I had so much trouble booking Rajeshwari…wait a minute, I'll call you back.'

He put the phone down and opened the beige telegram from Sundaram that stood apart in the pile. He read its contents but could not figure out what had happened. He picked up the phone.

'Prema, it's Bhaskar. Is Arun there?'

'He is asleep. I don't want to wake him up. Is this about the photo in *Cinemalaya*?' she asked.

'I haven't seen it.'

'Who is this Kalyani?'

'Why don't you ask Arun? But don't believe what they write in the magazines. These journalists have no sense.'

'Ah, okay. I don't care about it anyway,' Premalatha said.

Ambi entered the wedding marquee, took a look at Kalyani and looked stunned for a moment. Then, he went up to the groom. 'Visu,' he said, 'I have to show you something.'

14

VISWANATHAN, THE GROOM, LOOKED AT the picture in *Cinemalaya* and could not believe his eyes. Was that the girl he was going to marry? 'What's this?' he asked Ambi.

'Visu, did you see?' Ambi replied. 'It seems your would-be wife is famous.'

'What do you mean?'

'Look what is written below!'

Visu looked at the caption: '*Is she asking: Is it fair to reject me and marry someone else?*'

'Oh, hell!'

'I think it is safe to inform your father,' Ambi said.

'If Appa hears about this now, he'll say "Stop this marriage at once!" Let's talk to Sundaram first. Why don't you bring him here?'

'But we must leave for the temple as the wedding procession. How can we all sit here like this?' someone from the wedding troupe piped up.

'Hey! There is a bigger problem at hand—just relax for a moment.'

Sundaram arrived just then and saw the magazine at once.

'Mr Sundaram, I have to ask you something.'

'Is it about the photo?'

'Yes. Why didn't you tell me about this before?'

'I saw it only today myself.'

'I don't mean the photo. I mean this stuff...'

'What stuff?'

'This thing between your sister and Arun. I feel embarrassed to even mention it.'

'Aah! Do you really believe this bilge?'

'They can't be lying, no?'

'Viswanathan, let me ask you something. Are you from Mannargudi?'

'Yes, of course.'

'When you were a student, weren't there any girls in the house across yours? Think about it.'

The groom thought about it: *'Visu, will you put on this hook for me?'*

Aloud, he said, 'Naturally, there were. You can't have a town without women.'

'You know, in all our schooldays, we had these kinds of friendship, innocent stuff. They call it calf love. That is just how it was between Arun and my sister.'

'They were familiar with each other? Played hide-and-seek and stuff?'

'I don't remember all those details.' Sundaram was a little angry. He could not see the trust he was looking for in Viswanathan's eyes, and he seemed adamant. 'At one point in time, Arun and I were growing up together. That's all,' Sundaram said.

'How do you explain this picture?'

'I have to ask you one more question, my dear groom. Have you ever been to a movie studio in Chennai?'

'I have no real interest in the movies.'

'You don't have to watch movies to go. Have you ever been to a studio to just watch a shooting?'

He had, but said, 'No.'

'Okay, let us say, for argument's sake, lots of people have been to studios for a lark. Suppose you go as well and perhaps you see a Sripriya or Sridevi during that shooting. And a photographer nearby takes of a photo of you together, publishes it in a magazine and slaps on a caption: "Sridevi and Visu have known each other since childhood." This is exactly like that.'

'Is Sridevi from Mannargudi?' Ambi piped up.

'Oh, shut up,' Sundaram said. 'I was only illustrating a point.'

But Ambi was off on a tangent: 'There is this guy called Mannai Mani from our town in the movies. He acts, does stunts and stuff.'

'Ambi, will you shut up for a while? We are having a serious conversation!' Viswanathan snapped at the boy. 'Sundaram, what are you saying? Do you swear there is no connection between your sister and Arun?'

'I am not saying that. They just happened to be with each other during a specific time period. How do I explain this now?'

Visu thought for a while. 'So you're saying that this picture is false?'

'The photograph is real, but what the caption says is wrong. It is fabricated gossip. I have sent them a telegram to stop such photos from appearing.'

Visu thought for a while and said, 'How do I tell my father about this?'

'If you ask me, there is no need to say anything now—it would be inappropriate.'

'You want me to hide this?'

'No, I just want it postponed a little. A wedding is an auspicious event, and we can talk about this at leisure after the ceremonies. But the main thing is that you should not nurse any doubts about this. You must start with a clean slate. That is vital, and that's what I am sincerely seeking from you.'

Visu thought about all this again. Kalyani's beautiful face flashed in front of his eyes. He recalled the rustle of her silk sari and the touch of the fabric on his body and how he had said that he would protect her all his life. *No*, he thought, purging his doubts, *those innocent eyes are enough for me. She is blemishless. Haven't I seen those women in Mannargudi? Haven't I ridden a bicycle to that sahukar's house hoping for a glimpse of Renuka? And that woman, Ramani, who had some facial hair—I'd had some strange pull towards her and I did feel a dangerous attraction towards her. There was also dusky Kamala, who used to fetch water from the municipal tap. If I was a celebrity, and someone linked me up with that Kamala…this is something like that.*

'Sundaram, I believe you. But you please do tell your sister when you think appropriate that I don't want Arun's name heard in my home again after we get married.'

It all seemed very childish to Sundaram, but he agreed.

Ambi started to say something, but Visu cut him short, 'Will you shut up for a while? Don't tell anyone about this.'

'Chee! Would I do something like that?' Ambi said. 'I just won't.' *But I must tell Thangam. Only her.*

Arun got off the bed, shook off the satin sheets and lit a cigarette. On the wall, three black women advertised 'Discomania' on a poster. Near the bedside lamp with a coarse cotton shade, Premalatha's favourite comics lay scattered: *TinTin*, *Archie*...

'Do you read *Asterix*?'

'Hmm, I don't like it.'

'The only comic I like is Charlie Brown.'

'That is also boring.'

'All right. Do you know the joke about the maharaja and forty-eight women?'

'I don't want to hear any jokes.'

He looked at her, her eyes were shut. She quickly threw open the bedsheet as if to reveal her attractive contours, and covered it again. Giggles.

'We are one of the first couples in history that celebrated a honeymoon before the wedding,' Arun said in a laconic tone, as if there was nothing to celebrate...

'So, are we going to Switzerland for our honeymoon?'

'Yes, but we are going to do the same stuff there as well.'

'Heyyyyy!' she chided him. She called him to her and played with his hair; she drew sketches on his back, pressed her head on it and said, 'Arun, Bhaskar had called.'

'Bhaskar is much older than me, please call him sir.'

'You know, a picture appeared in *Cinemalaya*.'

'Okay.'

'You and Kalyani are looking at each other with love in your eyes.'

Arun got up with a start. '*What*?'

'Yes. And if that is acting, you are the world's best actor. Arun, who is this Kalyani?'

'Is there a photo?'

'Will you take a look at it?' She drew out the magazine from under her pillow. 'I think it is page nineteen.'

He flipped the pages quickly—and there they were.

With her head on his shoulder, Premalatha read aloud, 'But it is true that Arun made a special trip to see her before his wedding.'

'So, when did you go to Trichy?'

'That Gnanasekaran has done this,' Arun said. 'You bastard, I will kill you,' he swore under his breath.

'Easy, easy,' Premalatha said. 'You don't have to pretend to be so angry for my sake.'

'This is not for you, Prem. It is about these lies—it's all bullshit.'

'The picture looks fabulous.'

'Oh, *you*!'

He picked up the phone and dialled furiously. 'Bhaskar! What the hell is this? Did you see *Cinemalaya*?'

'I did. There is a telegram from Sundaram—an angry one.'

'What does he say?'

'"Don't take undue revenge and create mental agony"—he thinks you are responsible.'

'Oh! First, call that journalist and threaten him. And whatever the cost, slap a defamation case on him. Strip him to his underwear.'

'Come on, Arun, relax! I won't whisper a word about all this,' said Premalatha, trying to cool him down.

'Shut up, Prem. I am not thinking about you now.'

'You know, she is pretty, but her nose is a bit like Mumtaz.'

'Shut *up*, Prem.'

Premalatha suppressed her laughter, pouted and sat cross-legged on the bed.

'Bhaskar, do something,' Arun said. 'Call them up as soon as the courts open tomorrow. Summon that Gnanasekharan here. We can give him a piece of both our minds.'

'I think you are overreacting,' said Bhaskar.

'This doesn't affect me, Bhaskar. But won't that girl's life be ruined by such a thing? She is getting married tomorrow and this picture appears. Read out Sundaram's telegram now.'

Bhaskar read it out.

'Send a reply.'

'I've done it, saying, "There is no connection between this article and me whatsoever."' Arun read out the message. He added: 'I don't think we need any legal action right away. Anyway, no lawyer is going to help you at midnight. Think over it in the morning. You know, the whole thing would have died down a bit.'

'It won't, and it shouldn't. I must file a case in the morning. What do these guys think of themselves?'

Premalatha took off her sheet once more and giggled.

'Look here, Prema. We haven't been married for even a day yet, and we have to be husband and wife for quite a while now. Don't tease me like this now, it is irritating.'

'How then?' she asked. 'Like this?' she burst into a spasm of uncontrolled laughter.

'*My God, what have I done, I say? To marry a woman like this!* Bhaskar, look for a divorce lawyer as well tomorrow.'

'Arun, you have no idea what to make fun of and when,' Bhaskar chided him.

Premalatha, still laughing, was swishing the sheet on and off.

'What, di?'

Her mother had come to the police station. Selvakumar from the union was also there, as was Saraswathi Ammal, her neighbour. Manonmani wept when she saw her mother. 'That taxi driver deliberately made me get inside and offered to drop me home. They fooled me. There was a policeman in mufti inside.'

'Who is the taxi driver?'

'I don't know his name. But his face looked familiar.'

'Who was it? Durai? Gopal? Pandurangam?'

'I don't know the name, sir.'

The mother ranted to the police inspector. 'What, saar? My daughter has done no harm. She is innocent. Why have you tricked her and locked her up like this? To hell with you.

Don't you have a wife or sister? May the pox get you! May you suffer from diarrhoea.'

'Shut up, you,' a policeman shouted. 'This case was directly caught by the SP—it's not a frame-up.'

'Can we tell our local MLA?'

'That guy himself was going to get caught in all this. Go away, man,' the policeman said. 'If we revealed what this girl did there would be a big stink. Just take her to the magistrate's court. They'll slap a fine, and you just stay in there for four days. What's the matter? Never eaten sambar rice in the jail before?'

Manonmani's mother was persistent. 'She is an innocent girl,' she cried out loud and slapped her own mouth. Manonmani had stopped crying and was speaking to Kumar. 'Kumar, please talk to them. We only have to give them something. We can sell off a jewel or something.'

'I have done that already, but the buggers won't come around. They keep saying it is the superintendent's catch. How did you get caught like this, Mano?'

'I had gone to ask for a part.'

'From whom?'

'Lakshmanan.'

'Which one? The one from LV Pictures?'

'Yes.'

'Did he give it to you?'

'Do you think he ever will?'

A policeman was taunting her. 'Hey Kannagi, virtuous one, come on. Some bangles are waiting for you,' he said.

'Mano, don't you worry,' Kumar said. 'I'll get hold of some lawyer first. Then, I'll haul that Lakshmanan up and yank some cash out of him and get you bail. Stop worrying. It's election time, and no one likes to be strict at this time—they'll release you soon.'

It was then that Manonmani saw the young man for the first time.

15

MANONMANI HAD NEVER SEEN THE fellow before. But there he was, coming towards her, without taking his eyes off her.

'What's the matter, ma?' he said.

'They caught hold of a girl walking on the street and locked her up. Thambi, what kind of injustice is this?' said her mother.

The man was still peering hard at her, and she looked away, unable to bear his scrutiny.

'Who the hell are you?' a policeman asked him.

'I am from the union,' the man replied. And then, he said, 'Why do you cry, ma? Is this your daughter? Stop worrying, I'll get her out.

'Hey, yettu ayya, has the case been registered?'

'Will you get out?' the constable said. 'This is something that the SP has nabbed. You don't stand a chance.'

The man came to Manonmani and said, 'My name is Manikkam, and everybody calls me SM. I have just taken charge of the union.'

He was about thirty years old with lots of black, curly hair, a square face and a large forehead. There was a hint of feminineness in his eyes. Beneath his sharp nose and thin moustache, his lips were large and pronounced.

'So, you are Manonmani?'

'Yes, saar.'

'Don't call me sir. Are you a member of the union?'

'Yes.'

'Where is your card?'

'It's at home, sir.'

'But it is to avoid such problems with the police that we gave you a card, no?'

'Will they let me off if I show the card?'

'It is the superintendent who has caught you, and he won't. What really happened? Tell me?'

He lit a beedi that looked inappropriate on him. As she glared at him, he dropped it and extinguished the butt with his feet. 'Listen, there may an odd one here or there who has gone astray. But just look at the way they dub all junior artistes as prostitutes—it's not fair.'

'I did not do anything, sir. I just went to the hotel to seek a role.'

'From whom?'

'Lakshmanan—*Ilanthalaivan*.'

'You know there is a whole group looking for a part in that. We can see about that later. First, I need to get you out of here. You'll need to just wait for a while.

'Hullo sir, has the case been registered?' Manikkam asked the policeman again.

'We'll know after the circle inspector comes.'

'Just you wait a while,' Manikkam told Manonmani. 'If I bring a smart lawyer, he'll get us the bail fast.'

'Thambi,' Manonmani's mother cried in gratitude. 'You have arrived like a saviour at the right moment.'

'When the cops came to inform you of her arrest, I was at the paan shop across the road. I'll first get your daughter out, and then I need to talk to her,' Manikkam said.

To the policeman, he said, 'Brother, why are you dragging this? Just settle the matter with a fiver or tenner, no?'

'Hey you!' the angry cop said. 'You want me to shove you into the lock-up as well?'

'I'll be back, Manonmani,' he said to her. 'Don't you worry.'

After he had left, something he had said still hung in the air.

Then I need to talk to her.

The Rockfort Express was all set to leave from Trichy Junction. In the corner of a second-class compartment, Viswanathan and Kalyani sat across each other on window seats. On the platform stood a huge send-off party, including Kalyani's parents, Sundaram and an assorted bunch of friends and relatives from Sannidhi Street, Kuppammal the maid, and Achuthan the convenience shop man. On the berth across, cotton dhurries from Bhavani rested in a roll, holding large cotton bed rolls. Kalyani, with her hair braided in a long, single plait, with lots of kadambam flowers in her hair, was weeping gently.

'Don't be crazy, Kalyani, you are not going far away,' her mother consoled her as her father was setting his watch to the station clock.

Sundaram told the family's new son-in-law, 'She reads and writes a lot, draws pictures and does some embroidery as well. But she is still a child, you know. If you see any flaws in her, don't stay silent. Just tell her and she will correct herself. If she does anything wrong at all, it would be on account of ignorance. She is innocent, you know.'

Viswanathan peered outside and said, 'There's still five minutes to go for the train to leave, no? By now Mother and Father would have reached Mannargudi, right? We haven't told him about that stuff yet.'

'What stuff?'

'You know—that thing.'

Sundaram's face fell. 'It seems like you have not yet forgotten the matter yet. This is a small matter, Viswanathan. Its shadow should not fall on your life.'

'Chee, chee! After all, you had explained everything so clearly.'

'Viswanathan, how do I explain? My sister is a gem. Taking good care of her is your responsibility, your duty.'

'I have also been brought up in a very disciplined way, Mr Sundaram,' the new son-in-law said. 'I do my sandhya vandanam regularly. I don't read those dubious books. I don't watch movies at all. I have read *The Voice of God*, the complete volume. I read *The Hindu*, *Bhavan's Journal* and *Science Today*. I don't even *touch* Tamil magazines. Do you know what kind of serial stories they sell? Awful! Whenever you pick one up, it's either love or sex. I have better things to do. I have to study for my banking exams as well.'

Sundaram had a mild headache now.

At the other end, Kalyani and her mother were in a hush-hush conversation.

'Don't talk back to him, okay? And find out about his likes and dislikes. When your in-laws enter the room, always stand up in respect. Answer their questions properly. Get pregnant soon, and don't take those godforsaken pills. You still have that wheezing cough. So, have that Waterbury's Compound regularly. I have given you enough vattal to fry for three months. Write to me before the stock get over. I'll have some sent through Paaccha who works in the railway mail service. Write to me once a week anyway. And give up that habit of putting in an extra dash of salt in the rasam. You must watch that the smell of the rasam powder…'

'Amma!' Kalyani said. 'I am scared, Amma.'

'Don't be silly,' her mother said. 'When I was your age, I had already given birth to Chandru by then…you know, I went to my in-laws home while I was still in a half-sari.'

'Ma, will you visit me in Madras?'

'Ask my son-in-law to invite me, and I'll come.'

The station bell rang out, the engine hooted and the train was off.

'Kalyani, Kalyani! Be good, okay? Write letters,' said Sundaram to his sister. He controlled his tears with great effort.

Kalyani felt a strange mix of laughter, tears, joy, sadness, pain, fear and a heaviness in her stomach all at once. As the train moved off the platform, those close to her moved away as well. She felt a huge burst of tears surging within.

Viswanathan was not looking at her. He was reading a magazine called *The Accountant*.

The lady in the seat across consoled her. 'Don't cry, my dear. At first, it feels depressing. It becomes all right over time.' Then she popped the question. 'Are you from Trichy?'

'Yes, maami,' said Kalyani, sniffing a little. 'Trichy district, Uttamarkovil.'

'I think I have seen you somewhere.'

'Uttamarkovil?' the boy in the next seat said. 'Isn't Arun Vijay from your town?'

'Do you know Arun?' the lady now asked her.

As Kalyani hesitated, Viswanathan looked up and said, 'We don't know him, maami.'

'I have seen this girl somewhere,' the lady said.

Viswanathan glared at Kalyani. '*I told you so*,' his eyes said.

The next morning, as the Rockfort Express moved towards Egmore Station, Arun got off his bed, half-asleep, and wondered who was next to him. *Oh, Premalatha. Oh my God, I am married now.*

Premalatha was wrapped up like a ball in a sheet, and there was a gentle snoring sound. He moved the sheet gently. He could hear a small growl from under the sheet. '*Grrrrrr.*' It was her pet. The puppy eyed him with a clear message: 'I don't like you.' He grumbled in disgust and went to the wash basin and opened the glass cupboard. There was something bundled up there. Premalatha's wig! He looked for his toothbrush, which he found amid a plethora of womanly pastes, creams, waxes and colours. A bra hung nearby, and lots of hairpins and bangles as well.

He slapped an inch of paste and started brushing. *Arrrgggh*! That was not toothpaste. It was some other cream. 'What the…'

'Prem, wake up,' he hollered from the bathroom. 'Where did you put my toothpaste?'

He immediately buzzed Bhaskar on the intercom and snapped 'Bhaskar, come on up at once. There is no goddamn toothpaste in this wretched house.'

Premalatha, awake now, said, 'Good morning, Julie!' to her puppy and patted it gently.

'*Hffff*!' Julie said.

'What happened, my dear?' she asked Arun. 'Do you have a cold or something?'

'Where is my toothpaste? I can't find it. I put something in my mouth and the damn thing is icky,' he said.

Prem clapped her hands and laughed out loud.

'What's so funny?'

Bhaskar, in the meanwhile, had come in with a tube of toothpaste.

'Chee, no! Bhaskar, it is not proper to come in without knocking any more, and that too when we are still in our pyjamas,' Premalatha told him. 'Arun, tell him. These old habits have to change. We are married now.'

'Sorry,' said Bhaskar, moving away.

'Can't you put that cream somewhere else?,' Arun said to her. 'Did you have to put it only in my cupboard? Couldn't you find a dressing table for yourself?'

'But there is no other place in this house.'

'What are you blabbering about? It's such a big house.'

'The house is big all right,' Premalatha said. 'But the place is occupied by your relatives. Look at the room my mother has—it's insufferable. And why does Bhaskar have a special room all to himself?'

'Hfff!' It was Julie again.

'You know, Julie can't stand this AC. Let's switch it off tonight. It's so damn cold anyway—how on earth do you manage to sleep?'

'If you're feeling cold, why don't you sleep in another room?'

'It's not even a week since we got married. People will laugh at us if we sleep separately,' she said. 'Okay, what's on the call sheet today?'

'Must ask Bhaskar.'

'I am free today, Arun. Shall we go to Mahabalipuram?'

'No. I've got a shoot today.'

'Cancel it!' she said and pressed the intercom button and barked into the speaker. 'Bhaskar, what's Arun's schedule today?'

'He is at Prasad all day. In the evening, he's at KM Hospital and then dubbing at 9 p.m. after that. At 11...'

'Cancel everything,' she told Bhaskar.

'Bhaskar, don't!' said Arun. 'Don't cancel anything.'

'Bhaskar,' she insisted. 'Cancel everything. We have to go to Mahabalipuram.'

'Prem, listen to me,' Arun said. 'Bhaskar, send me some coffee. I'll be ready by 8.30.'

Premalatha now had her hands on her hips and wore an 'Oh-is-that-so?' look.

'Prema, be reasonable,' he cajoled. 'I don't have a shoot on Sunday. We can go then.'

'But I have a shoot on Sunday.'

'Cancel it,' he said.

'Why? What for?'

'Hmm, but that's how it would work for me as well, right? Oh, come on! Let's not fight so soon after our wedding. We haven't even had our official honeymoon yet.' He switched off the intercom and said, 'Prem, come, give me a kiss.'

Before he could kiss her cheek, she said, 'Don't you have to get Bhaskar's permission first?'

'That's not funny.'

'Do something to change my mother's room.'

'Where do I change it to?'

'Bhaskar's room. Why does he need a room in this house?'

'Don't be ridiculous. Bhaskar looks after everything here.'

'I'll take care of it from now on.'

'Don't talk nonsense. You don't know how to handle everything in this house.'

'So what? I can learn.'

She pressed the intercom. 'Bhaskar, will you come here?' she said.

'No, Bhaskar, stay put,' Arun said.

Bhaskar sighed at the other end. Palanisamy was sitting across him. 'What, saar? A fight?'

'Nothing of that sort. They always speak to each other like this. So, what brings you here?'

'For the April call sheet. You know we booked it early.'

Bhaskar looked at his diary and said, '20 to 27 April, full day for eight days.'

'I know that, sir. But there is talk about whether he is going to continue acting or not. There are rumours that he has gone back on two contracts after his marriage.'

'Who said that? It is all bloody false,' Bhaskar said. 'We don't go back on our word.'

'If you're planning anything of that sort, please tell us in advance,' Palanisamy said. 'We need time to make alternative arrangements.'

'The question does not arise—it won't happen, Palanisamy. You stop worrying.'

'Thanks so much, sir.'

Bhaskar stared at the man's back as he was leaving. He could not see the letters and other stuff meant for Arun's attention on the table. He was, in fact, waiting for an important document from the auditor.

He went up slowly to the first floor and knocked on Arun's bedroom door. This was a place he could once walk in to at any time without knocking. A lot had changed in two days.

The door opened and Premalatha appeared. 'What is it? You again? Doesn't look like you'll leave our bedroom.'

Bhaskar's face showed no expression. 'I have to see the letters.'

'What letters?'

'The ones Arun receives. I am expecting an important one from the auditor.'

'Okay, I'll get it for you.'

'I need it at once. An income tax statement for advance tax has to be sent urgently.'

'I told you I'll get it ready.'

'When?'

'Come back in the afternoon.'

'Can you call Arun?'

'He is in the shower. You want to enter the bathroom?'

'You are sounding indecent.'

'And what about your behaviour?'

Bhaskar looked unperturbed as a vein at the corner of his forehead moved a little. He flashed a sneering smile at Premalatha and left. He could hear her giggle behind his back.

He climbed down the stairs slowly, walked to his table, picked up a paper and a pen and wrote, 'My dear Arun…'

He stopped, thought for a couple of minutes and then tore up that incomplete letter.

16

Arumairajan felt goosebumps all over his body at the mere thought of his being a lyricist. It seemed wonderful that a mere eight lines scribbled on a piece of paper could be set to tune amidst a large band of musicians and turned into a song for the silver screen. He was dreaming about the day when one of his own songs would come of age in such a studio ambience.

The instrumentalists and engineers would be sitting with equipment and unidentifiable machines behind soundproof studio panes—what an enchantment! There would be a drum tapped there, a string caressed here, and some Western instruments being strummed somewhere with a strange assortment of percussion drums being played. He imagined S.P. Balasubramaniam and S. Janaki with their headphones, waiting for the recording to start, and everything suddenly coming to a halt with someone crying, 'Arumairajan sir has arrived.'

'Hey, man, move aside! They are ready for the take. If you want to listen to the song, go into that room!' A voice shook him out of his reverie outside the recording room.

Arumairajan wanted to open the doors and go inside, but he did not have the courage. From behind closed doors, sweet music wafted out, and he stored it in his heart and played it back in his head. There was no sign of Kittu. Despite the elaborate security, that man managed to enter whichever place he wanted. That influential man had said that with two hundred fifty rupees more, he could actually craft two songs out of his lyrics. But where was he going to get that amount from? He had already sold whatever he could sell. Kittu had made it clear that he had already given his word to record two songs at seven hundred and fifty rupees each. With the extra money, the composing could begin! Arunmairajan could give the balance later. If not, Kittu was ready to return the thousand rupees he had taken. Such a magnanimous man this Kittu was, he thought. 'I am so unfortunate—only two hundred and fifty rupees stand between me and fame.'

For now, Arumairajan stood beneath a tree outside the recording studio. The short palm trees in the compound outside seemed to be keeping a watch on him like quiet sentinels. He walked slowly, and in the small buildings around, many men were going about their busy routines. He sat in the shade and realized that he still had not eaten anything. Pangs of hunger struck him. He would get some rice if he reached home. Kittu, who had gone inside, showed no sign of coming out. Arumairajan was waiting for some news so that he could leave. He, was, after all, trying to see if one song could be fixed for seven hundred fifty rupees. If he could not, he would have to arrange that extra two hundred fifty. He thought of donating blood at the general hospital, which would fetch him twenty rupees. If Mary also agreed, that would be forty. Six times that, he would be home. But they didn't usually allow blood donations at short intervals.

He even thought of asking Mary's cousin to join but felt confused. He was already a guest in their home and a burden on them. He was getting free meals, though Mary did help them with their housework, cooking and all sorts of chores. She was still weak, having given birth only recently, and was also dealing with the sorrow of having lost an infant. 'Poor Mary,' Arumairajan said to himself. 'One day I am going to earn much from my poems, wipe your tears, make you ride in cars and deck you up with jewels.'

'Hey, where are you? I've been looking for you all over the place. I asked you to stay put where I left you…'

Arumairajan was startled to hear Kittu's voice. 'Sorry sir, but they would not let me in.'

'Who said that? Did you say Kittu sir asked you to come in?'

'No, sir.'

'That's where you goofed up. Look here, Arumairajan, I was talking a lot about your poems inside. "This is a poet of a high standard, and it is unfair to charge him instead of paying him," is what I told them. I just let them have a piece of my mind. But what do they know about poetry, these blokes? Apparently it is their norm. Aspiring lyricists have to pay to get in.'

'But I have paid the money, sir.'

'That is not enough, no? You only gave a thousand.'

'I just wanted one song.'

'Hmmm, no! I've asked them. They never do one at a time. They insist on two.'

'So you need two hundred fifty rupees more.'

'No, five hundred rupees.'

'How is that, saar?'

'Two songs cost fifteen hundred. You've paid one thousand. How do you say two hundred fifty?'

'Oh, I did the calculation wrong, sir.'

'I am always clear in my calculations. Anyway, you think it over and decide. If you can't give the money right away, you can do it in instalments. If you can't do that either, tell me clearly and I'll refund your money. But do tell me one day in advance. I'll have to go to the bank and withdraw it.'

'May I have your contact address, sir?'

'I am always on the move, Arumairajan. But if you enquire at this number, 446666, they'll tell you my whereabouts. Have you eaten?'

'No, sir.'

Kittu whipped out a ten-rupee note from his pocket. 'Keep it,' he said. 'Have a good meal. You look like a man living through a famine.'

Arumairajan took the ten-rupee with some trepidation. Kittu rushed to where a number of cars were parked and hollered: 'Now who is the LV Pictures driver here?' As one man answered, he opened the door and asked Arumairajan, 'Where do you have to go?'

'Perambur.'

'Perambur? That's far. I am going towards Triplicane. Get in, and I'll drop you off at Mount Road. Eat at some decent place there and reach home safely. Take care of your health. That comes first. Poems can wait.'

'You see, sir, there's been a tragedy in the family.'

'Aah, keep going straight, no?' Kittu was now speaking to the driver.

Kittu, much in quiet command and not saying much further, dropped Arumairajan at Mount Road and sped off with a wave and a smile. Arumairajan really liked him. How sensitive of Kittu to realize he had no money and give him a tenner! He was touched. He walked on the road bustling with traffic, under large movie banners bearing names of stars like M.S. Viswanathan and Kannadasan and Babu…

MSV, Arumairajan, Babu—he replaced Kannadasan with his own name in the middle in that banner and it seemed to ring true. He stopped at a bookstore and his eyes widened in wonderment.

He stepped in, enquired about the Tamil section and gaped in awe at what he saw. So many books, so many poems! He felt like buying the entire collection of Bharathidasan—he had already read them. Kannadasan? He knew the legend's lyrics by heart. He was craving something new. There were ten rupees in his pocket, and he thought a meal would not cost more than two rupees. Maybe two and a half. The bus fare would cost him a rupee or perhaps one and a half. So, he had a budget of five rupees to buy himself a book. He stepped out with a collection of poems by Abdul Rahman.

He grabbed a bite in a roadside eatery after which he changed buses, and throughout his journey, he was reading the book non-stop.

'Come to me as the rain, my love,
Turn the seeds sprouted in my hearts
to flowers that blossom,
Speaking pollen secrets, my love,'

He thought of Mary. As he reached home, he saw that his wife was sitting at the door in tears.

The European honeymoon turned out to be a big disappointment because Arun and Premalatha had chosen the wrong time. In spite of layers of woollen clothes and overcoats, and despite the central heating they had in most places, it was no match for walking tropical streets, munching popcorn and peanuts, eating ice cream and looking at the world going by. The Sistine Chapel and St Peter's Cathedral in Rome turned out to be boring. Mona Lisa's billion-dollar smile at the Louvre in Paris did not quite charm them. Nor were they impressed by the shows at the Moulin Rouge or the Lido. Switzerland only seemed like a huge, frozen city. Premalatha had a headache every day for a week. She felt like returning home within ten days of their arrival. This was the only thing on which they had no disagreement. In everything else, they were polar opposites.

Arun wanted to watch some X-rated movies in Paris. All Premalatha wanted was to go around the city.

'In this biting cold?' he asked her. 'If you spit, it comes out as ice, and if you piss...'

'You are telling me this joke for the eighth time,' she said.

'Well, we do many things over and over again, no? How is this different? Are you going to join me for that movie or not?'

'No!' she said. 'And you can't leave me alone like this. I have been horribly bored since we reached here. You brought me here in the dead of winter, making things miserable for me. In Switzerland, the hotel guy said that we were the only tourists around as the place was always empty during this time of the year. That Bhaskar must have made these arrangements.'

'What can Bhaskar do? He only made the bookings for the days we wanted. I had planned on April. *You* insisted we go now!'

'Me? Don't lie, Arun! It's your call sheets that were full through the year. Bhaskar said you could get leave only in December.'

'Bhaskar again! Why are you so upset with him?'

'He doesn't behave like an employee, much more like a dictator. It was because of him that Kalyani and you...'

'Kalyani and me? What about it?'

'Forget it!'

'You might as well tell me. Don't hold back. Come on, be frank!'

'You'll get angry.'

'I'll be furious only if you leave things incomplete like this.'

'It was Bhaskar who got you to meet Kalyani frequently and made the two of you close. That's what they are saying in the industry anyway.'

'And what else are they saying?'

She giggled. 'You are angry—your lips are quivering.'

'Prem, do you believe all that you hear?'

'As far as I am concerned, the two of us are married. It is not proper for you to think about her anymore.'

'Who said I was?'

'I saw you.'

'Saw what?'

'Saw you taking her name in your sleep. Kalyani…'

'You are lying!'

'Okay, I am lying. And it is also a lie that you met her one day before the two of us left for Europe.'

'Don't be ridiculous!' Arun said. 'I have no clue what happened to her and where she is. I know nothing about what she is doing at all. And I don't care either.'

'Good.'

'You don't believe me, do you?'

'I don't care about her. Even if I say we shouldn't talk about it, you always bring her up again. I think it is all because of Bhaskar. I don't like the way he looks at me—as if I were an uninvited guest. He doesn't behave like a secretary. I have my doubts about whether you are in a position to sack him.'

'Why?'

'Because he knows all your secrets.'

Arun now grabbed her shoulder and turned her towards him. 'Look here, Prema, whether I keep Bhaskar or not is my wish, my business. I am not going to decide based on what you say. Understand this: Whatever you think of me, even if you call me a male chauvinist pig, I am the boss in my house. If you live with me, you have to do as I say—I am the one who is earning the money.'

'*What?* As if I don't earn, is it?'

'You can't be working for long. You'll have to give up acting soon.'

'What for?'

'Why are you talking as if you don't know?'

'Is it because I am pregnant?'

'Yes.'

'It's not even two months yet—I am going to abort the child,' she said in a nonchalant tone.

'Oh no, Prem! Don't be silly. It is a sin to think like that. Why do you want an abortion?'

'My career will be affected. Shouldn't I be acting for a little while longer? If I have a baby so soon, my looks and body will be ruined. I don't want a kid now. Let's think about it after a couple of years, maybe three. Becoming pregnant is pretty easy, no, and you're very good at it.'

For a moment, Arun felt like grabbing her, shaking her and slamming her into the wall.

17

The Airbus jet crawled slowly like a python that had just swallowed its prey, had ladders attached to its body, opened its doors and spewed out two hundred and fifty passengers. Arun and Premalatha, wearing dark shades, walked out on to the tarmac.

Bhaskar was waiting behind the glass pane in the airport terminal, and with him were two production assistants and some fans clutching garlands. A magazine reporter who had nothing better to do stepped out of the toilet. Bhaskar offered to carry Premalatha's hand baggage but she refused his assistance. Her mother had also come to receive her.

'Hi Bhaskar!' Arun greeted him. 'They gave us hell at Bombay customs.'

As Bhaskar returned the greeting, the fans garlanded Arun, who immediately took off the smothering piles of flowers. 'There is a shoot in the aferrnoon, thambi,' said an elderly member of the reception party.

'I'll be there, Annachi,' Arun replied in respectful reciprocation.

'Prem, you carry on. I'll come in the next car,' Arun said. Premalatha, without saying anything, walked beside her mother. The fans surrounded Arun and were joined by airport staff. The reporter asked, 'I hear three of your projects are off and they are casting Kamal or Rajini instead.'

'Why are you grilling me so soon, brother? I have just arrived from a long trip,' Arun said.

'The reports are all false, of course,' Bhaskar offered a denial to the journalist.

'Let him confirm that.'

'He is tired.'

'Why did Premalatha leave alone?' the reporter persisted.

Arun said nothing and got into the car. Bhaskar took the baggage collection slips from him and handed them over to an assistant, asking him to follow in a van. Bhaskar got into the driver's seat, and the fans chased the car a bit as it sped off.

'How was the honeymoon?' Bhaskar asked.

'A disaster. We went all the way abroad and spent a lot of money only to fight. The bloody cold made it worse.'

There was a silence and then Arun spoke. 'I thought I had adjusted my call sheet before leaving. Has some movie been cancelled?'

'Yes.'

'How many?'

'Four.'

'But why?'

'The problem is not your call sheet, Arun. Three of your films have flopped in a row. After *Vayasukku Vandha Ponnu*, not a single one has done well at the box office. *Malarcharam* is a super flop. They took it off the halls after a week.'

'It was a good movie—that's why it didn't do well.'

'You need a hit, Arun.'

'Bhaskar, I have an idea. Let's make a film on our own. In cinemascope, colour, like *Dharam Veer* in Hindi, in which horses gallop and go *tak-tak-tak-tak*. The audience would love it. We can bring in Parveen Babi from Bombay and ask Salim–Javed to write the story.'

'It will cost you at least a crore.'

'Won't distributors fund that?'

'How? They are getting squeezed for 10 lakhs now. They are making village movies these days by the dozen and making heroes out of any Tom, Dick and Harry walking the streets. The area-wise exhibition rights get sold easily. Arun, the market is ebbing for stars like you.'

'I think they are tired of my face.'

'That is not the reason, Arun. Your indifferent acting may be a better answer. Have you seen *Udhiripookkal?*'

'No.'

'Watch it—these are new folks, doing a very sincere job.'

'Is it running well?'

'Reasonably.'

'Don't you worry, Bhaskar. I'll bounce back,' Arun said. 'With a bang!' he punched the car's dashboard. 'But Bhaskar, make sure you don't do one thing.'

'What?'

'Don't leave me'

'Who is even thinking about that?'

'Prem.'

'Well, I know she hates me.'

'Whatever she says, you mustn't leave me—promise me!'

'Hmm.'

'I don't have anyone in this world, really. All those relatives surrounding me and now my wife? No one really cares about me.'

'Don't say that, Arun. You are wrong.'

'Bhaskar, I need a child—it's a gift a wife can give so easily. But she says she is not ready for one. Bhaskar, she wants to abort the baby.'

'I am sorry.'

In the car speeding ahead of Arun's, Premalatha told her mother: 'Ma, I have to see a doctor this evening.'

'Why?'

'Let us talk about that later.'

'What happened, my dear?' Arumairajan asked a sobbing Mary.

'Let's go back to Bangalore,' she said. 'I can't stay in this house anymore.'

'Why? What happened? Tell me what the hell is going on.'

'Let's go find a hotel to stay in, Arumairajan.'

'But tell me what happened first,' he said in an irritated tone.

She felt hurt by his tone. She cried some more.

The woman's voice came from inside the house. 'Look here, Arumairajan, when you are not at home, some not-so-good things happen here. They may be cousins, their uncle's kids, and there may have been a tragedy in the family, but he has been buying her a sari and tiffins. He's been asking her if she has eaten and bathed and what not. I don't see this as a good sign.'

'Listen to this!' Mary sobbed. 'Look at what a woman who has just lost a child has to go through here.'

Arumairajan woke up slowly to the crisis and looked stunned. 'What are you saying, ma? This is ridiculous—preposterous!' he told Mary's cousin's wife.

'This is a strange relationship, and I don't like the way it is going,' the woman said. 'Forgive me, thambi. I am a woman who knows her husband, and if he learns that I told you this, he will whip me.'

'Why are you standing there doing nothing?' Mary told Arumairajan. 'How can you listen to such an accusation? Don't you know me? Am I someone that base?'

'Who said that, Mary?' the lady told her. 'I am the one who does not trust my husband. I have been hurt in the past.'

'What do you think we should do?' Arumairajan asked.

Mary, in agony, said, 'What is this? Why are you tolerating all this? Let's get out now.'

'But where to, Mary?'

'Wherever. Where…ever. Come, let's go!'

They stepped out soon with their tin trunk and bed roll, walked in the blazing afternoon sun, got into a rickshaw and reached the nearby stop.

'Mary, have you got any money?'

'No. Let's get into a train somehow. We just have to reach Bangalore. That's all.'

Arumairajan stared at the two rupees and twenty-five paise in his hand. What was he going to do now?

'Brother! Don't you have a younger sister? An elder sister? A mother? Think of them. Aren't they all women?'

'They are women, but you are a different kind of woman.'

'Leave me! Leave me alone! Brother, I say in the name of God, this is a sin.'

'Why are you calling God? He is asleep in heaven above.'

The door was bolted from inside and they were shooting inside for *Ilanthalaivan*. The only people inside were the director, Lakshmanan, the cameraman, his assistant, the actor playing the villain and Manonmani. Venugopal stood in a corner.

'Now, Balagopal, what you say is, "You are a different kind of woman" and rip off her sari. Mano, you run around the bed and fall on the bed. Come on, let's have a trial…'

Then the director told her, 'Don't fold your hand in prayer. It hides your breasts.'

'It would seem apt that she folds her hands when she says "…in the name of God"', the assistant suggested.

'Okay, let her do it just once,' the director said.

'Do I have to fall face down on the bed?'

'No, you have to fall on your back. At which point, Balagopal takes off your blouse.'

'Why are you calling God? He is sitting in heaven above,' the villain spoke his line.

'He is asleep,' the director corrected him.

Her blouse was torn, and Manonmani was wearing a bra with a flowery print.

'How many times do I have to tell you not to cross your hands over your breasts?' the director chided.

'Sorry, sir. It happens on reflex.'

The director now told the villain, 'I did not tell you to tear off the blouse. Did I?'

'Sorry, sir. It was in the heat of the shoot. '

'Is there a replacement blouse? We'll need it for the re-take.'

'Durai, tell the costumer to get one. You sit down, girl,' the director said.

Manonmani wrapped the sari around her torso, as if she was inside a cocoon.

'Sir, will the censors allow this scene?' Venugopal asked the director.

'You see, it fits into the story. This is just thc beginning. In fact, he rips off the whole thing. His character is like that. What can we do? We have shown him as a lusty bastard right from the beginning.'

'I somehow get the feeling they'll chop this off at the censor board.'

'Don't worry about that,' Lakshmanan said. 'We'll see the superintendent and separately handle the Assistant Censor Officer (ACO). They'll get the pliable members in for the screening.'

'Even then...' Venugopal said. 'Will they let the scene go this far?'

'They will,' Lakshmanan said. 'It's going to be a massive hit in the B and C towns. Did you see *Sarithiratthil Oru Rathiri*? This is not more forward than that.'

The conversation turned to Manonmani.

'What, Mano? They say you are acting in some art movie? Same guys who made *Kudisiai*?'

'No, saar. This is a new project. The director studied at the Adyar institute.'

'What institute, bah!' Lakshmanan said. 'By the time they finish one line of dialogue, I can finish a cigarette, it's that slow. You call that cinema? You know, good films carry a message for the people. You take our story here. Balagopal is a bad fellow, and we show him sinning, doing bad things. Why do we show him like that? You see, he goes to jail later and has a change of heart. Yes or no?'

'Is that how the story goes?' Venugopal asked him.

'What else?' Lakshmanan said and turned to Manonmani. 'Mano, listen to me. Don't hang out with those arthouse boys. They just have ten thousand rupees in their hands and then go begging to shoot every reel. Let my film be released. You are going to get big opportunities after that. I told you I would make you the second heroine. Did I do it or not? Where was the need to tell the union? That man came and screamed at me. Where was the need for all this? You know, I am the only one in the industry who does not go back on his word. Balagopal, come here. Why are you so hesitant? Act with force, okay?'

'That is his first rape scene, that's why,' the assistant explained.

'You'll get used to it,' the producer replied. 'Has the blouse arrived?'

Mano was asked to put the new one on.

'Just a minute,' the cameraman interrupted. 'Saar, the blouse is a green one. She was wearing a red one earlier. We have a continuity problem here.'

'Oh my God. How much have you shot?'

'She comes in, stands in the room, Balagopal closing in from behind—all of that is with her wearing a red blouse. We can't change it to green now. The critics will give us hell.'

'Who reads the reviews?' Lakshmanan asked. 'In those village tent talkies, they are not going to check out green and red.'

'But still, sir…' the cameraman persisted. 'We can't be shooting like this.'

Lakshmanan, irritated now, gave in to the request and hollered to someone: 'Saavu kraaki! Change the colour now and get a new one…and you, Mano, sit down.'

Manonmani sat in a corner. She was scared now. They would first take her sari off in front of the camera. They would then ask her to remove the blouse covering her breasts and they'd want even more. So much had already been done in this closed-door set. The lens eye would soon be ready to crawl over her body again, and with its whirring noise bite off her body parts. Pairs of roving eyes would follow her eventually. The rape scene filmed inside closed doors would spread out on the screens and travel from city to city and to villages.

What kind of life is this? Manonmani asked herself. *Can't I get married like others, feel shy and experience intimacy in a special, sublime way, between two souls?*

'Come on, dear, the blouse has arrived,' the producer said.

Manonmani went to the side and put on her red blouse.

Anney, don't you have a younger sister?—She spoke her rehearsed line.

Slowly, her scene was filmed, in minute detail. 'And turn around once,' someone instructed her.

'Let's make two prints,' Lakshmanan announced.

The shoot was over. Manonmani stepped out of the set. Vans were summoned to drop people home and cars sped off. Doors were banged. Beedis and cigarettes were lit. Manonmani was given a car.

'Where to, ma'am?' the driver asked. 'Virugambakkam?'

'No,' she said. 'Mambalam.'

'Where in Mambalam?'

'You get there first, I'll tell you,' she said.

At the same time, on Car Street in Triplicane, in a corner of a large, old house in which many families lived under one roof, Kalyani was sobbing away, lying on a bed in the corner of a room.

18

KALYANI WANTED TO SEE HER mother. She felt like writing a letter to her brother. The man who could not understand her, meanwhile, sat in a corner reading something about accountancy. The intensity of his bespectacled face in the glare of a table lamp assaulted her. On the floor below, a film magazine lay open. The breeze through the window opened it to a page that had a picture of Arun.

The fight had begun around 9 p.m. after he had seen it and thrown it down.

'How many times have I told you not to read these wretched magazines?' he shouted, flaring up.

'It was Vanaja who gave it to me. I was bored, and I just was looking at the pictures.'

'If you have nothing better to do, you can always read the books on the shelf, no? There are many of them. Mercantile law, banking...and *Deivathin Kural.* You can read any of them!'

'Sorry,' she said. 'I looked at it by mistake.'

'Then why did you hide it under the pillow?'

'Because I thought you'd get angry when you saw it.'

'You already know that, no? Then you must avoid doing that kind of thing.'

She felt pinpricks, a methodical acupuncture of sorts, as he pierced her with his words.

'Why did you look at it? It's because you have many secret desires—that is why.'

'No, no, not at all.'

'There is no point in just ogling! You are pining for him.'

'Chee!' she said. 'Don't say such horrible things.'

'What's horrible about it?'

'It just so happened that his picture was in this magazine. There are so many of actors in it—Kamalahasan, Rajnikanth and all. That doesn't mean I am thinking about all of them.'

'But Arun is special to you, no? What did he do in your childhood? Did he take you to the backyard and take off your half-sari?'

'Ayyo!' she cried. 'Why are you taking his name over and over again? What am I supposed to say? You seem to take everything I say in a wrong way.'

'You can stop touching such magazines?'

'Do I have to listen to so much abuse just because I flipped through a magazine?'

'You are talking back again and again,' his voice got louder, his eyes wider. 'I'll tell you what is bothering me. Whenever you hug me, I feel as if you are thinking it is him you are hugging.'

Kalyani burst into tears. 'Amma, amma!' she cried. 'Oh my God!'

'Why are you crying?'

She wept some more and he stared at her for a while. 'You can keep crying!' he said and walked out. And his voice chased her from the next room: 'I will forgive you this time. Make sure this does not happen again.'

She crouched on the bed for a while and wept some more.

He came back after a while and said, 'Have you finished crying?'

She stayed silent.

'Kalyani!'

There was still silence.

'Don't talk to me if you don't want to. I said what I did for your own good.'

He sat in a corner of the room and started reading. Kalyani lay down on the bed, turned to the other side and dozed off. He read till 11 p.m., let out a big yawn, snapped his fingers, switched off the lights and lay down beside her. 'Aeyy!' he said, shaking and waking up Kalyani, who was curled up like a worm. 'Come!'

It was quiet. She felt a stupor, and she felt it was someone else experiencing this. Warm breath hit her breasts. His hands roamed as they pleased on her body. Later, as he lay tired next to her, she asked gently, 'Are you angry with me?'

All she could hear was gentle snoring.

Manonmani got off at the street corner. 'You carry on!' she told the driver.

'Okay, ma'am,' he said.

She did not care about the I-know-what-you-are-up-to tone in his voice, and she walked on. The door of Prema Dry Cleaners was shut. She could hear the swish of the brooms as they swept clean the floors of Nehru Cafe which had closed for the day. She crossed a wicket gate, an apology of a garden, and climbed up a staircase in the backyard. Fortunately for her, it was not locked. She knocked.

'Who is it?' said a voice.

'It's me, Manonmani.'

The door opened after some hesitation, and Manikkam emerged. 'What is it, Mano? Why are you showing up at this odd hour…'

She went into the room with a sense of ease and asked for a glass of water. He brought her one from a narrow-necked mud pot, and she drank it at one go. 'Tell me,' she said.

'It was I who was asking what brought you here at this time…'

'Just like that,' she announced. The room was clean. A couple of trousers and shirts, properly folded, hung on a string. The underwear lying nearby were starched and clean. There was a shelf full of books in Tamil and English.

'So you are an educated man.'

'Yes,' he said. The Bhagavad Gita rested with the New Testament and another tome called *The Thirst for Beauty*.

'Really!' she said. 'Looking at you, no one could have guessed you are so educated.'

'Must be the handiwork of the beedi I smoke,' he said.

'But you smoke cigarettes in your room?' she said as she eyed a packet on the shelf.

'It is cigarettes until the fifth of every month.'

'How long have you studied?'

'BA in Direction at the Adyar Institute. And after that, I came to Kodambakkam with dreams. I wanted to shake up the world of Tamil cinema, but it all went phut in a year. I am a junior artiste now, but an A-grade at that.'

'How did you become a junior artiste?'

'I had no food to eat. What else do you expect? To get fifteen rupees for a call sheet is a big deal, and I fight to get it. I fight on the screen and off it. That's why they made me the secretary of the union this year. There's lots of hassles, but it would be a big achievement if I end this agency system where these middlemen eat up our share. We don't even know what the producers are actually paying for our work. I once acted as a police inspector in seven scenes in a movie. The producer paid three hundred rupees for that. What I received was seventy, the rest was all swallowed by the agent. We will do well only when we have the right to do our own billing. Never mind all that! Did you get a role in *Ilanthalaivan*?'

'I did. I am coming from the shoot. It seems I have got a promotion. I did a rape scene. They ripped off my sari fifteen times.'

'Did they shoot further than that scene?'

'Yes, they did...Manikkam, I feel like running away from this and getting hitched to the old man from Pondicherry who my father wanted me to marry. What happened to your film project?'

'I am preparing the script.'

'Why do you need that? Look at *Ilanthalaivan*—no one bloody knows the story.'

'My film is not like that. I am writing it frame by frame.'

'Why don't you make a film out of my story?'

'What's so great about your story?' he said. 'Like many here, you must have run off secretly to make it here. This is the story of Virugambakkam, after all.'

'There's more to this, saar. You know, my story includes an A-rated scene that my own father enacted in front of me when I was a child, and there was my uncle who showed me some disgusting magic when I was at an innocent age, and there's this bit about how they fixed a rate for me to be packed off to a good-for-nothing thug from Pondicherry. After that, my escape from all that, and how my mother joined me in my escape…there is a lot in my story.'

'Tell me at leisure someday,' Manikkam said. 'What I am writing now is my story. The only story I really know. Here, take a look…'

He took a red bound notebook from the shelf. It had clear, beautiful handwriting with small sketches nearby.

Full shot. Dark, pitch-black night.

Voice: 'Leave me. Leave me alone, master.'

Full sky to day

Lap dissolve to long shot.

Schoolkids, aged 11, 12, 13

Pan towards little boy. A scar on the cheek where he has been branded with a rod.

'I don't really understand this, but you look like someone who knows his stuff,' Manonmani said.

'There's a party waiting to fund my movie, and the actors and actresses are all new. But some area rights will still be sold. It is a career progress for me in some way. There is a man who wants to put seven lakhs into it, and he will take care of the production. We can shoot outdoors and finish it off in two or three schedules. But I insisted that the camera should not stir until the entire script was ready.'

'Do I have a part in your movie?' she asked.

'I told you I'll give you one. You remind me of a woman who made an impression on me. But you die in the story.'

'I am happy to hear that,' she said.

'Isn't it getting late? You won't be able to catch a bus at this rate, and the taxi guys won't agree to drop you.'

'I can leave in the morning,' she said.

'No, that won't look good. The Iyer across the street has already peeped in eight times.'

'Don't you want anything from me in return for your freeing me from jail?' she asked.

'You can do something for me,' Manikkam said, 'in broad daylight.'

Mano glared at him and then laughed out loud. He walked a step away from her until he dropped her off at the bus stop.

'Cut!' the director shouted and made a face.

Arun scratched his head. 'Sorry. I'll do the next take better,' he said.

'Okay,' said the tired director. As he puffed at a cigarette, the clapper board was corrected again: Scene 55, Take 8.

'Sound. Is the camera running? Action!'

Arun walked into the camera's focus and spoke his lines.

'Look here, Meena. We make all sorts of mistakes in our lives. You can't be so upset over such a small mistake. Am I not your brother?'

'Cut it!' the director said again. 'You forgot to say "Aren't you my dear sister?"'

'Sorry, sir, it is difficult to stare into nothingness and act without the sister in front of me. Where is this sister?'

'She is in Hyderabad. She had call sheet problems. We are just taking separate shots. What happened to you anyway? Thinking about your wife?'

'Wasn't this take okay?' Arun said. 'So what if I didn't say "Aren't you my dear sister?" Why don't you okay it?'

'Okay then,' said the director.

'That's all for now, right?'

'No, stay. Don't leave. You have a couple more bits to do here. In the fifty-ninth scene, you get a telegram saying your father has died. You get extremely upset...where is that telegram?'

They looked for a telegram, but there was none on the sets. 'Do you think this will pass?' Someone offered an inland letter.

'Oh, hell,' the director said. 'They don't send news of deaths in an inland letter. What kind of production are you guys running? Can't you even find a simple telegram?'

'There is one in the office,' someone said. 'Let me bring it.'

As they waited for the telegram, Arun stepped out of the floor, lit a cigarette, and thought about the stuff that was chewing him inside.

'Prem, please. Don't do this. Please listen to me.'

'Look, Arun, I have to bear the child and deliver it. In my current busy schedule, that is not possible. I have more movies in hand than you do. Why are you so worried? We have not been married for even forty days yet. We can have a baby next year.'

'Prem! Please. I need that child now.'

'And I don't. Don't be silly.'

'Arun saar,' a voice sounded. 'Shot is ready.'

The telegram in his hand bore some commercial details, but he read other things in it.

'Action!'

'Your first child has been aborted,' he saw the telegram saying. He burst into tears and wept copiously.

'Okay, cut it!' the director said. 'That was vintage Arun—a superb shot!'

At night, as he returned home in his car with tinted glasses, the sadness inside had not entirely left him.

'Don't I have my own individual freedom, Arun? Don't I have the right to decide when I want to have a baby?'

On reaching home, he rushed into Bhaskar's room, where the secretary was typing something.

'Bhaskar!' he said. 'I have to find out where Kalyani lives.'

19

Bhaskar stared at Arun, stunned. After a few moments of silence, he said, 'What has gotten into you?'

'Where is Kalyani? Find out for me. Get hold of her wedding invitation and get me her husband's address.'

'What on earth for?'

'I want to see her, talk to her. If you can't do it, I'll do it myself,' Arun said, and started rummaging through piles of paper in the almirah, scattering them everywhere.

'You are thinking about something else and fuming inside.'

'Where *is* the wedding invite?' he snapped at Bhaskar.

'I have it safe somewhere. You won't find it.'

'Bhaskar! Give it to me.'

'First tell me what the matter is.'

'Did Prem come here?'

'She is in her room.'

'Did she visit the clinic?'

'Yes.'

'The bitch!' Arun banged the table hard. The typewriter moved with a trrring.

'Why does she have to earn now? Am I not earning enough? Isn't it adequate?' He was shouting at the top of his voice now.

'Can't this situation be different from her point of view?' Bhaskar said nonchalantly in direct contrast to Arun. 'Maybe she does not even want to have a baby. Maybe she is afraid of bearing a child. Have you ever discussed this calmly and patiently?'

'Oh, come on, Buddha!'

'You have to have everything exactly your way. If it does not work out, you just lose it.'

'Where is that letter?'

'To get in touch with Kalyani now is sheer madness. It will ruin both your lives.'

'My life can't get worse than this.'

'What has really happened? Why are you overreacting like this?'

'All of my four recent releases have flopped, my career is waning. Those small guys are going up the ladder. The myth, "Cast Arun and it will run for days" has been busted. They don't need a star like me anymore. They just need a gramophone and some random face. Just one hit song will do. The hero does not have to know anything, not even the language. The voice can be dubbed. The hair, the brows, the moustache—everything can be faked. Where is the room in such a place for a classical actor like me? My magic is over, Bhaskar. They are asking me to vacate this place.'

'The cycle can turn again. Even if it doesn't, you have to be prepared for it. What do you want?'

'Fame. More fame.'

'You've earned enough fame.'

'But it's not enough.'

'It is not that—what you want now is something else.'

Arun hesitated for a while and then said, 'Kalyani.'

Bhaskar made a weary face and said, 'You are as stubborn as a mule.'

'Are you going to find her address or not?'

'I won't.'

'You are fired!'

'Okay!' Bhaskar laughed.

'I'll find it myself.'

'You can't. You can't do anything all by yourself. The fame that you have earned will leave you with no time or room to do anything on your own. Arun, I'll tell you something if you won't get angry.'

'I'll get angry, but tell me anyway.'

'You say your career is sliding and what your wife did is wrong. You only want some reason for self-pity and a feeling of being wronged to justify some sin you are up to. You are only preparing the ground for that.'

'That's just stupid stuff. Keep your pop psychiatry to yourself,' Arun said and left.

'First go and take care of your wife,' Bhaskar replied.

Arun went upstairs and opened his bedroom door. The air conditioner was switched off, and Premalatha was lying on the bed, a handkerchief thrown over her shades, sleeping because of the anaesthesia. He went closer, touched her softly and said, 'Prem!'

Her dog growled. Arun picked it up and threw it off the bed. It made a squeaking noise and hid under the chair. But Prem did not get up.

He gently rubbed her stomach and spoke to his aborted child. *Sorry, my son. You were a little ball of life born in the passion of a moment, in a chromosomal swarm, hiding in that DNA magic were her features and mine, wrapped in a single drop...with a desire to emerge as a small nose, a small pair of ears, little fingers and nails. What you went through was also a kind of death. Did it hurt, my son?*

Arun stared expressionless at his wife, who was fast asleep. He came down the stairs again and tiptoed back into the room. As Bhaskar was looking at Kalyani's wedding invite, he quickly snatched it away.

Arumairajan walked slowly in China Bazar. He had his trunk in hand and Mary beside him. In the glare of neon lights, thermocol mannequins were grinning in strange assortments of clothes. There were so many garment shops! He was wondering if all of them managed to sell their stuff. But his own worries weighed on him now. Three hundred clocks were swinging their pendulums in another shop. What was the time? 7.40 p.m. or 12.40 a.m.?

'Where are you going?'

'We have to walk straight, and we will reach Central. Just a little further, Mary.'

'Let's go to Bangalore.'

He was, in fact, walking towards the station with exactly that idea. The last bit of money he had was the ten-rupee note that Kittu had given him. Pangs of hunger gripped his stomach. They reached the railway station. *Must get on the mail that leaves around 9 p.m.*, Arumairajan thought. No one seemed to be checking the tickets, and deaf-mute girls were selling coffee and tiffin packets. Hundreds of people milled amid the rush of handcarts as porters went back and forth in their red shirts. Across the road, a hospital was calling out to people to donate blood.

He stood still, hesitating at the thought of travelling by train without a ticket. Police whistles sounded now and then, a sea of cars stood outside the station, some whizzing in and some out. Yellow-topped taxis managed to sneak in through difficult passages. Bed rolls and suitcases were all around.

Where should we go?

Arumairajan felt like he was actually on the streets now. The anxiety about his next meal only sharpened his hunger. Where would he sleep tonight? He sat near a staircase with Mary.

After the Madras Central Station despatched all the trains at its disposal, and as the platforms fell somewhat quiet, Arumairajan realized that there were a whole lot of people around like himself without a roof over their heads. The reservation counters were shutting fast. As he saw two people rolling out a bed in a dark corner, he sat nearby with some trepidation. 'Sit, Mary,' he told his wife. She put the trunk down and joined him.

One of the two strangers there asked, 'Who are you, brother? You look new here.'

'Sir, my name is Arumairajan.'

'Who is that kutty with you?'

'She is my wife.'

'Why did you come to my place?'

'I have no other place to go.'

'You are going to sleep here?'

'Yes, sir.'

'If Kalimuthu comes here, he'll thrash you—just watch out.'

'Kali has gone to Puraswalkam, boss,' the stranger's sidekick informed him.

'I'll stay here until he comes,' Arumairajan said.

'Okay then. Lie down,' the man said and asked his assistant to massage him.

As the obedient boy massaged him, he lit a beedi. He had a handkerchief around his neck and a taveez to ward off the evil eye around his arm. Mary looked around.

'Will you have a bun?'

'I have no money, sir.'

'Kabali,' the man told his sidekick. 'Get four buns on my account.'

After Kabali left, he eyed Arumairajan. 'Tell me, what's the matter? You look like an educated guy.'

'I came here to write songs for movies.'

'Wow! That is fantastic.'

Kabali returned with four buns and the man punched him on the back and announced to him: 'Look, kid, this man writes songs it seems. Come on, write one for me.'

'I can't write without a paper and a pencil, sir.'

'Daai,' the man called the assistant. 'You have a pencil stick?'

'Nah,' the boy said.

'Look here, boss,' the man told Arumairajan. 'Let me sing a song for you. You can use it in your movies. It was written for my mother's death. Hey Kabali, can you play the beat?'

As the boy sounded a rhythmic beat, the stranger sang something about his sufferings, and his comrade returned his favour with another sad song as he clucked his mouth in a bizarre kind of percussion:

'Beyond the river
a telegraph pole stood alone,
No shade to rest under
No one to call a home.'

The man made some artificial noises that resembled weeping. Then they fed Arumairajan some buns.

Arumairajan tore a bun into two and offered half to his wife. 'All this for you,' the host announced. They finished the buns off in silence.

'Now, it is your turn to sing,' the man said.

Arumairajan hesitated, thought for a while, and spoke a poem in a soft voice.

'How many days I waited,
For a son pure as a pearl,
Just a few days ago,
He left this cruel world.'

'Awesome,' the man said. 'This song is so good! But why do you cry? Look, you either sing or cry. And why are you crying, sister? Don't cry now.'

'We lost our son, boss.'

'Aah, he died? Sorry, brother. Lie down now. Sleep well.'

As he lay curled up, a policeman's stick woke him up. 'Giddaaap!'

The sky turned a pale white, signalling dawn. 'Mary, Mary!' Arumairajan shook his wife awake.

She reached out to touch the trunk but there was nothing. 'Where is the trunk?' she said.

'It was here!'

They hunted everywhere. Their comrades from the previous night had vanished. Mary froze in fear. 'The trunk is gone,' she said. The policeman was also gone.

Arumairajan stood stunned. 'What was in the trunk?'

'Saris. Trousers. Paper, pens and an empty purse.'

'Where are we going to look for it now?' Arumairajan said. 'Mary, couldn't you have been more careful? Please don't cry now. Just stay here, don't go anywhere.'

'Where are you off to?'

'Stay here, I'll be back.'

Arumairajan walked out of the station. The place was buzzing with morning sounds in a crowded hub. He crossed the bridge near the Central and reached Moore Market. He could not figure this city out. Were the men he'd seen last night good guys or bad guys? They had fed him and sung songs with him. But he could not remember their faces now. They had been so enthusiastic—they could not have been thieves. It must have been somebody else. He had actually planned to sell their clothes, and even that was not possible now.

Arumairajan was now a complete pauper.

Some people were waiting for a bus. They all looked like they had jobs to go to.

Arumairajan approached them, but he didn't know how to begin. He felt the same pause he felt each time he started penning a poem. Slowly, his hand stretched out.

'Brother! My wife and I have not eaten properly for two days. I lost my child recently. Please help. Sister! Brother!'

The first person he approached looked angry and backed away. The lady next to him put on her shades. The third one said, 'I have no change, go away.' The fourth one, with an irritated expression in her eyes, took out a small purse from a handbag, opened the button and used her thumb and forefinger to pick a coin and dropped it in his hand.

It was a five-paisa coin.

There were only three people seated in that projection theatre, and the small, air-conditioned hall had twenty-five very comfortable seats. On the screen, the rape scene from *Ilanthalaivan* was running in rush shots.

'What do you think?' Lakshmanan was asking the man next to him.

'Will the censors let this go?'

'They'll give it an A certificate, that's all. I'll fix this. You stop worrying.'

'Who's the girl?'

'Manonmani from Virugambakkam. Should I send her over?'

'How much are you asking for?'

'For her? Just a small note will do.'

'I didn't mean her. I am asking about area rights.'

'You give me two and a half lakhs.'

'Don't be greedy, Lakshmanan. This one is not worth more than one.'

'Naah! One won't work out for us. Didn't you watch the scene? Isn't it top class?'

'Does it have a Jayamalini dance?'

'I didn't get the call sheet for that, sir.'

'How much have you shot?'

'Well, it is nearly finished. Just a song, the climax and some dubbing to go.'

'What is the story?'

'We have done some kind of a set-up.'

'I've heard of a good story called *Karayellam Thamaraippoo...*'

'This is different. This one is a hero-centric story.'

'Let us finish this deal at one and a half.'

'Okay,' Lakshmanan said. 'Should I send the girl?'

'Not right now,' the distributor said. 'I can't. I am going to Sabarimala this year.'

On the screen, Manonmani was resisting the villain's advances.

20

ARUN SNATCHED THE INVITATION FROM Bhaskar. 'You got it? Viswanathan, Indian Bank Head Office, Madras…'

'Arun, what you are doing is utterly ridiculous.'

'What do you think I am going to do?'

'It's not a good idea to go and see her now.'

'Tch! I have no such plans. This is something else.' He looked at the invitation again. 'Kalyani,' he said aloud. 'Kalyani Viswanathan.'

Bhaskar stared at Arun for a while and let out a big sigh. He picked up the phone, dialled quickly and spoke into the receiver. 'Is Mr Durairaj there?' As someone spoke at the other end, he said, 'What, saar, you said you would call me. You didn't like the terms?' He fell silent for a bit.

Arun flipped through the papers on the table in a disinterested sort of way, Bhaskar went on with his negotiations, humming and hawing away to the man at the other end. Arun grabbed the only banana left on the table and slowly peeled and ate it. Bhaskar put the receiver down and announced, 'Arun, we have to do something.'

'How much did you ask for?'

'One and a half lakhs, half of that in black.'

'A total of one and a half?'

'Yes.'

'Look here, Bhaskar,' Arun said, 'when did you slash my rates?'

'Recently. We are not getting any new projects, Arun.'

'You can't just cut the rates like that, Bhaskar. They'll say this chap's films are flopping and he has cut his rates—that's how they'll sideline you. Don't just cut the rate. All I need is one hit and everything will be alright.'

'Where is that hit? We have had four flops in a row.'

'Just wait a bit, boy! You know, Arun is like a phoenix. I will rise from my ashes. The only stupid thing I have done is this marriage. You know, my glamour quotient has ebbed a bit after that. But you never know. I'm doing a double role in one movie—I am the hero and the bad guy. I think it will catch fire.'

The intercom buzzed. 'Bhaskar, is Arun here?' It was Premalatha.

Arun piped up, 'He has come, madam.'

'Arun!' she said. 'Please come upstairs, please. Quick.'

'Aah, the lady beckons,' Arun said. 'I'll see you.'

When he went upstairs, he found her on the bed, awake. Her brows were knit together and she seemed to be in some sort of agony.

'Arun, come close, please!' she said and gave her hand to hold. 'It hurts, Arun.'

'Where?'

She put his hand on her tummy and he rubbed it. 'Will I be okay, Arun?'

'Hmmm, no chance!' he said. 'This is a serious infection. I can say only after midnight,' he joked.

'Stop playing, please. You know, I am really in pain. You have no idea.'

'Pain!' He shook her hand off. 'Do YOU have an idea how much pain I am going through? Not in my tummy but a few inches above. What right did you have to kill it? It was a bloody living being! When they poked a weapon into him, don't you think he would have felt some pain? Don't you think you could have to gone through a bit of agony just for that?'

'Arun, don't scold me!' she pleaded. 'You know I also want a baby.'

'When?' he asked. 'After you are as old as a grandma?'

'No, no, Arun—just not now. I am scared. I am not ready. I am scared I will die in childbirth.'

'Fear! That's a new excuse. Your reasons keep changing. Earlier, you said it would ruin your career. Now, you're scared. Bloody fear! Just go to the local Kosha hospital. They take one baby out every minute there. Prem, you have really cheated me. I had even asked Bhaskar for application forms for the convent school for this kid. I was so keen and you spoiled it all in a second. I wanted that child, Prem. A kid all of my own, my blood, my face, my heir. I don't even have siblings. I don't have a mother or father. Everybody around me is a bloody leech, sucking away my blood.'

'We'll pack them off.'

'Hmm, that's all you can do.'

'You only want kids, no? C'mon Arun,' she humoured him.

'Bloody hell! I am not going anywhere near you for three months. Let the wounds heal,' he said. 'My wounds!'

Arumairajan sat hesitantly on the chair. 'Sit down, Mary,' he said, as Mary sat on a corner of the chair across. A man wearing a huge turban brought in a tray of pastries with red and green toppings and placed it in the centre of the table. The delicacies looked inviting. Mary asked, 'How much does one of these cost?'

'Seventy-five paise,' said the waiter.

'I don't need this,' she told her husband. 'A bun and some tea will do.'

As the waiter left, Arumairajan counted the change in his pocket.

'Where did you get this money?' she asked.

'I earned it.'

'Did you beg?'

'No.'

'You begged!' she cried out. 'Please don't beg again.'

Arumairajan looked around and said, 'Look here, why are you crying? What happened now?'

'What have we done to deserve this? Let's go, let's go to Tuticorin. My akka is there. They'll feed us. Or let's go back to Bangalore. You can still do a hotel job like you used to. What have we come to? We are begging now!'

'Stop crying! Everybody is looking at us,' Arumairajan chided her. 'I don't have the money to return to Bangalore.'

'But you sold off all the jewels.'

'That chap said he will give me a break. We just have to hold on for a few days.'

'Let's travel without tickets.'

'That's wrong, Mary. Please bear with me. Now, please drink this tea.'

'What about you?'

'I don't want anything—you have it.'

He poured the tea in a saucer and pushed it towards her with much care. She sat there like a zombie and sipped it. He tore a bun into two halves and ate one, dipping it into the same cup.

'Where is he?' she asked. 'Do you know where he is at least?'

'We can try looking for him. He gave me a phone number, but I forgot it.'

He went to the cashier and gave him the money he said he had earned. The restaurant owner glared in irritation at the small change and said, 'This five paisa coin is not valid. Give me another one.'

Arumairajan paused. 'I don't have another other, sir,' he said. The owner glared at both of them again, at Arumairajan's stubble, at the dust on his wife's hair, and at the sweat on his chest.

'Okay, keep it. I don't want the money.'

'Why, sir?'

'I don't want it. It's okay,' the owner pushed the coins towards him.

A bit stunned, he scooped up the coins, pushed them into his pocket and walked out. They just stood there for a while. What should they do now?

'Let's first find that man and get our money back,' Mary said.

'But the studio is so far, Mary.'

'Let's walk, then.'

'Wait. Let me ask around. We can go some of the way by bus.'

When they reached the gates of the studio, cars and taxis buzzed past the generous path that led inside. A Hindi-speaking guard sporting a dark green military shirt was checking who was entering.

'This is where he often comes,' Arumairajan told his wife. 'His name is Kittu. He comes in a taxi. Slightly bald, large build, fair skin.'

They waited for an hour. When they nearly lost attention because of their fatigue, a Fiat drove in and Arumairajan spotted Kittu stretched out on the backseat. 'Kittu saar, Kittu saar,' he yelled and ran after the cab. 'Aeyy,' the guard stopped him and said in Hindi, 'Andar jaana mana hai—you can't go in.'

'I need to meet that man,' he told the guard. 'He owes me money—they have called me in.'

The car had disappeared by now into the leafy interiors of the sprawling studio lawns, and the guard held him back.

'Ayya,' Arumairajan pleaded with the Hindi-speaking guard. 'Please let me in. I know that Kittu. I have to meet him.'

'Yahin khade raho!' the guard barked in Hindi.

'I have to go in. Please let me go, please.' Arumairajan broke himself loose and ran in, and the guard grabbed him again. Mary was sobbing. A small crowd gathered.

'What happened, ma?' one of them asked.

Mary recounted her plight between her sobs. 'We have lost all our money. I sold my jewels and we gave the money to this man—we have been cheated.'

'Don't talk like that, Mary. No, please,' Arumairajan said. 'We weren't cheated. We gave an advance to somebody, and we just have to meet him. He has gone inside, and this guard is not letting us in.'

Someone interjected on their behalf. 'Let him go, no? How does it matter to you?'

Another person countered that. 'The guard is only doing his duty!' Turning to Arumairajan, he said, 'Hey you! Do you have a pass?'

Meanwhile a stern voice sounded. 'What's the problem here?'

The guard stood up and saluted the newcomer. 'Andar jaana maangta hai yeh!'

Another voice piped up: 'You, speak in Tamil. This is Tamil Nadu, not your own area.'

'He wants to go inside,' the guard explained.

'Who are you, sir?' the man who had just received the salute asked.

'Ayya, there is this man called Kittu who has my money. He has gone inside, and I have to see him, and these people won't let me in.'

'Kittu? How much money?'

'One thousand rupees, saar.'

'Why did you give him so much?'

'So I could write lyrics.'

'Aha!' the man said. 'What's your name?'

'Arumairajan, sir. This is my wife, Mary.'

'Come with me,' the man said. 'My name is Manikkam. We shall first meet your friend Kittu. He will be gorging on tiffin on the fifth floor now.' And then to the guard, 'You, cat-face! Let them in. You come, and you too, ma.'

Hesitantly, the husband and wife walked behind Manikkam in the studio premises, crossing rows of trees and treading past manicured grass and giant-sized sheds. People on the way greeted the man who was taking them inside. 'Vanakkam, Manikkam anney!'

Mary, in a feeble voice, said. 'We chucked up a regular job in Bangalore, and we have just lost our child. We are on the streets here, ayya. If you could just get our money back…'

'That's difficult,' Manikkam said. 'If you have given it to Kittu, it is not easy to get it back.'

'No, sir. He has made arrangements for recordings and has even given some advance.'

'Look here, Arumairajan,' Manikkam said. 'Do you actually write songs?'

'Yes sir. I have written a many.'

'Where did you say you are from?'

'Bangalore, sir.'

Manikkam counted on his fingers, 'Coimbatore, Madurai, Tirunelveli, North Arcot, South Arcot...a hundred lyricists land up here every day from these districts. Everybody wants to be a Kannadasan in a month. Look at that group standing under that tree! You know who they are? Poets! Pawning their wife's jewels and then pleading for a chance in the film world until their money runs out, and then they go home.'

Mary interjected, 'We'll go, too, sir. We need that money back somehow, that's all.'

'I am not too hopeful,' Manikkam said, 'but let's have a go at it.'

'Ayya! You are...?'

'I am an actor.'

'Oh, that's why you looked familiar. Did you recognize him, Mary?'

'You don't have to lie,' Manikkam said. 'I am just a junior artiste, an extra, the type that appears in a corner of the screen or at a distance. We have a union, and we plan to straighten out guys like Kittu.'

'Anney, vanakkam!' a voice said. They were in front of a huge, imposing door that was shut. A red light was glowing above. 'Anney, take is on. Please bear with us.'

Manikkam peeped through the cracks and announced, 'No take-shake! They are just changing shots. Come on!'

Inside the large door was a smaller one. Manikkam opened it and went inside, and it was dark. A confusing array of cables were strewn on the floor. A voice sounded, 'Let's have a sun gun on. And I want a baby.' The lights then glowed unexpectedly, and they could see real men above them, supervising the lights. At the centre of the floor, in an island of shining light, an actor and an actress stood chatting.

'Aha! Arun!' Arumairajan exclaimed. On a sofa inside the set, Kittu was seated comfortably.

Manikkam approached him. 'Kittu, saar! Can you come here a bit, please?'

Kittu narrowed his eyes in the dark and shaded them with his palm. 'Who is that? Manikkam? Come on, man! I heard you are producing a film. Who is doing your PR?'

'Kittu saar! Do you know this man?' he said, pulling Arumairajan and propped him up in the front.

Kittu's eyes looked puzzled for a moment and then brightened up. 'Oh, Arumairajan! How can I not know him, Manikkam? He is a very good poet. Arumairajan, where do you expect me look for you? Everybody was ready that day: orchestra, director...all of them.' And then to Manikkam, he said, 'Only the lyricist was missing. Half that call sheet was wasted.'

'Kittu saar!' Manikkam butted in. 'Keep the lies away from me. Just return this chap's money first.'

'Who are you to mediate in this?' Kittu said. 'Arumairajan, if you wanted the money back, you could have simply asked for it, no? Didn't I tell you the other day?'

'Meeting you was so difficult, sir! I thought if there was no song recorded, I could get my money back.'

Manikkam interjected. 'Song? Recording? Look here, Arumairajan. This guy is one big fraud.'

'Don't shout like this on the sets!' Kittu said. 'What do you want? The money, no? Sure, that can be arranged. Just ask him if he is ready to accept a cheque—wait a minute, they are ready for the take.'

There was silence. 'Where's the dupe for the younger sister?' someone asked.

'I am here, sir.' Manonmani stepped out of the dark recesses of the studio set.

21

MANIKKAM DID NOT EXPECT TO see Manonmani there. 'Really, Mano! You have graduated to playing Arun's sister. Good for you!' he said.

Manonmani came near him and smiled gently. 'It's my back that will play Arun's sister. Since the other actress did not give her call sheet, I am playing the dupe.'

'Are the continuity clothes okay?' the director's voice came from somewhere.

'It's fine, sir.'

'Arun, please come. You, too, amma.'

Mano went and stood in front of Arun. He did not notice her at first. When he did, he took a second, closer look. 'Excuse me, are you playing my sister?'

'No, sir. I'm the dupe.'

'Aah, that's what. I got a bit confused. What is this, director saar?'

'You don't seem to be comfortable without a character in front of you. This woman has the same height, same build. It is only her back that they will see.'

'Why don't we make her my sister for the rest of the film?'

'How is that possible? What do we do with all the scenes already shot?'

'How about the original sister dies and becomes a ghost and comes back in this girl's body and kind of helps her brother. We can change the story. How about it? Where's the writer?'

'Stop joking!' the director said and shouted, 'Is the shot ready?'

'Ready, saar.'

Flash, flash, flash! Suddenly, a bank of lights blazed on the set and the camera started whirring from behind Manonmani. Arun placed one hand on her shoulder and touched her chin with the other as he spoke his lines. Manikkam's watchful eyes took in the scene. Arumairajan felt a sense of wonderment, and Mary, cringing in shame as she looked at her worn-out sari and dusty hair, hid in the shadows.

When they finished shooting one round, in the short break, Arun sat on a chair in a corner of the set. Somebody towelled his face. Someone else inserted a cigarette between his lips and a third person lit it. Kittu smoothly perched himself nearby and said: 'Viju, my dear, do you know who this is? It's Manikkam, the secretary of the Junior Artistes Sangam, powerful man. He is making a new film.'

Arun looked up at him and gave him a half-smile. 'Is that so? What film is it?'

'Low-budget movie, Arun. Will you play a guest role in that?'

'Why?'

'It will be a change for you.'

'That's not the issue. You need me for the publicity, right? You need a star to splash across your posters.'

'Indeed!' Kittu echoed Arun in a slavish tone.

Without losing his poise, Manikkam said, 'I think you have misunderstood my saying that you will play a guest artiste. The role is a good one, but you would have to act without taking any money.'

'Sorry, but I don't have such a serious income tax problem.'

'Can't you act for free in just one film? For art's sake?'

'I think you are still in junior school in filmmaking. That's why you speak of art. Don't you know art is a dirty word in Tamil cinema?'

'I think you are letting go of a good opportunity.'

'Thanks, but I don't have the time,' Arun said.

'Arun, please come,' the director beckoned and Arun moved back into the spotlight.

'The creep!' said Manikkam. 'Kittu, I am actually here to see you.'

'You want Arun's call sheet? An adjustment perhaps?'

'No way! You, why are you cheating these poor people? Please give this guy's money back.'

'Did I say I won't return the money? Manikkam, Arumairajan himself asked me to keep a thousand rupees as advance for two songs and he said he would bring five hundred more. The money is still lying untouched. Isn't that right, Arumairajan?'

'Let that be, Kittu,' Manikkam said. 'Just return the money—the man is on the streets.'

'Isn't there always a struggle in the beginning? Haven't we all gone through some tough times?'

'Will you give him the money right away, please?' Manikkam was insistent.

'Wait, let me see.' Manikkam flipped open his purse and took out some cash. 'Here, Arumairajan, keep these forty rupees. I gave you ten the other day, and that makes it fifty. I will throw a cheque for the rest of the money on your face tomorrow!'

'A rubber cheque won't work,' Manikkam said. 'Make it cash. What say, Arumairajan?'

'Many thanks, ayya. If I don't get the money back, I need a work opportunity.'

'Listen, this is the stuff you should avoid. Just don't take this guy's words seriously. Take your money and head back home.'

'You are being mean, Manikkam,' Kittu said. 'Arumairajan, you don't want that chance?'

'Please don't wait here and deal with this man,' Manikkam told them. 'Where do we take the rest of the of the money, Kittu?'

'On this very floor. Tomorrow.'

'Let's see, Arumairajan. Come tomorrow, and if you don't get your money back, tell me. Give me a piece of paper—I'll write out my address.'

As he wrote out the address, Kittu piped up. 'Look, Manikkam, this is not fair. You sound as if I go around cheating people. Why don't we have a private chat? You carry on, Arumairajan.'

'Thanks, ayya.' Arumairajan left with a look of satisfaction.

Kittu dragged Manikkam aside and said, 'What's this, man? Why are you shaming me like this in front of others? Where's the money going to go?'

'Look here. That guy is a good Christian, an innocent man. If you cheat somebody like him, you will roast twice in hell. Just pay back his money quietly, okay?'

Manonmani joined them. 'Ennamma! I heard you got a fine role in Lakshmanan's film. Is that so? Can we have an interview of you in *Cinema* magazine?'

'No, sir.'

'I saw a still. Fantastic!'

'What happened to your film, Manikkam?'

'I am furiously writing the script, and we are having the poojai on Friday. We are going to make it a simple affair.'

'Who is the director?'

'Me, of course.'

'Wow! Why don't you give Arumairajan a couple of songs to write? We can adjust our amount.'

'There won't be any songs in my film. Just one title song, and that will also be a folk tune.'

'Oh! That's a recipe for disaster!'

Arun ended the conversation abruptly and stepped out of the set, wiping his face clean after having removed his make-up. Premalatha was on the next floor, acting in a Telugu movie, and he made his way to her set. She was wearing a bright, brocaded princess outfit, a princess from the past. As she stood in the middle, an actor stood with his chin on her shoulder, his arms around her waist. Some Babu he was. It seemed to Arun that all Telugu lead actors looked alike. That Babu spewed some Telugu lines—'*Nee kosam, naa kosam*'—as he rubbed his very Andhrite nose on her cheeks. Arun took all that in for a while.

As she saw him, Premalatha greeted him. 'Hi Arun!' She came near him. An orchestra of jewels made jingling noises from her body.

'Would you be long?'

'It will be 9 p.m. by the time I pack up.'

'How are you feeling?'

'I am okay now. Would you wait for a while? Should I cancel the schedule? I'll say I have a headache.'

'Naaw, you carry on. I'll see you later.'

'Are you done for the day?'

'Yup. I'll see you.'

'You are going home, no?'

'Where else?'

A journalist who had rushed up asked, 'Arun, there are rumours in the industry that all's not well between you and Premalatha. Why aren't you snuffing out those rumours?'

Prem came close to Arun. 'Here, take a picture of us,' she said and kissed Arun on the cheek. 'Publish a big one, okay?'

'Of course!'

As the thrilled reporters moved away, a voice called out in Telugu, 'Premamma, ostha va?'

Arun stepped out of the set. He walked towards a solitary telephone in a corner and thought for a while.

'Is this Indian Bank? I want to speak to Mr Viswanathan.'

'Which Viswanathan? G.S. Viswanathan or R. Viswanathan?'

'The one who got married recently.'

'Oh, you mean R. Viswanathan. You'll have to wait. He is in the advances department.'

Arun wondered if he should put the receiver down. *What can I possibly talk to him about? What should I say? What kind of madness is this! Arun, south Indian superstar—why the hell should he be calling a clerk sitting in the corner of a bank adding numbers?*

'Hullo, advances.'

'I want to speak with Mr R. Viswanathan.'

'Oh, he has gone out on an audit.'

'Where?'

'Out of town.'

'May I get his home address?

'Who would you be, saar?'

'I am a relative from his wife's side.'

'Wait a moment.' There were some gentle noises at the other end. They were asking around about Viswanathan. 'Rajagopal, do you know RV's address?'

'Theradi Street. I think it is 78, near some medical store.'

'Many thanks, sir.'

'What did you say your name was?' the voice asked at the other end.

Arun put the receiver down. He left and sat in his car. 'Hasn't Bhaskar come?'

'No, sir. I have dropped him in Nungambakkam,' the driver said. He spoke very little and waited quietly for Arun's next order.

'Head towards Theradi Street in Thiruvallikkeni,' Arun told him, and the car set off towards Triplicane.

What are you going to do there? Can you even get out of your car on Theradi Street? Can your car even go slow there? Your face will give you away. Why the hell are you going there anyway? It is not just fair. Do you even have a clue about what complications you will cause by going there? Why? Why? Why?

Arun rolled up the tinted windowpanes of his car. It turned into a lane, crossed the Parthasarathy Temple, its mandapam, its green pond, and crawled on Theradi Street.

'Should I stop now, sir?' the driver asked.

'Go straight.'

The car moved past little boys, milkmen, cycle rickshaws, Venkata Lodge, a stainless steel utensils store and dolls dressed in silk. Then there was Ananda Medicals.

'Go slow now, pa.'

Andanda Medicals, 79, Theradi Street, the address read.

'Okay, let's go home,' he told the driver.

The driver's face was expressionless. He obeyed his master.

Kalyani and Vanaja stepped out of the sanctum sanctorum, having worshipped the tall and well-built Lord Vishnu sporting a moustache at the Parthasarathy Temple in Triplicane. They crossed the murals on the corridor walls adorned with the lyrical poetry of the Alwar saints, prayed to Lord Narasimha and came next to the mandapam, where they bought themselves a small wooden box to store kumkum, and walked on.

Vanaja did most of the talking. 'Why are you so scared? What hell will break loose if you step out for a morning show?

'He will kill me.'

'Only if he finds out, no?'

'He will find out somehow—he does not like the smell of cinema.'

'Not my husband,' Vanaja said. 'Once I have done the cooking and set it up for him, he serves himself and washes all the dishes and arranges them back neatly. He even makes the advance bookings for movies for me.'

'Everybody is not the same in this world, Vanaja.'

Kalyani had lost some weight. The kumkum that she had been given at the temple was applied close to the bindi she already had. Her voile sari was neatly wrapped around her shoulders, and her wrist bore a single bangle made of some kind of a steel wire. Viswanathan's instructions to her rang in her ears. ('Don't wander around wearing any jewellery when I am not around. I have arranged for a locker at the Triplicane branch.') On her feet were a pair of rubber chappals. ('It is enough to wear rubber chappals to the temple. Your better sandals can be worn for a wedding or for some festival. They will be maintained well and shine.')

'Why are you dressed like this? It's a Friday. Why can't you dress a little brightly? You know, wash your face, put on some talcum powder on? You are quite beautiful, you know.'

'Po di!' Kalyani fobbed off her friend. ('You should not be dressed in bright clothes when I am away, and there is no way you should stand outside on the street, okay?')

'He is not in town, no? Should I bring all those magazines?'

'No, Vanu.'

'So what the hell are you going to do in your room?'

'He has bought a lot of plastic beads. I am making a bag out of it. I also have some embroidery to do.'

'You still have your periods?'

'Mmm.'

'I was only asking because of this embroidery thing you mentioned.'

'No, Vanu, nothing like that yet.'

She crossed the wrought-iron gate, the dark passage and the dimly lit courtyard where the other tenants were waiting near a water pipe. She climbed up the backstairs to her room and opened the lock with a key. ('Make sure your key is always attached to your thaali with a safety pin. Don't take it off—ever.')

On the table was a letter Viswanathan had written to her from his outstation trip. She read it once more.

Many blessings to you. I have reached here safely. Since there was a lot of audit work, I could not write to you earlier. The room here is comfortable, but the food is extra spicy. I forgot to pay the electricity bill before leaving. I have put it on the top rack of the almirah, under the book on mercantile law. Please take it and tally the reading in the card attached to the bill with our meter (ours is the fourth from the left) and give it to Srinivasavaradan next door. Please ask him to pay the bill and tell him that I will return the money on my return. If I recall correctly, the amount is eighteen rupees forty paise. Don't go anywhere on your own. Take care of your health. Reply on receipt of this letter. I have kept a postcard on the second rack of the almirah in the left-hand corner.

Yours – R. Viswanathan

Kalyani looked around. There was a Westclox alarm clock on the mantle and a framed copy of her husband's B. Com degree from the University of Madras with its wavy calligraphy on the wall. The paramacharya of Kanchi Mutt smiled from a calendar. A mattress lay firmly rolled up on the cot.

Somebody knocked at the door.

'Who is it?'

'It's me, ma. Ananda Medicals.'

'What is it, pa?' She peeped out through the window.

There stood a little boy. 'You are Kalyani, no?'

'Yes. Why?' She had seen that boy in the medical store.

'There is a phone call for you at the shop.'

'Who is it?'

'I don't know, ma.'

'Who could it be?' she wondered as she locked the room again and followed the boy.

The telephone receiver was lying flat on its back atop a glass box.

'Give me a strip of Dacron. Who is that call for?' a voice called out.

'Here she comes.'

'Hello?' she said, pressing the receiver to her ears.

'Kalyani?'

'Yes. Who is this?'

'This is Arun. Do you remember me?'

22

Kalyani suddenly felt a wave of fear sweep over her. *Oh, what kind of trouble is this?* she thought. She wanted to hang up at once.

'Kalyani, please wait. There is no harm in talking to me on the phone. Look how I have traced you down, Kalyani. Are you all right?'

'Mmm,' she said. 'And you?' she wanted to ask him but restrained herself.

As if he had heard her thoughts, he said, 'I am getting by—somehow.'

'Shall I hang up?' she asked.

'Don't. I must talk to you.'

'Hmm. What is it?'

'Kalyani, I have to see you.'

'He is not in town.'

'It is you that I want to see.'

'No. Let him come back.'

'I have to see you. I am only going to talk. Don't be scared, don't be scared.'

'You have already spoken to me.'

'I have to meet you and talk to you, Kalyani. I am still thinking of you. And you?'

There was silence.

'I am restless. In my life, there is no solace, Kalyani. Don't you talk to that guy from the medical store? You can talk to me like that, no? There is nothing to be afraid of. There is nothing wrong in this, there is no harm in talking. Look, this evening at 7.30 p.m., there is a road that leads to the beach from the pond near your home…'

'I won't be coming.'

'Listen to me, you just have to be at the corner where that road meets the beach road. I will be coming in my car. 3366. It is a Fiat.'

'I am not going to be there.'

'You will come. You must come. You have to come.'

'Let me put the phone down.' She quickly put back the receiver.

Her hands were trembling. 'Who is it, ma?' the shopkeeper asked with a smile.

'Somebody we know,' she said, finding her balance. She wanted to say, 'Sir, please don't tell my husband about this call.' But she did not. She walked back to the room, disturbed. She locked the door from inside at once.

What? He will come as far as here? What kind of problem is this? What kind of ordeal! What am I going to do, God! Should I write a letter to him? No. He won't understand. Maybe I can write to my brother? My dear Anna, I am in a state of deep confusion…no, I can't write a letter. There will be a reply and he will open it—he has the habit of opening all letters.

Tick-tock-tick. The table clock seemed louder. It was 7 p.m.

How did he find out where I live?

'You will come. You must come. You have to come.'

'Kalyani, you are so beautiful.'

Chee! I should not be thinking like this. It is wrong. It is a sin. I should not go there.

She fastened the other latch of the door from inside, pulled the chair and placed it near the door. Her heart was beating fast. Her husband's letter was lying on the table. She opened it and read it again. The electricity bill! Not a word asking how she was. Not a word of love. The meter reading and eighteen rupees and forty paise. *That's all?*

Why the hell couldn't he write, 'Oh my love, I am so far from you and thinking of you constantly.' What evil would befall him if he wrote something like that? *What can I do now? Read* Deivathin Kural, *perhaps.*

The right way is to help uphold the dharma of the Vedas, to birth future heirs to that dharma such that in the coming times, the world has citizens who have that high attitude…

She looked at the clock, got up, took away the chair, opened the door and, clutching the letter her husband had sent, went to meet the neighbour, Srinivasavaradan, about the electricity bill.

Arun drove slowly to the beach road around 7.30 p.m. Mercury lamps were illuminating the entire stretch. He could not find a dark spot to park his vehicle. *This is the corner where I asked her to come. She will come. She has to come.*

There were small groups of people making their way to the sands. Petromax lamps shone brightly as hawkers sold raw mango slices, bhelpuri and chilli bajjis. Madras was merrily munching peanuts, unmindful of the sea roaring nearby.

He wanted to walk along with them. *Dear friends, I am just one of you. Why don't you take me along with you? Let me whistle and fly those balloons. Let me play kabaddi with you. But there is no way. The traffic would come to a standstill. The crowd will engulf and swallow me up.*

He crossed the spot and took a U-turn near the Gandhi statue and glided along the side of the road slowly. Kalyani was nowhere in sight.

Could she have come and gone? Would she have turned up in the first place? What strong faith I have! Arun, how can you even think another man's wife will come at your beck and call? No, she knows me well. She would not have forgotten the memories of the day we were together. After all, I am not calling her with any evil thought…she knows that for sure. There! Is that her?

He stopped the car. That girl looked back and called out to someone on the other side of the road with a smile. No, this was not Kalyani.

'Vaadhyaare, isn't that Arun?' a voice called out.

'Adeyy, yes da!'

'Hi Arun!'

'Hey Dhanapal. Come running—get here fast. It's Arun!'

In a few moments there were about fifty people around them.

'Bring the panes down. Let us take a good look at you.'

There were a series of palms, five fingers each, stamping their fandom on his car's window panes. *Dum, dum, dum.* There was a drumming on the bonnet. He pressed the horn. No one stirred. 'Open up!' they shouted. 'Open, open!'

He half opened the window and said, 'What, man?' The sound of clapping hands drowned out his voice. A ten-rupee note came his way for an autograph.

'You,' he said. 'Don't touch me.'

'What, brother, your films are all flopping these days.'

'Boring,' another said. 'What was that new one?'

'Big Brother has come loose, man. His game was over after he married that Premalatha.'

Arun got out of the car in a ferocious mood and grabbed the collar of the man who had mocked him. 'What did you say, da?' The crowd backed off a little.

'You, leave that shirt, man!'

He slapped the man who had provoked him and pushed him into the crowd. Before that man could get up, Arun had sprung back into the car and started it up. He nearly drove it into the crowd and got away. The last thrashings of the crowd landed on the car's rear. '

'What arrogance this man has!'

'Note his car number! We have to register a police complaint.'

'I think if we write about this, all the magazines would be ready to publish it,' said a man who was a regular contributor of snippets.

Blood rushed to his head. Arun drove the car like a possessed man. The car whirred past the television tower at eighty kilometres an hour and reached Mount Road. The colourful hoardings were looming above him. *Ramayee Vayasukku Vandhutta, Pennukku Yaaru Kaaval, Ullasa Paravaigal…*

None of them had his face. Oh, the number of new faces in the film world! *I used to be smiling all along this road,* he thought. *Do people forget stars so fast? What brother, your films are flopping these days! Come on, you guys! I am going to make a hit that will swallow everybody. I will put my heart and soul into it. It will be a superhit. Who do you think I am?*

As the car turned into his house, the rear bumper hit a corner of the wrought iron gate. The car growled to a halt in the portico.

'Where have you been?' Bhaskar asked. 'I have been hunting for you, phoning every damn studio in town.'

'Bhaskar, let's make our own movie. Make an announcement to the magazines tomorrow.'

'Are you joking?'

'I have never been more serious, my dear secretary.'

'What is this? All of a sudden…'

'We have to show them who Arun is.'

'You can do that even in the films you are acting in now.'

'There is no scope there. Who is the best heroine face in town? Sridevi? Rathi? Radhika? Or let's cast them all together.'

'Premalatha,' said Bhaskar.

'Nah, let's not. Who is the best writer? Who is the best director? Get them all at ten above the current rate. Just make them offers.'

'Can we talk about this in the morning?'

'No. Let's do it now—right now.'

'Arun, will you listen to me?'

'I won't.'

'It is not that easy to make a movie, Arun. We don't quite have the machinery and the manpower.'

'If we don't, let's build it. Why do you think I am paying you a salary?'

'Okay, I'll get it done. Take it easy now and go to sleep. There is clearly something else bothering you. Shall I get you some Scotch?'

'No.'

'What else do you want?'

'I have not got what I wanted.'

In a corner of the editing room rested an archaic Moviola machine. Little round cans were strewn about, loaded with film rolls, labelled something or the other. On a tray nearby were film rolls stacked to fit the intended sequence. On the right-hand side was an editing table with a splicer, a viewer, a synchroniser and other gear. To stick them all together, there was some Mylar tape.

Ilanthalaivan had just reached the editing table. Lakshmanan and the director stood in a corner. The editor

Rangan, wearing with a long, red naamam vertically streaked across his large forehead, was previewing the rough cuts on the Moviola. On the small screen of the machine, a pint-sized Manonmani was running for her life as the villain chased her.

'Ayyangar! Just make sure this scene doesn't meet your scissors. I don't want a single frame of it touched,' Lakshmanan said.

'Swamy, this is not in sync, what can I do?' Rangan Ayyangar responded as the sound-track on the celluloid film on the left refused to sync with the visual on the right.

'Adjust it somehow. Who is going to look at the editing quality? Only this *Vikatan* critic will scream as if the world will end because of this movie.'

The Moviola turned out to be in a cranky mood, and Ayyangar gave it a kick. 'This is an ancient machine. You have to kick it for every ten feet of film. Why don't you tell your owner to buy a new machine? I am stuck with this like it was a godforsaken harmonium.'

'That's where your skill lies, Ayyangar.'

'What skill? You should look at that Steinbeck console I saw in Bombay. What a machine! What I do in an hour here can be done in five minutes flat on that. Everybody just wants to save pennies…' he stopped suddenly and peered into the machine. Manonmani was lying flat on her back in that small viewer. For a fleeting second or two, her breasts were fully visible.

'Swamy, it is better to chop it off right here. Otherwise, I am quite sure this scene is going to come right back to this table.'

'Why do *you* have to worry about that, Ayyangarey?'

'What did you say was the name of the film?'

'Ilanthalaivan.'

'I have to tell my daughter not to watch it.'

Lakshmanan stepped out of the editing room. Venugopal did not like the air conditioning. He stood outside, pacing up and down with a cigarette in his hands. 'Will we be through with this by tonight?'

'Give me five hundred rupees first.'

'I have been showering these five hundreds without count. Have the censors set a date yet?'

'Aah, no! We have not even got a copy of the script in yet.'

'Look, my interest payments are shooting up, and you have already announced the release date. Have we booked the theatres?'

'Don't you worry, sir. We will do it. All we need to shoot is a horseback scene, but we can't find the damn horse.'

'What is a horse doing in this social drama?'

'This one involves a zamindar, no?'

Venugopal seemed to lose interest and let out a loud belch.

'We still haven't sold Coimbatore.'

'It doesn't matter. We'll sell them. The film is sure to be a hit. We can recover the cost in just one area.'

Rangan stepped out. 'I have fixed it all somehow. The lip sync is a bit jerky but I have given it some jump cuts here and there. Want to see it?'

'You are a smart fellow, Ayyangar!' Lakshmanan beamed. 'There is nothing you can't do.'

They both went inside.

'Ah, you are so punctual,' Kittu said. 'They let you in?'

'I gave Manikkam's name and they let me in,' Arumairajan said. Kittu looked around and lit a cigarette. 'Do you need the money right away?'

'Yes, sir. We can't even stay two nights in a hotel on the forty bucks you gave me. I have left my wife there. If you give me the money we can go back to Bangalore tonight.'

'Why, man?'

'I am done with the film world. Please, please give me back my money. That would be very kind of you. I will leave at once.'

Kittu looked at his watch. 'It's 2 p.m. now, and the bank will be closed. Will you take a cheque?'

'What will I do with a cheque?'

Kittu thought for a while. 'Can you wait a bit? It will take an hour and a half for me to arrange the amount.'

'I'll stay right here with you.'

'There is some composing going on inside. You want to watch it? Come with me.'

Arumairajan, looking crestfallen, walked behind Kittu. They walked past an asbestos-covered corridor next to the recording studio.

There were eight people in the room. There was a man with a harmonium, another with a guitar and a third with a tabla. Across them, leaning on a fat round cushion sat a huge man. An assistant squatted on the floor, writing stuff on sheaves of paper in a neat, calligraphic style. Torn up sheets of paper littered the ground nearby.

'*Thanthana, thana-thana, thanandam*' the composer sang the opening notes of his tune.

The lyricist thought for a moment and asked, 'What's the theme?'

'It describes a woman, saar,' the composer said sang again. '*Thanthana, thana-thana, thanandam.*'

'*Her laugh is such you can't capture in lines*,' a lyricist offered the first line of the song.

'Wonderful,' the composer said, gesturing to the squatting scribe. 'Note that down.' Then he warbled the tune of the second line, '*Thanadham thana-dhana, thanandham.*'

'That sounds complicated,' the lyricist said.

'The tune's like that. You can fix it with your skills,' the composer cajoled him.

The lyricist furrowed his brows and pondered a while. The harmonium player now played the tune on his instrument. '*Thanadham, thana dhana, thanandam.*'

There was some hesitation in the air now. Everybody was looking eagerly at the lyricist's lips, waiting for words to tumble out of his mouth.

Arumairajan, standing in a corner of the room, spoke in a clear voice,

'Her laugh is such you can't capture in lines

My words stumble...Her smile glows like a sky filled with sunshine.'

23

THE ROOM FELL SILENT AND everybody was now looking at Arumairajan. The lyricist standing in the middle was visibly irritated. 'What's this, ayya? Who is the lyricist here? Me or some passer-by?'

Arumairajan heard someone chiding him. 'Why did you butt in here, man?' Arumairajan looked scared and started walking towards the door.

'*My words stumble...Her smile glows like a sky filled with sunshine*—it fits so well,' the composer said. He fiddled with his harmonium and tried out the tune and the line again.

The lyricist spoke up. 'Let's drop it. I have changed the first line anyway. Let's change it now to, "*Words can't capture the beauty of her teeth.*" Let's drop that "*Her laugh is such you can't capture in lines.*"'

'So, it is now "*Words can't capture the beauty of her teeth,*" right?' the clerical calligrapher called out from the floor.

The composer was playing it safe. 'Let's keep both the options in stock.'

'Okay, let's have the second line.'

The harmonium played the tune of second line again. The lyricist furrowed his brows again and thought some more. They all waited for a while. Arumairajan stood near the door.

'*Words can't capture the beauty of her teeth*—and then?' The composer looked around and caught Arumairajan's eye. 'What says our roadside poet? Can you think of some line, brother?'

With much hesitation, Arumairajan spoke, as if he was saying something grossly inappropriate: '*They are diamonds that buy out the heavens in a smile so sweet.*'

While everybody looked stunned, the composer asked, 'Who is this man? He plays so wonderfully with words.'

'His name is Arumairajan, and I introduced him to the industry,' Kittu piped up.

The lyricist was furious. 'Kannabiran, how much advance have we taken?' he asked his aide.

'Just one song.'

'We have done one song already, no? So let me go. I can't be writing lyrics for these godawful people. Roadside amateurs are interrupting my songs. There is no respect for experience anymore. To top it all, there is this whole crowd here, like it is some village fair.'

'Sorry, anney. You! Get out everybody!'

'Let me leave before they do. Come, Kannabiran. It was not for nothing that Kamban wrote, "Did I learn Tamil for a person like you?" Vaayya.' The lyricist shook the cotton tippet off his shoulder and moved out in a hurry.

After he had left, someone asked, 'Why is he leaving in anger like this?'

'He has a point, no? How will you feel if somebody interrupted like this? What a big poet he is! Let's first get this man out. If one is here to watch, the thing is to keep one's trap shut. Off with you! Go!'

As Arumairajan started out, the composer spoke. 'Wait!'

'His name is Arumairajan. He is my find, Raja,' Kittu said.

'Please complete this song for me,' the composer said. 'I won't get a call sheet from this poet again so easily. Your lines have fitted in quite well so far.'

'What are you saying?' Arumairajan said. 'Are you giving me the chance to write a song?'

'Yes sir. Please take a seat.'

Arumairajan, feeling elated, froze in his tracks.

'Come here, now. Why are you kneeling?'

With tears in his eyes and hands knitted together, Arumairajan looked up and said, 'Our Father who art in heaven, hallowed be thy name. May your kingdom come.'

'Wow!' someone exclaimed. 'Even these lines sound so good. Can we use it in our film?'

'Kavignar Arumairajan, please be seated,' Kittu said with an air of confidence. Arumairajan's name was uttered with a title that announced the official arrival of a poet. 'Come, sit in this chair. Who goes there? Get a coffee down here. Anney, are you the production guy? Can you give me five hundred?'

Arumairajan's shirt was drenched in tears.

Lakshmanan paid the censor fee at forty-five rupees per one thousand feet of celluloid film through a demand draft and submitted alongside eight copies of the songs, eight copies of the synopsis of the story and a laboratory certificate—all neatly packed in a big envelope. He now went to the censor board office. Before he entered through the gate, he told his driver to get change for a hundred rupees. There was a small crowd outside, but the office bore the distinct hallmarks of a central government office: a toilet that had not been cleaned for a week, with a door that they had not been able to shut for the past one year. A notice board was hanging inside a glass casing. There were official notices typed in off-white paper in English and in Hindi which no one seemed to find use for. The peons, as usual, were ruling over the corridors. Lakshmanan approached one of them squatting on a stool. The man was puffing a beedi perched on an upright knee. 'Muthuswamy! How are you? All well?'

'Vaanga,' the peon greeted the producer, without getting up.

'Is the superintendent in?'

'He is in the toilet. Let him come,' said the peon.

His tone changed when a five-rupee note came his way, and he said, 'Just wait. Let me see if he is back.' He peeped in and shooed him in. 'You may go in.' Muthuswamy sat on his stool again and shot off a question to a colleague seated across the corridor. 'Is it possible to take a provident fund loan on the grounds that your sister-in-law is not well?'

Lakshmanan entered the office. Some clerks did not see him coming in. The superintendent was sitting in a corner, reading a copy of *Ananda Vikatan* behind a huge pile of files, and he promptly hid it on seeing Lakshmanan. The Godrej almirahs blocked the windows and let no air in. There were ink stains everywhere, near wooden tables that seemed to be well past their prime, and there seemed to be no chair in proper working condition. There was a hole in one, a broken arm in another and a third had a shaky leg.

'What's the matter?' the superintendent asked.

'I've come to get a date,' Lakshmanan said, submitting the fat envelope. The superintendent pulled it up carelessly and took out the stuff. 'Vinayakam, make an entry,' he said.

'Shall we meet the senior officer?'

'Oh, certainly! If you go straight down, he is in the corner room,' the superintendent said before trying to pay extra attention to the files at hand.

'Er...we have set the nineteenth as the release date.'

The superintendent looked at the calendar. 'The nineteenth? Impossible! The screening can only take place on the eighteenth.'

'But we have decided on the nineteenth.'

'And who did you ask before fixing the date? Are you joking?'

In a rare moment, the superintendent's top drawer was quietly opened and it witnessed the surrender of a hundred-rupee note. The superintendent, with no change in his facial expression, said 'Hmmm. No, this is going to be difficult. If you insist, we can have the screening on the seventeenth and if there are no cuts, the certificate can be given on the eighteenth. What did you say the film's title was?'

'*Ilanthalaivan*.'

'Come with me. Why don't you see the RO anyway? The film is clean, no?'

'Hmm, sort of,' said Lakshmanan with much hesitation.

The regional officer of the Central Board of Film Censors, who was sitting somewhat idle, responded to Lakshmanan's ear-to-ear grin with a grim face and looked at the superintendent. 'What's the matter?'

'They have set the release for the nineteenth. They are asking for a date now.'

'When do you think it is possible?'

'I think the seventeenth is possible.'

Lakshmanan chimed in. 'Please, somehow you have to…'

'He has already said the seventeenth, no? Why do you think we have published a proper booklet on this? Aren't the rules and regulations clear to you?'

'The date is too close. If there is a cut or something, we will be late.'

'So what? You can postpone the release.'

'Come,' the superintendent signalled, and as they stepped out, Lakshmanan slurred. 'What can I…?'

'He is a strict man.'

'There is one more thing,' Lakshmanan said. 'If the board members are meek, it would be great. The film is a bit offbeat. We don't mind an A certificate, but just make sure there is no Balachander or KVJ at the screening.'

'We'll see about that.'

'Okay.' Lakshmanan was cheerful as he left the office of the censor board.

Arun had not given up on Kalyani. He phoned the medical store again. 'Could you please call Kalyani from next door?'

'You are the one who phoned yesterday, no?'

'Yes.'

'The boy is not here. Could you call after ten minutes? It's a busy time at the shop.'

He banged the phone down in a frustrated mood. 'Bhaskar! Bhaskar!' he called and went into the next room and then the main hall. No one seemed to be around. The walls were decorated with framed photographs of him in various moments of success: as a young boy in Sarojadevi's lap; his first film; his first one as a hero; a shield for his first movie to complete one hundred days; his first Malaysia trip; one taken for a lark with white men and women on an overseas trip; more rewards and shields; twenty-five-week mementos. He walked to the backyard of the house. No one seemed to be around. *Where the hell had everybody gone?* He came back to the front and climbed the stairs up and knocked on the door of Premalatha's bedroom. It opened to reveal Premalatha's mother in front of a mirror. She was applying Lacto Calamine on her face.

'Where is everybody gone?'

'Who?'

'My relatives.'

'I don't know, ante.' She spoke in Tamil mixed with Telugu. 'They said they were going out of town.'

'Have you driven them away?' he snapped.

'Ayyo, no! Varalakshmi! Varalakshmi! Ikkada raa,' she called for her daughter.

Premalatha emerged from the next room. 'Emamma?'

'This Arun is saying strange things. I am scared.'

'What is it, Arun?' she asked.

'The two of you have conspired to drive all of my relatives away, right?'

'Who says so?'

'Then where the hell are they?'

'How do I know? Do they ever talk to me or Amma? They treat us as if we are untouchables. Ask Bhaskar. He'll tell you. He is the be-all and end-all in this house.'

'You didn't drive them away?'

'Why would we do that?'

'Hmm, they have the same rights here as you do. You know that?'

'We know that only too well. You don't have to keep repeating it.'

'You can't touch them, understand?'

Premalatha looked tired and frustrated. 'Ask yourself, Arun, if how you are behaving is right.'

'I am just telling the truth.'

'Why do you have to shout? Why are you so angry? Arun, I know that you are just angry that your film has flopped. I am the only one in this house that you can take it out on. Is this a home? My mother and I have got a room here. That's all. We have no right to ask for anything more. What right have you given me here as the woman you are married to?'

'Hah! Wife! Don't talk about that!' he raised his voice again.

'Amma, you please go inside,' she told her mother. 'I have to talk to him alone. Arun, don't go anywhere.'

'Eydukondlavaadaa!' Premalatha's mother said, invoking the lord of Tirupati and went inside.

He asked in a tired voice, 'What is it now?'

'Arun, I want to ask you something. Why do you phone Kalyani now?'

He was startled. How had she found out? What could he say now?

'Why are you quiet?'

'Is eavesdropping your profession?'

'Why do you have an extension for your phone in my room, then? I picked it up by chance and heard you. And look at this!' she said, throwing a daily newspaper at him.

'Famous Actor Arun in Beach Ruckus and Violence, Scuffles with Fans!'

'Rascals!' he muttered.

'You had gone to see her, right?'

Arun kept quiet. *How do I tell her?* He didn't want to tell her all that was on his mind.

'I have not met her.'

'You want me to believe that?'

'How does it matter to you where I go? That is my wish.'

'Can I also behave like that?'

'Do it! After all, you have seen and done everything.'

'Arun! Don't be cruel!' Her eyes were glazed with tears now. 'Just think of what you are doing. Is it proper to phone a married woman and meet her?'

'Why? Can't we be friends?'

'By all means. Why don't you call her here, and I can also join you? We can talk together.'

'You can't match her.'

'What's to match? Whatever she has I do, too,' her voice was trembling now.

'Tchai!'

'Arun, this is not good for anybody. How *could* you, Arun? How can you think on these lines when you have a wife? What do you look for in her? What are you seeking? Tell me. Let me also know. I feel so hurt.'

'You won't understand even if I tell you. Only your career is important to you—not your family. A child is not important to you. Prem, you have really let me down.'

'But why did I do that? You only have to ask Bhaskar to know how many of your projects have been cancelled. Do you know what is your bank balance today? Arun, your earnings are coming down. I have to be the one earning now. If I get pregnant now, do you think I would be able to act in eight films at a time? Do you have any idea how much it costs to run this house each day? Ask Bhaskar. Petrol, groceries, food, servants, salaries...where do you think the money will come from if every film is a flop? Think about it!'

Arun could not stomach the truth of what she'd said. 'I am going now,' he said tersely and left the room.

Viswanathan, who returned from his official tour soon after dawn, got out of the autorickshaw and went to the medical store to get some change. As he gave the man a ten-rupee note, the shopkeeper spoke. 'There were two or three phone calls to your house when you were away.'

24

After tendering the exact change to the autorickshaw driver, Viswanathan went back to Ananda Medicals. 'There was a phone call? For me?'

'No, sir. It was for Amma. She attended to it.'

'Did the person say who?'

'He didn't say, sir.'

Viswanathan picked up his suitcase and air pillow and went inside. *Who could it have been? Sundaram? But why would he make a phone call? And two or three times at that?* He climbed the stairs and went towards his wife.

'Who is it?' her voice asked from the other side of the door.

'It's me, Viswanathan.'

The door opened. She had not yet taken her morning bath. 'Ada! You've come home? I was just writing a letter to you,' she smiled.

He went in quietly and sat down.

'Just a minute. Let me get you some coffee.' She went inside and her voice came from the other room. 'Did you get a good place in the train? Did you sleep well?'

Viswanathan got up and took a good look at the almirah. He looked for something like a half of a movie ticket or movie magazines or a letter. She had inserted the letter he had written inside *Deivathin Kural: The Voice of God*.

He took a sip of the coffee and put it down.

'Why?' she asked. 'Is the sugar not okay?'

'Who called?' he asked in a composed voice.

Kalyani stood there, looking stunned. 'What?'

'It seems someone called for you two or three times when I was not here. I am asking about that. Do you understand the question?'

She stood there, silent.

'Sundaram?'

'No,' she said in a feeble voice.

'Was it your father?'

She shook her head.

'Then who was it?'

She took a hesitant step back. Deep down, she had the feeling he was going to hit her. Her hands were trembling, but she could not bring herself to lie. 'It was Arun,' she said.

'What did he say?' he asked in a soft voice.

'He asked if I was well, and I just put the phone down. That's all.'

'Do you expect me to believe that? How did he find out that we were living here. How did he get the medical shop's number?'

'I don't know what to say,' she said.

'So, all three times he only asked if you were fine?'

'Illainna! Illai, he telephoned just once. I didn't say anything. I swear on my father, mother, brother and God. That's what happened.'

'Where did you go and meet him?'

'Ayyo! Nothing of that sort happened.'

'So it was you who first phoned and asked him to come, right?'

'Chee! Why are you torturing me like this? It just happened the way I said. If you want you can call him and ask.'

'You know his number?'

'No, I don't know it,' she said, in tears.

'Why should I phone that dog? You shameless woman! You had to call him and ask him to come when I was away for just a few days! Which hotel did the two of you go to? Did he give you any money? Or did he profess undying love?'

'Ayyo! This is atrocious. It's a lie. Why do you treat me like this?' Kalyani was now weeping aloud. Her face turned intense, the tip of her nose turned red and a river of tears flowed down her cheeks. Her body shook. 'Oh God! Deivamey! What should I do now? What can I say?' She cried some more.

'Chee! I don't want you or your coffee!' He threw the tumbler at her, and brown stains drenched her sari. 'I am leaving, I am disappearing somewhere.' He walked out of the building, out on the street, towards the temple. He bought himself a pouch of betelnut powder and popped its contents into his mouth. He sat in the mandapam, near the shrine's dwajasthambam that towered above and chewed on the betelnuts in an awkward manner. He was not used to this but somehow felt like doing it today.

He was lost in thought. *What will she do now?* Kalyani's pleasant face and her distorted, crying face flashed in turns in his mind. *She will write to her brother. Let her write. Let him take her away. No! Let me pack her clothes in a bag…how much money would she have? Will I have to give her some? She used to talk about some distant relatives in this city—will she go there? Does she know the way? Does she even have the address? No! She will only go to Uttamarkovil. No! She will write a letter. No! She must have started out by now. Will she run away?*

He got up with a start and walked quickly towards his home, climbed the stairs in a jiffy and threw open the door.

Kalyani was still there, with her hands on her cheeks. Her tears had dried up and she sat there with a vacant expression on her face. The coffee tumbler was still upside down, and she did not even see him coming in.

Viswanathan bolted the door from inside, caught her by the shoulder and drew her up.

'It's all right. Get up!' he said. His fingers touched her breasts. She was limp. He took her near the bed, unrolled the mattress, put her to bed and lay down beside her.

A small crowd clapped. On a stool in the middle waited a thick notebook with a red kumkum mark. 'Manikkam Creations Production Number 1,' it proclaimed.

Manonmani stood in a simple sari with no make-up on. 'Lights! Camera! Action!' Manikkam shouted. The camera whirred, a spot boy in half-pants did the clap and Manonmani walked slowly with her head down and smiled gently at Manikkam.

'Okay, cut it!' said Manikkam. A soft round of applause followed, and sweets were distributed in small packets. Kittu came to Manikkam and ate some sweets. 'What, Manikkam, what kind of a poojai is this? No pictures of any gods? Not a priest in sight!'

'There is no need for all that. The poojai is for hard work.'

'What is the name of the film?'

'*Thiruppumunai: The Turning Point.*'

Kittu counted his fingers. 'Six letters. Not bad. If you had used *Thirupppina Munaigal* in plural that would add up to nine.'

'I don't believe in that.'

'So the launch has been simple. Have you sold any areas yet?'

'No.'

'So where is the money coming from?'

'I've found someone.'

'It's a colour film, no?'

'Yes. We can make it powerful in black and white. But as you know, black and white is dead now.'

'But that will cost you seven lakhs'

'I am not bothered about that now. The first schedule starts tomorrow and runs for fifteen days. Everybody is new, they're folks from the institute. Sharp guys. I have a proper script, and I am also having some backup help ready.'

'How is that enough?'

'Why don't you wait and see if I do it or not?'

As Manonmani neared them, Kittu said, 'Mano! I saw the rushes for *Ilanthalaivan*. Everything's top class. Should I ask them to say "Another Seema in the Making?" in the headlines? Classic rape scene!'

'Mano, please come straight to the location tomorrow,' Manikkam said. 'There won't be any pick-up.'

'No public relations for this?' Kittu asked.

'Everything is just me,' Manikkam said.

'I am worried, Manikkam.'

'Don't you worry about it, Kittu. By the way, did you return the money to Arumairajan or not?'

'I did that, and I have taken the advance for three more songs too. That "*Virippu–Sirippu*" song! Wow! What a tune it has. They just killed it. He is sitting in a composing room now. He will get booked for three more films this month. He is a king—you should see him playing with Tamil. And then he met the big poet whom he had made angry in that recording with his own verse. He walked up to him and said, 'Ayya, I need your blessings. The two have made up now. Just wait, this man is going to be big. Okay, I will be off. I have another poojai to attend on the fifth floor. They are going abroad for a location shoot.'

As Kittu sauntered off, Manonmani stared at Manikkam.

'What is it, Mano?'

'They have also asked me to come to VL. It's a small part.'

'Look here, you have to decide now. If you are in my movie, you can't be doing that. You have to let me know.'

'I have taken the advance.'

'Give it back.'

'But I have spent it all!'

Manikkam thought for a while. 'Mano, I have some money now, but I have to spend it on a thousand things. It is a fifteen-day shoot—the outdoor unit, film rolls, the wages for technicians—there are loads of expenses. I don't have enough for all that. I am not in a position to give you any advance now. I am sorry,' he said.

Mano thought for a while and said, 'It's okay. I'll manage.'

'You'll come tomorrow, no? It is a good role, Mano. It's real acting, not just your body! I have lots of things to do, so shall I take your leave? Please come, okay?' He smiled and left.

Manonmani stood there pointlessly for a while and then walked away. A top-ranked actress got off from a car. Three people rushed to touch her feet. Photoflashes littered their glitter as she smiled and showed her famous dimples. Manonmani stared at this for a while and then looked for Ganesalingam.

Production manager Ganesalingam was dialling one of the many numbers scribbled in his dirty notebook. Manonmani stood near him for a while. He looked through her as if she was not there and spoke into the phone. 'Has the van arrived?'

'Send it along at once to the director. Take some food along and ask Mastan to get a snake.'

The voice at the other end was not audible.

Ganesalingam raised his voice. 'I said snake...*a snake!*' And he went on with his conversation on the phone, oblivious to Manonmani. 'You don't have to take it with you. Who said it had to be you? A boy will bring it along in a basket. Just don't forget, okay?'

He finally looked at Manonmani. 'What's it, ma?'

'Mmm...I won't be able to make it tomorrow, sir.'

'What's this, ma? You have taken your advance, no? What's the point in telling me this now? Where am I going to find another person?'

'I am so sorry, sir.'

'You are from Virugambakkam, no? Just wait...' He thumbed through his notebook. 'Saraswati, Chandra, Baby, Usha, Tamizharasi, Nithiyamalli, Suguna, Nirupama...'

'You know Nirupama, right? Just pass on your money to her and ask her to come in your place.'

'The money...' But before she could finish, he got into a car that sped in and left immediately. Manonmani stood there for a while, frozen.

Lakshmanan and Venugopal stood outside the small screening theatre like expectant fathers outside a labour room. Inside, in a place that could seat about twenty people, four censor board members and the regional officer were seated separately on seats designed to help them take notes. They were connected to the projection room by a switch that they could use to light a bulb in the projection room so that they could ask for repeats of scenes. On the screen was *Ilanthalaivan*, and in its gentle glow sat four elderly men and a woman in glasses, viewing the film with tired looks on their faces.

As the hero ascended a white horse, one of the members spoke, 'I bet there will be a bathing scene here. I am wagering ten rupees on that.'

As the screen beauties giggled, the hero slowed his horse with his '*Huv, huv*' sounds. The water fell *glug-glug*. 'What's this?' the hero exclaimed in wonderment. The scene showed mountains and a pond and then focused on what looked like a waterfall engineered in a studio.

The beauties, as predicted, were bathing. Everybody was giggling. The camera closed up on them. They all had their chests covered with tight saris, knotted in the middle. As the ladies, covered till their breasts in the blue waters, splashed water on each other, you could see the nipples through the wet clothes. A red light flashed inside the projection room, asking for the screening to be paused.

'What's this, Nithyanandan?' the lady asked. 'Do you think we have to see this film any further?'

'This scene has to be chopped off.'

'The film is not even into its fifteenth minute yet. There are already eight cuts. I don't think this is going to make it.'

The censor board officer took notes.

'I don't want to see this movie. You could have put someone else in my place. It's a disgrace.'

'This is nothing compared to *Satyam Shivam Sundaram*,' said a younger censor.

'Let's give it an A,' the officer said.

'No, it can't be an A. This deserves an X rating. It's like a blue film with no head or tail. A bathing scene all of a sudden!'

'Let's see the whole thing anyway. We can tell them there are lots of cuts. Is the producer around?'

The lady was persistent. 'Why should we certify this film? We can give it a "Not Suitable" tag.'

'No! Let's order the cuts and give it an A rating and be done with it,' said the younger one.

'Let's watch the scene again. Are the breasts clearly visible? It doesn't seem that way to me,' said another member.

As the regional censor officer stepped out, Lakshmanan approached him. 'How is it going?'

'Lots of cuts,' he said and went back in.

'How can that be?' said Lakshmanan. 'We'll apply for a revision. In a way, this is good. We can spread gossip around in the magazines. If we get some publicity about it being roasted by the censors, we can easily sell one more area.'

25

ARUN STOOD IN FRONT OF the mirror. When he took the comb off his head, he was startled to see some hairs sticking to it. He noticed dark circles under his eyes and some sagging in his cheekbones. He looked at his stomach and tightened his belt to control the beginning of a paunch. He looked again at his face in the mirror. Like a much-travelled trunk, it had some dents here and some scratches there. He plucked off one grey hair—it didn't hurt—stared at it for a while and stuck it on to the mirror. He heard his secretary knock.

'What is it, Bhaskar?'

'Lakshmanan is here.'

'Ask him to wait. I am coming.'

'Did you ask him to come?'

'Yes. He is financing our production.'

'Do you know what producing your own film means? A clear downfall.'

'Shabaash! Sage advice so early in the morning. It must be experience talking. How many movies have you made?'

'I have not made any but have seen a lot.'

'Bhaskar, I am not like the others. I still command a name and respect in the industry. The one I am producing is a sure-shot hit. Three heroines, colour, cinemascope, the perfect locations, super direction and music. I have asked Rathi, Sreepriya and Sridevi. "Arun, how can we refuse you a call sheet?" they said. No, Mr Bhaskar, I am not going to miss this mark.'

Bhaskar did not show even a fraction of Arun's enthusiasm. 'I will be in the hall. You're coming there, no?'

'Where is Prem?'

'Hyderabad—on a fifteen-day schedule. She will be back only on the eighth.'

'Isn't anybody home? Peace! Why are you here? Why don't you leave, too?'

Bhaskar glared at him as he left the room. 'Arun, don't speak like that again. One day, I will actually leave. '

'Hooo!'

Lakshmanan was waiting in the drawing room and with him was a fair-skinned young man smoking a cigarette. He smelt expensive and looked as healthy as a newly baked loaf of bread.

'Vanakkam, thambi,' Lakshmanan greeted Arun. 'I believe you sent for me? Bhaskar, can I have a glass of buttermilk? I had some brandy last night and it has not gone down well. I am belching away.'

'Sorry, there is no buttermilk, sir.'

'Send somebody to get it,' Arun said. As Bhaskar moved off quietly, he asked Lakshmanan. 'Who is this gentleman?'

'You don't know? This is Chimanlal Seth, the owner of Maheshwari Circuits.'

'Oh, so this is him.'

'Hi!' the young businessman greeted Arun.

'He understands Tamil but has difficulty speaking the language. But he can say "Switch off the lights" in Tamil clearly. Why seth?' Lakshmanan laughed loudly and punched Chimanlal in the stomach. The man smiled coyly like a newly married bride.

'So, you're making your own film now,' Lakshmanan said.

'Yes.'

'Good show. Do it. You have the call sheets? Of course, no one will say no to you.'

'There's no problem there, Lakshmanan. But I'll explain the situation. Since I was not on to good projects, a couple of my films have not done well. I need to do a big one to establish myself again. But I don't think I can pick up the entire cost. You know this, you are an experienced man in this business.'

'How much have you budgeted?'

'At least thirty lakhs. It's an all-star cast. Cinemascope. I also want to shoot in Europe.'

'Splendid. Then it may go beyond that number.'

'I can only muster two or two and half now, but that won't fund a single set that I have thought of.'

'But why do you have to put in that amount? Even just one lakh will do. I'll take care of the rest. Why do you think this seth is here?'

'I don't understand.'

'Thambi, when you are making your own movie—or any movie for that matter—you should never put in your own money. This is a lesson you learn in the nursery class of the film industry. All I have to say is that Arun is producing a cinemascope movie and shooting overseas, and I will sell area rights like they were chilli bajjis. You keep the city rights and stop worrying. We'll splash an acre-sized ad in *Dina Thanthi*, hold the inaugural poojai and shoot a song. We'll finish it somehow.'

Bhaskar presently appeared with a glass of buttermilk. Lakshmanan finished it off in one glug and announced, 'Nothing like stale rice for brandy. But we are making do with buttermilk instead.' He gushed on about seducing Seth for business.

'Look at this seth now. He came rushing in his car the moment I told him about this. All he wants are the Salem–Coimbatore rights. Why settu?'

Chimanlal Seth smiled his coy bride smile once more.

'Who is the director?'

'Our man Pasumarthi Satyanarayana Rao is doing it. It's being shot in both Telugu and Tamil.'

'Oh, that fellow? Brilliant. Heard that, seth? He is a king in the industry. Whatever he touches becomes a jubilee hit. Arun, why don't you accept this? What day is it today? I hope there is no mess with a Rahukaalam or Yamakandam.'

Chimanlal Seth took a sheaf of papers and some bundles of fifty-and hundred-rupee notes out of his briefcase.

'This is for starting expenses, please take it. You have to provide three signatures.'

The stamped paper was neatly typed.

'This is just an agreement to sell area rights.'

'Bhaskar,' Arun said. 'Give me a pen.'

Bhaskar, who was watching it all silently, spoke for the first time in a while. 'Read it first, Arun.'

'It will all be fine, I am sure.'

'May I read it?'

'Why?'

'Why not? Let him read it,' Chimanlal Seth said. 'This is a routine agreement that we do all the time. It is a receipt for taking an advance for area rights for two cities and the prints.'

'No, sir,' Bhaskar said in a firm, casual tone. 'We can sign only after reading the whole thing.'

'What's this? You are being a spoilsport right at the start of a project?' Lakshmanan said. 'Where are we going to run off? If you want any revisions after reading it, you can always tear it up and change the damn thing. It all runs on trust, no?'

'No, sir. Why should it be that way?'

'Lakshmanan, give it to me,' he said and snatched the papers from him. He grabbed a pen from the roly-poly young businessman's shirt pocket, scribbled his signatures and gave the papers to Lakshmanan.

He took it and extended a copy towards to Arun. 'Here, this is your copy.'

'Give it to Bhaskar. Let him read it.'

'Thambi is moving as fast as lightning! If we maintain this speed, before we finish the poojai and start the shooting, we'll raise two lakhs!'

'So what happened to *Ilanthalaivan*? I believe it got bloody wounds at the censors?'

'Don't ask! First they said that they wouldn't give it a certificate. We pushed here and there, got a quick revision, moved some cuts and patched it up, and somehow managed to release it. They chopped off the bathing scene. The press called it vulgar, but it's running housefull in all centres for the past fifteen days. We have already done the poojai for the next one called *Paruvakkulam*. Now, may I take your leave?'

Arun was smiling and joined his palms in a courteous greeting.

Lakshmanan stopped at the door, paused a little hesitantly. 'Thambi, I'll say something, but don't get angry.'

'Go on.'

'On this very doorstep, when I came to you six months ago, you ignored this old man. Do you see how things have changed now? I think there is a lesson for both of us here.'

Arun's face fell. 'Yes sir. I have changed now—I have got married.'

'So, I'll take your leave?'

'Vorren,' Chimanlal Seth spoke in broken Tamil and smiled his shy smile again as he left.

The stamp papers and currency bundles were resting on a low table. Bhaskar stared at Arun for a while. 'You are being foolish,' he said patiently.

'Bhaskar, I am tired of your Boddhisattva advice. You are a good secretary, I admit. Income tax, audit, transport, call sheet, this and that—you manage all that just fine. But your expertise stops there. You don't have vision. You know, Prem is right when she says "You are overestimating Bhaskar and giving too much of a free hand."'

'No, Arun, I am just a servant here. I'm sorry, I may have overstepped my brief. Let me first make the preparations for the new film's poojai. Keep the money safe. Let me set off now,' Bhaskar said as he left the room.

'Pessimist!' Arun said, talking to the door. He picked up the bundles and caressed them with his thumb. The notes were a bit old. 'This must be black money!' he told himself. A chill swept through somewhere inside him.

Is this courage or foolhardiness? he thought. He felt like talking to someone. He looked at the clock. It was 8.05 a.m. Prem must have woken up. She always stayed at the Chalukya in Hyderabad, and she always wanted room number 9. He wanted to tell her about this. *I need some of her money. She is my wife*, he thought.

He wondered if Hyderabad had entered the STD list, but he also did not know the hotel number. He called the trunk call booking service. 'Hello! Can you book a trunk call to the Chalukya Hotel in Hyderabad? Yes, a number call. And my number is…'

He waited to be connected. Prem would certainly be happy to hear the news. He had to tell her about the first time he decided to do something without consulting Bhaskar. He had made up his mind now. He had put his best foot forward. He must involve Prem in this now. She could always be given a guest role. She could be the village belle he marries at the end of the film after rejecting all the leading heroines. Great idea! Village belle! Prem…

Kalyani…in a bright sari with a kudam on her waist, walking towards the village stream, her head bent down, her anklets jingling. Memories came flooding back.

'Come Kalyani…'

'Maami! Amma asked me to get Amrutanjan.'

He rushed to get the Amrutanjan and hid it upstairs.

'Where did it disappear? Viju, where is the Amrutanjan?' asked his mother.

'It's here.'

'Bring it down'

'I am having a shave.'

'I can't climb the stairs now. Why don't you do something—why don't you get it from Viju?' He could hear his mother.

'Shaving? Ha! Look at the liar!' Kalyani muttered

Upstairs, he twisted Kalyani's hand gently, and her bangle broke. He pulled her close and gave her a kiss that left a stamp.

She jerked away and ran off. He saved that broken bangle as a souvenir.

The telephone rang. 'Hotel Chalukya? Room number 9, please!'

'Just a minute.'

That piece of bangle was still in his box.

'Hello, Prem! Hello, hello…Prem?' There was a silence.

'Wrong number,' said a male voice.

At 11.30 p.m. that night, a car door shut and then there was the sound of sandals on the floor. A gentle whistle broke into a song. It was '*Kadhal Vandhirichu*'—a tune that heralded a love affair.

'Anney, please be ready at 8 a.m.!'

'Okay.'

A knock sounded at the door. Sagaya Mary quickly wiped her eyes, straightened her hair, adjusted her sari and opened the door.

Arumairajan came in. His hair was tousled, and his net half-sleeved vest showed through his jubba. A paan sat in a corner of his mouth. 'Have you eaten, Mary? he asked, covering his nose with his hand.

'Illeenga,' she replied in the negative.

He went straight to the phone without the dial and pressed a button. 'Cottage number 16. Please send one Bombay meal,' he said.

'No,' she said. 'I don't want it.'

'But I have eaten. Why did you wait for me?'

'Have I ever eaten before you?'

Arumairajan came near, took her hand and placed it on his cheek.

'Please touch me, Mary. Forgive me, I am sorry,' he laughed. He was slightly unsteady. 'From morning to night, we did four songs. Look at this,' he said and took out a bundle of hundred-rupee notes and rained them down. 'From just five paise on that platform…' He went to the sink and spat out a wide, blood-red stain. '…we had begged for. Look now!'

'I can smell something on you.'

'Nothing like that, Mary. I don't drink.'

Two polite knocks sounded at the door. A white-liveried waiter walked in with an excess of food filled in an array of bowls and waited for a signature from Arumairajan.

'Are you connected with the film world, sir?'

'Why do you ask?'

'I just heard something like that. Are you an actor?'

'No. I write songs.'

'Sir, what is your name?'

'Arumairajan.'

'Her laugh is such you can't capture in lines?'

'Yes, I wrote that.' He looked at Mary now.

'Is that so? I saw that movie three times just for this song.'

'I am so happy to hear that!' He looked at Mary again. 'Let's shake hands, brother.'

'How can you write such lines, sir? What are those words…"*They are diamonds*"?'

'They are diamonds that bring down the heavens in a smile so sweet.'

'Wow! Let's shake hands to that.'

'Arumairajan was also a waiter in a hotel—just like you,' said Mary.

26

After the waiter left, Arumairajan asked, 'What is this, Mary? Must you tell him about our ancient history?'

'How is it ancient history? Have you forgotten everything in six months? We were struggling on the streets.'

'Does that mean we are struggling now?'

'We should not forget such things,' Mary said.

'How can one forget it?'

'Looking at you, it seems like you have forgotten it all. Your attitude has changed. Everything about you seems new. That smell, this jubba, the chewing tobacco—everything!'

'I won't change, Mary, whatever wealth comes my way. These are small things.'

'Nothing has changed for me because of this money,' Mary said. 'I used to wait for you in Bangalore before. Now, I wait in Madras. You used to bring packed food from the hotel then. We used to open it and eat together. Now you are ordering food. What has not changed is my waiting. I was at my cousin's home, waiting for a chance in the movies for you. I was carrying my son in my lap, waiting at the doctor's place. After you got that chance, as you write songs all day, I am now waiting for you in a hotel, wondering when you will come home. Nothing has changed for me.'

'Why are you being so cynical, Mary? Kittu has told me he will get us a rented house here soon—on Mahalakshmi Street.'

'It's okay. Then, I will be waiting there.'

'What is it that you want now?'

'I want you,' she said.

'I am right here, in front of the mirror,' he said in a tired tone.

'I want to see you in the daytime,' Mary said.

Arumairajan whipped out an imported cigarette. The lighter made a clicking noise.

Dear Anna,

Many namaskarams to you. Both of us are well here. Please write and inform us about Amma and Appa's well-being.

Anna, I write this to you with much hesitation and much thinking. Of late, his behaviour with me has not been proper. He doubts me about everything and talks at tangents. He taunts me greatly about that matter concerning Arun. I just cannot put up with it sometimes. That Arun, in his crazy way, telephoned me at the neighbouring shop. He found out, and without properly asking what and why and imagining all sorts of things, he is harassing me to no end. At this rate, I feel like jumping into a lake. Sometimes, he speaks well. But somehow that matter concerning Arun does something to him. I don't think I can stay with him much longer. I am writing this to you in sheer confusion. Why don't you take me home for a few days? Or find a way out of this mess for me? Please don't say anything about this to Amma and Appa. They will feel really bad. Come here yourself. I will explain everything to you. I had told Amma to re-make my silver golusu. He does not want me to do that now. It seems that the price of silver will rise further. How is the joint pain that Appa was suffering from? Is it better now? When you come here, please bring two copies of your horoscope with you.

Sincerely, your loving sister
V. Kalyani

'What are you writing, Kalyani?'

Startled, Kalyani hid the letter under the book. 'I am writing a letter to my anna.'

'Is that anna or Arun? Why are you hiding it like this?'

'Have you started about that again? It is to my brother.'

'Let me see!'

Her voice fell. 'It is to my brother, and it is about a personal matter—stuff concerning our home.'

'Can't I read it? Am I not your husband?'

'I have not finished writing it yet.'

'You are lying. It seems like you have not written to your brother.'

'Ayyo! Look here!' She showed him the first lines of the letter. 'My dear Anna…'

'Read the whole thing.'

'Why should you read my personal letter?'

'Because you would have told him some canards and made accusations.'

'Ayyo! Am I not entitled to any personal space? Oh God!'

'Why should anything be confidential for you? Are you going to give that to me or not?'

'I won't!'

'Give it to me!' He pounced on her.

Kalyani quickly tore the letter into little pieces.

Viswanathan was dumbfounded for a moment. This was the first time Kalyani had truly resisted him. He raised his hand to hit her. There was a strange, new hostility in the way she stood in silence, glaring at him with her moist eyes. Viswanathan picked up the pieces of paper carefully, put it into a bag and moved to the next room.

Kalyani was still standing there. She could not understand all this. 'Do such people really exist in the world?'

'I'll read it—I'll read it all. I'll stick it all together,' she could hear his voice. Disturbing thoughts ran in her mind. *So there is this kind of complication in life. Can a husband and wife fight like this? How do I prove the wretched truth that I have not been thinking of Arun? Why is he behaving like a stubborn horse who simply refuses to budge? Can't I write a letter to my own brother? I just have to somehow tell my brother about all this and bring him here. I can't handle this on my own. Let the men talk and settle this.*

In the next room, Viswanathan was patiently putting the words together. 'His behaviour with me has not been proper…' he read out. 'Shabaash!' he said.

He left the room. 'I am going to the office. I will eat outside.' He shut the door, stood by the window and stared. 'Kalyani, there is a lot of theft these days. I am locking the door from outside,' he said.

The lock clicked shut.

'Arun Vijay invites you…'

An invitation card of a significant width and length lay on the table. Arun's photo was printed on both sides, and golden letters shone on the card inside: 'You are cordially invited to the inauguration ceremony…'

'Have all the invitations been sent?' Arun asked.

'A week ago—the press conference is today.'

'Where?'

'Right here.'

'Shouldn't Prem be here by now? Is the flight late?'

'No, it is on time. Arun, I need some money. Twenty thousand for the musical orchestra, set designer and then…'

'The song is sounding great, I hope.'

'Hmm.'

'Bhaskar, what do you think of Prem?'

Bhaskar thought for a while and replied calmly. 'If I must honestly answer that question, we should not be enjoying a difference in status between us. I am a secretary working for you. I don't think I have any right to give you a frank opinion on your wife.'

'As a friend, you can.'

'I'm sorry—these days, I'm kind of confused about when you are my friend and when my boss.'

Arun heard the car door shut and turned around. Premalatha almost ran towards Arun to hug and kiss him. 'Hi Arun! I missed you.' Then she threw an apology to the secretary for her public display of affection. 'Oh, Bhaskar, you are here? Sorry!'

Arun brought her down from her hug. 'How was your schedule?'

'It's over, only dubbing to go now,' she whispered into his ears and laughed gently. 'Court, dancer, colourful outfits and shiny stuff on my boobs...SPB sang a song in the Malayamarutham ragam—it's great! After *Shankarabharanam*, all the Telugu films are going Carnatic! Hey, where is Julie?... *Joo...leeee...*' she cried, calling out her dog.

'Prem, let's go upstairs. I need to talk to you.'

'The poojai for our film is tomorrow, right?'

Bhaskar called out, reminding him for the money, 'Arun, Arun!'

Arun threw his keychain at him. 'Take it yourself,' he said, climbing the stairs.

'Do I have a part in your movie?' Premalatha asked Arun.

'Guest artiste.'

As they entered the room, Prem shut the door with the back of her foot. She caught Arun's hand and rubbed it on her chest. 'It's been so long,' she said. 'Let's make love.' She drew his hand towards her waist. But Arun broke free.

'Hey, are you angry with me?' she bit his earlobe.

'Prem, which room did you stay in at the Chalukya this time?'

'Nine. As usual. Why?'

'I called you the other day in the morning. There was a male voice, a blank sort of voice, on the line. He said it was a wrong number.'

'When was this?'

'I don't remember exactly. I think it was four days ago.'

'Could have been the director.'

What was the director doing in your room so early in the morning?'

'He must have come for a discussion.'

'Why did he say it was a wrong number, then? Did you really have a discussion, or did you do something else?'

'What are you saying, Arun? You've seen the director Chella, no? He is my father's age.'

'Who is your father?'

Her face turned a darker shade. 'Arun,' she said in a firm tone, 'so you know how many things run on trust? I can ask you same question as well.'

'What question?'

'Who is your father?'

He fell silent.

'I can also start imagining all the things you did when I was out of town, right?' she said.

'Please do! Look here, you go your way and I'll go mine. You can go to Hyderabad and do whatever with that Whatshisname Babu. But you have no right to ask me anything—just remember that.'

'Arun, I see how clever you're being. You are inventing things about what happened in Hyderabad so you can get an excuse to do what you want anyway. Arun, you may have met Kalyani and talked to her. I have done nothing of that sort. I swear upon Baba and Lord Venkateswara...'

'All right, come clean. Swear on Baba and Lord Venkateswara.'

'Okay, you swear first that you did nothing while I was gone.' Premalatha was assertive.

'I asked first. Come on, swear upon God! You'll rot in hell if you lie! I have seen as many people as you have. That's it, right? We are even now, okay?'

'Why do you behave so cruelly, Arun? Is this how you talk to your wife who is home after fifteen days? Chee!' she started crying. As Julie watched her, wagging her tail, she gently blew her nose into her handkerchief and wept.

There was a knock at the door. 'The press is here,' Bhaskar announced.

As they came down to meet reporters and photographers in the main hall, both Arun and Premalatha were smiling, looking like fresh flowers. Lights flashed as Prem locked her hand over his shoulder. 'Take your photos, gentlemen!' she told the eager lensmen.

Questions buzzed all around them.

'Is Prem going to act in your film, Arun?'

'Can you do it without Prem?'

'*Adhu Oru Rahasyam*, that is a secret,' he replied.

'Isn't that the name of the film?'

'Prem, are you the joint producer?' a reporter asked.

'No.'

'Smile, please!' said a photographer. 'I need some colour shots now.'

As they both smiled, the cameras clicked away, their shutters adding to the rhythm.

27

To,
The Chairman,
Central Board of Film Censors
Chennai

From
R. Thiruvengadam
8, C.P. Koil Street
Chennai—600 004

Dear Sir,

When I visited Tirunelveli recently for some personal work, I happened to see the film called Ilanthalaivan *at the Royal Talkies cinema. I was very shocked to see some of the scenes in the movie. In particular, some women were bathing in a manner that clearly showed their breasts in the process. I am baffled as to how such a scene escaped the censors. The number of youngsters whose minds can be polluted by such a scene is a matter of deep concern. When I came back to Chennai, another surprise awaited me. My friend Parasuraman (9, C.P. Koil*

Street) told me that this scene was not being shown in the theatres in Chennai at all. I am truly puzzled. I urge you to immediately look into the matter and do the needful. I have also written a letter to the editor of The Hindu *concerning this matter.*

Yours truly,
R. Thiruvengadam

Below the letter was a note from the chairman: 'RCO, Pl. verify. If true, arrange to seize prints through magistrate order, suspend certificate.'

Arun was restless as he picked up the phone. 'Where has that man gone? He said he would be here by 8.30 a.m. and it is 10 a.m. now!'

The telephonic message conveyed to him from the other end did not seem to be of interest to him. He simply said 'Okay' and slammed the phone down. Bhaskar showed no emotion as he waited, his arms folded on his chest, like Aladdin's genie after it had been summoned.

'Why are you standing like that? Do I look as if I want to be mocked?'

'Chee! What's going on, Arun?'

'There is no sign of Lakshmanan! We can't figure out where the hell he is. And he told me he would bring some money this morning.'

'I believe the police are also looking for him.'

'What?'

'They have sealed all prints of *Ilanthalaivan*, it seems. The movie is off—the certificate is gone.'

'Bloody hell! What will happen to me now?'

'Arun, I don't want to irritate you by saying "I told you so", but don't expect anything else from Lakshmanan. He will take at least year to recover from the losses of *Ilanthalaivan*. He is going to face many court cases.'

'Ayyo! I need two and a half lakhs now. I have a fifteen-day schedule starting tomorrow.'

'Just put it off—that is the best you can do.'

'Impossible! I'll be able to get those call sheets again only after a few months.'

'How about asking Prem?'

'Prem! She'll have the money, no?'

'I would not know.'

'I think she is asleep upstairs.'

He went upstairs, opened the door and drew aside the curtains. She was fast asleep.

'Prem...' He softly blew on her ears, and she moved slightly. He patted her cheek. As she lazily opened her eyes, he smiled. 'Good morning. Rather, good afternoon,' he said.

Prem got up and said, 'What's the time?'

'10 a.m.'

'Oh my God! I was supposed to be in Vijaya at 9.30.'

'Let them wait! Prem, wash your face. I have to discuss something important with you, darling!'

'What's this darling thing?'

'Aren't you my darling?'

'Don't butter me up! What's the matter? Come to the point.'

'I need some money.' He felt small asking his wife for money.

'How much?'

'Two and a half lakhs.'

'Ohhhh!'

'We have a schedule tomorrow. You know that, don't you? I need the money urgently for that.'

'I thought Lakshmanan was supposed to give the money.'

'That guy is now underground.'

'I don't have that kind of money.'

'How much do you have?'

'I'll have to ask Amma—she looks after everything.'

'I am done talking to your mother in Telugu. Why don't you ask her? I need the dough! Tell her Dabbu Kavala. You are acting in eight films. Where have you kept all the money?'

'Arun, shall I tell you the truth? For the past six months, this home has been running on my money, and I don't command the high rates that you do. I am just getting thirty or forty thousand per movie. Besides, they don't give me everything in advance. I am certain I don't have as much money as you want.'

'You don't have the money, or you have it but don't want to give it to me?'

'There's nothing of that sort.'

'Why don't you ask the producer for some money upfront?'

'I'll do it, but on one condition.'

'What's that?'

'You have to cast me as the heroine.'

'Uh-oh! What happens to all that I have shot with the others?'

'Arun, do you know what the talk is in the industry? They say we are heading for a divorce. They say that's the reason why you aren't casting your wife even though you are producing your own film.'

'Why do you believe all that gossip?'

'Well, in order to end that speculation once and for all you have to cast me as your heroine.'

'That is not going to work.'

'In which case, don't ask me for any money.'

'Are you trying to blackmail me? I'll make those rumours they are spreading come true.'

'What will you do?'

'I'll divorce you.'

'That is not so easy, Arun. You'll need money for that as well.'

'Are you going to give me the money or not?'

'I told you I will arrange it—on one condition.'

Arun stared at her and she stared right back. 'All right,' Arun said. 'I don't want your peanut money. I know how to raise money. I'll show it to you this evening.'

'Do whatever you want!' Premalatha said.

Arun went to the door and turned around. 'But perish the thought of acting with me in that movie. We are simply not compatible.'

'Yessssss! I agree, the hero sucks!'

Bhaskar was waiting in the living room. 'So what is the alternative?'

'What?'

'I can see on your face that Prem said no.'

'Wow! My secretary is a genius. Can't raise a single rupee. Bhaskar, get that Seth boy's number. I am going to ask him for a loan.'

'Arun, please! Whatever you do, don't borrow. He will ask for forty or fifty per cent interest. And he will deduct the interest first. He will trap you among the loan sharks.'

'Get me that number!' Arun shouted.

The village was about eight miles off Ramanagaram. Though the name, Devarayapatna, sounded majestically big, the only easily identifiable building was a concrete structure. A tractor stood in front of that building while the landscape comprised of thatched huts, a Kannada-style Ayyanar temple of large village deities and an expanse of green with paddy and sugarcane fields. The lushness zealously guarded the village from the townspeople.

Manikkam Creations' unit was camping there for its shoot. There were tin squares, an Arriflex camera and some budget-friendly lights near the extension boards. A diesel-laden van stood nearby. A Bengali cinematographer and a host of assistants were enthusiastically cooperating with the director. They all were staying the night in the same village house. The hero, a newbie, had not yet acquired any of the film world hang-ups and was reading some poetry between shots, while the heroine was chit-chatting and smiling without any fuss. Manikkam was liberal with praise with the smallest of things as he got things done. *Thiruppumunai* was progressing at low costs with a definitive screenplay, with no loss of film rolls.

Manonmani was supposed to shoot there on Tuesday. They had pored over the script the night before and scheduled the scenes after fixing some holes for the morning shoot. Manikkam had written to Mano, asking her to catch the early morning train to Mysore and had made arrangements for her to be picked up at Mandya. Mano had eagerly agreed and written back, assuring him of her arrival. The pick-up van went to the station. Everybody took a bath at a groundwater pump, ate fresh idlis for breakfast and was mighty pleased with the clear blue skies. They were all raring to go.

But Mano did not show up. The van that went to the station returned without her. They waited until 10 a.m. to see if she turned up in a bus.

This turned out to be Manikkam's first obstacle. The shoot had thus far proceeded like a hot knife through butter. This was the first glitch. Manikkam was furious. 'How can she promise to come and not show up? Could she not have sent a telegram at least?'

The cameraman was reading the *Sun* with a cricket cap on his head. The reflectors waited. It was a familiar Tamil film shoot.

'Durairaj! The only mistake I have committed is casting her. She was struggling as an extra and I thought I would give her a chance with a good intention. But look what happened!'

'Anney! Shall I tell you something?'

'What?'

'That girl won't come.'

'Why?'

'She takes a different route. Cinema is not important to her.'

'Aah! It doesn't matter what else she does or not. But she can't turn up for a three-day shoot? What does she think she is? A star or something?'

'Anney, you remember that schoolgirl who came to watch the shooting yesterday?'

'I noticed her, yes.'

'That girl's father has been nagging me. He wants a movie break for his hudugi. It is a small part, after all. Should we try her out?'

'Okay. Bring her along. We can take a quick audition.'

'She doesn't know Tamil.'

'Doesn't matter. Bring her along. I have to shoot this scene today.'

The little girl was biting into a raw mango as she arrived with her sparkling eyes. A girlfriend kept her company.

'What's your name?'

'Hesaru helu?' The friend did the interpreting.

'Thimmamma,' the girl replied, looking around and seeming to enjoy herself as she answered that question.

'All right, look here,' said Manikkam, 'why don't you walk from this end to that?'

That girl chatted with her interpreter friend for a while and then laughed enthusiastically. She was a little shy but did the walk. The Bengali cinematographer looked at her through the viewfinder. 'She's tops, Manikkam,' he certified.

Manikkam took a good look at the girl again. She was not wearing the half-sari worn by girls who had come of age in the village. A shirt and a green paavadai were all that she had put on. Above that long skirt, her breasts were fully developed for her age. Her moist lips were firm and protruded a little. Her teeth were gently visible, and her large, black eyes were prominent. Manikkam thought this girl would soon reach the status of the archetypal Hasthini in Vatsyayana's *Kamasutra*. It seemed that she would fit the role written for Manonmani in a youngish sort of a way.

'Let's cast this girl, Durai. Talk to that man and finish the deal. Ask her to wear a sari. Let's go for this. It's a risk but it is a small part.'

The shooting began in the afternoon. That girl wrote out her sparse lines in Kannada and frequently smiled at her friend as she unfurled and played with her newly acquired sari. In her first shot, she was supposed to cheerfully splash her legs in the stream that ran beyond the bund and then freeze in fear, staring into the camera.

'Okay, roll it!' Manikkam said.

As they packed up in the evening and returned to their village house, Manikkam saw Manonmani get off a bus and come running and panting towards them.

28

MANIKKAM LOOKED AT MANONMANI WHO stood with sweat on her upper lip. 'What's going on, Mano? You are so late!'

'They would not agree to let me go at VLS, and I did not have the money to give back. I went for their outdoor, caught a bus, took the Brindavan Express and then the passenger train. I dashed here,' she said with enthusiasm. 'Is everything ready?'

'We have finished the shoot,' Manikkam said.

'*What*?'

'Yes. We cast someone else in your place.'

'Someone else? But how?'

'We found a local girl here. How long could we wait? You know how much we would lose if we dropped a single day's schedule.'

Manonmani's enthusiasm fizzled in a second, and there was now fear in her eyes. 'Please don't say no. I came all the way just for you. What's this now?'

'We don't have the heart to say no to you, Mano. But all the film rolls used in the shoot with that other girl today will go to waste now.'

'What's this, sir? Could you not have put off the shoot by just one day?'

'How could we possibly do that, Mano? I told you right at the beginning, no, that we have a tight schedule, and you should come only if you could agree to that?'

'I said no to another film for this, sir.'

'I'm sorry, Mano. If you want, maybe we can pay you some money to compensate for the opportunity you lost.'

Mano stopped him with one look. 'The money is not important, sir. I thought differently of you. But you have proved that you are like everyone else.'

'Mano, don't judge me so unfairly. You are forgetting that I had explained all this to you before.'

'I had many expectations from this, sir. My life is full of such yearnings. "We have cast someone else. We have cast someone else" is all I hear. I have heard this so many times. I have missed the bus so many times.' Unable to control herself, Mano burst into tears and wiped her eyes with her sari pallu.

'Adadaa! Why are you crying? Look, what's the matter? It is only a small part. Okay, let's do something. Let's take a couple of shots tomorrow like you are that girl's friend who goes to her place.'

'No, sir. Let me go back. Let me plead with them to see whether they will take me back again.'

'No, Mano. Let's shoot here.'

'But why should you lose film rolls?'

'What can we do when you talk like this?'

'There are lots of friend roles available in Madras for twenty or thirty rupees. I don't have to go three hundred miles away and hang out all day for it. I thought this was a part with real lines and a chance to do some real acting. Then you have gone and cast this new girl out of nowhere. I am just not lucky. Does she even know Tamil?'

'She doesn't. She is a Kannada girl,' Manikkam said, his face falling.

'Okay, let me leave now.'

'Wait, I'll have you dropped. And please take the expenses for your coming here. I don't want to hear that you suffered a loss because of me.'

'I don't want the money, sir.'

'No, please take it.'

'How much will you give me? Whatever you give, I can earn three times the amount in an hour. That's not the big deal, Manikkam. Some compassion—that's the big thing. I'll see you.'

'Mano! Mano! Don't go. Stay!'

She turned back and walked off briskly.

'Look at her,' Manikkam said. 'Look at how angry she is! As if I don't have enough headaches in life…'

'That's true,' said a junior artiste.

Manikkam felt a sense of guilt deep inside. Although he was infuriated by what she had said, the underlying truth hurt. She had suddenly made it crystal clear, as if she had ripped off some veil, that the Manikkam who fought and argued for the rights of junior artistes and Manikkam the movie director were two different people. He told himself that he must pacify her when he gets back to Madras. He must give her a chance in his next movie. For now, he had plenty of other stuff to do and worries that were piling up.

Manonmani caught the bus to Mandya, walked to the railway station and bought herself a ticket to Bangalore. She got into one of the trains, in one of the coaches, and sat in one of the seats. A wave of self-pity swept over her. The same basic problem returned to haunt her over and over again. This or that? Oh, the choices! There was so much competition in this life. If she slept a wink, another woman took her place. When the shoot required four dancers, forty showed up! What about the chances that came after so many tussles? The chance to carry a bowl of rose water in a wedding scene. Or the heroine's fourth friend in college. Or the girl in the north-eastern corner of a group dance! And after a long time playing bit parts, all she got was a chance to speak real lines in *Ilanthalaivan*, but only as a damsel created for a short scene that required objectionable stripping!

Why was she fretting so much? She could not figure it out. Why was she struggling so hard for fifty or hundred rupees! What was that inexplicable urge to be featured in film magazines? Why? For some prince to appear some day and say, 'Here is Manonmani, the heroine of my next movie'? The addictive belief that he would raise her to new highs! It all seemed absurd. The path to stardom these days was different. A straight route for elite girls. Models, granddaughters of professors, girls who had graduated from the film institute...they all played the heroine in their very first film. People like herself waited forever, while there were so many who jumped the queue. *I am just a waitress of sorts in this industry, one who picks up plates for a living every day*, she told herself. To spend a hundred and fifty rupees to catch a train, to run like a dog and when told the part was not hers any longer, to say with a smile, 'It's all right!' and then onwards to catch another train to smile a plastic smile at another face. It was much easier to make the same hundred and fifty rupees in the 'other' life she led.

There was no need to act at all in that life, no need to smile even. The driver would give an address. It would mostly be a room number in a hotel. One had to knock the door by jingling her bangles. The door would open without anyone asking who it was. There would be a grinning face in front of her, and all she had to do was to sit on the bed. Without giving her much trouble, he would strip her himself, turn the sari into a ball and throw it away. As his eyes would glare fixated on the middle of her breasts, a snake-like tongue would dart out and wet the corner of his lips. He would come near, smelling of liquor. He would touch her. It would prick her like a thorn. Then, the first of the acid would ooze in her stomach. If she could manage that moment, it would only take a while after that. After that, the lustful glitter in his eyes would go away and a sheepish look would take its place. There would still be some time left at the negotiated rate. In that time he would speak of his wife and kids. 'I have two girls. They go to school. They are in a convent.' There were those who would worship her or put flowers in her hair. Millionaires who would crawl because she asked them to. How easy that way was!

Manonmani made up her mind to do something about all this.

Cumulous clouds loomed overhead like rolls of cotton balls in the sky. The foothills afar were swathed in green. Cameras, generators and vans stood ready for action. The director, the technicians and Arun were all were looking at their watches. There were some people playing cards under nearby trees. Nude women were smiling on the decks they held in their hands.

A sidekick told Arun, 'Anney, Amitabh Bachchan has sung in his own voice in *Natwarlal*. Why don't you try singing as well?'

'Hey, why don't you come along and sing with me! Let's make it a duet,' Arun shot back in irritation. 'What happened to that woman? I had asked you to phone and find out if she is coming or not.'

'Selvarajan has gone to find out. He should be coming any time now.'

Another factotum approached Arun. 'The tiffin is going cold, sir. Let's eat.'

'You eat and scram. All we have done so far is eat our tiffins.'

The director came and expressed his worries in Telugu. 'Enti idhi. What is going on?' He lit a Dunhill cigarette to ease his tensions.

He was smoking Charminars until last month, Arun thought.

'Rao garu, can we shoot another scene? It doesn't look like she will come. Is there anything in my part that needs to be done, Selvakumar?'

'We have shot all of your scenes, Arun. If this lady comes, we can finish the thing. It is just a day's work.'

'What happened to her?'

'She has not returned from her Ooty shoot yet. Maybe the car has had a problem. Hell, can't she at least send a telegram or something?'

'Selvakumar, what is the film's story as of today?'

'What, Arun? Don't joke like this. As if you don't know the story.'

'But we have made so many changes. We're no longer going to Europe and one heroine is out of the plot.'

'That lady said she would give us half a call sheet tomorrow. Maybe we can use that time at AVM and change it to an indoor scene and adjust.'

'We also have plenty of close-up shots from the same location in our stock. Shall we use that? The editor can handle putting all that together.'

'Why? Can't we kill her altogether? We can always show her ghost descending on someone else in her next birth!'

'That's a good idea, sir.'

Arun sighed. 'I used to joke about everyone doing things in a patchy, shoddy way. Now look at my own state.'

'The film has come along very well so far, sir.'

Arun glared at him.'En yaa? If you must suck up to me, isn't there a better way? You are crawling on all fours. Tell me the truth: is the film awesome or not? Do I owe you some money or something?'

Everybody fell silent. Arun turned to go back to his hotel room.

'So is that pack-up for the day, sir?'

'Ask the director.'

He walked out. The hotel building jutted out of the hills and towered over the expansive valley. Arun could see a cerulean sky, and Bhaskar was wearing a pullover and adding up some numbers through glasses perched on his nose.

'Bhaskar, I am ruined!'

'Why? She didn't come?'

'At this rate, I won't be able to finish this by the eighth. The interest payments will devour me. Show me a way out, Bhaskar.'

Bhaskar didn't say anything.

'Shall I call "The End" now and just be done with it?'

'No. Don't do that!'

'I am finished. Dead! The release date has been fixed. There are eight scenes left and there is no sign of that woman.'

'You know, it is wedding bells for her.'

'But I need money to take out the prints.'

Bhaskar remained quiet.

'Come on,' Arun said. 'Say something.'

Very calmly, Bhaskar replied: 'I'll tell you just one thing. Will you listen without pouncing on me?'

'No, but tell me.'

'Arun! Just leave. Scram. Quit.'

'What the…?'

'Your part is done, no? You go now. Just disappear somewhere. That's all.'

'And what about the unfinished parts? Who is going to finish those?'

'I will finish it. I'll get it released. Arun, the only flaw in this shoot now is you. Sorry, but I have to tell you this. Only I can tolerate your anger, your outbursts and your words. Just stay out of the way for a few days. We can finish the film—I'll finish it for you.'

'If this movie flops, my career is finished, Bhaskar.'

'We can worry about that later. First let us save ourselves from sinking. The main objective is to avoid a loss. Just listen to me. Stay away! Get some rest, and just forget about this movie. If it is not released by the eighth, you can just kill me! If you are around, nothing will get done. You are all strung out. You'll blow up anytime. You'll have a heart attack.'

'Where do I go now?'

'Go to Uttamarkovil, to the place where you came from. Go there just as a human being.'

'Who will I meet there? I don't have anyone for me there now.'

'Shall I tell you who's there? Kalyani!'

'What?'

'Yes. I have got news that she has gone there.' Bhaskar winked at Arun now.

'Bhaskar, you are a smart man.'

'The car is ready.'

'Just wait. Let me pack!'

'I've already done that for you.'

Arun rushed off to meet Kalyani.

29

ARUN DASHED FROM THE OUTDOOR shoot and did not stop in Bangalore. He paused only for fifteen minutes at Salem to grab a quick tiffin. When he reached Uttamarkovil, it was dawn. He recalled the dash he had made before his wedding to meet Kalyani. The same car, the same driver, the same place. The same Arun and the same Kalyani. But so many changes in the interim. After both had gone hither and thither like blind rats, what was the point in going to Uttamarkovil?

It was to escape some truths! It was a convenient hiding place for Arun. From the excruciating difficulties of making a film, stemming from the fear that it would definitely be a flop. He did not want to be in Madras at the time of its release. Everybody was waiting for him there with an axe to grind.

From the word go, it had gone wrong. Lakshmanan had come in, only to get into trouble with the censor board. After his prints had been seized, he had managed to evade a prison sentence by paying a hefty fine. And so, the money did not come to Arun. There were so many hurdles! He had borrowed so much at high interest rates, raised hundis, all in the fervent hope that he would be able to pay back the money in a short while. But that was not to be. His house had come close to being attached by creditors, and to escape this he sought refuge in Premalatha, who then took control. The story was changed, and a special part was written into the story only for her.

Rao garu, the much-revered director, turned out to be a disappointment. It took quite a while for Arun to figure out that this man's direction was fit only for Telugu movies. And so, if there was one man speaking a sentimental bout of lines in a scene, the director insisted that everybody around had to show a sad face and emote like they were swallowing castor oil. How was one supposed to tell him that it all sounded so out of date—like that mythological film *Bhakta Bhodhana*? When Arun finally got around to telling the director so, it had resulted in an ugly altercation between them.

Then there were those star actresses! When they were all required to be in Bangalore, one was found in Goa, one in the US and the third was in a village called Karundhattankudi. When they all came in their own sweet time, the shots were taken separately in medium close-ups and tight shots, with the uneasy plan of reconciling them on the editing table somehow. The outdoor shots did not have a single long shot. Even the name of the film was not decided yet. *Adhu Oru Rahasyam* seemed so close to *Adhai Vida Rahasyam* that it was abandoned at the eleventh hour.

'Oh, no!' Arun thought. 'This won't suit me. I just can't seem to handle these arbitrary adjustments.' A scene depicting absurdity from one of those Crazy Boys black comedies from France came to his mind—of a surgeon performing a complicated operation, with a troupe of doctors around him.

There are blood stains all around and the surgery is not going well, when all of a sudden the surgeon abandons his scalpel and simply walks off, saying, 'Alright, let's do this tomorrow.'

Arun thought of his own mood in much the same spirit. With blood stains on his hands, Bhaskar must be busy picking up the instruments fallen to the ground.

Soon, the car passed the granite mandapam of the temple at Uttamarkovil. There were people asleep at the Ayyanar shrine. The stream had run dry. The railway line had been altered. He entered Sannadhi Street and asked the driver to park in front of his house. Sundaram, who was reading the *Dinamani* in the veranda, disappeared inside after seeing him. Arun felt a stinging pain inside.

The driver opened the door. As he admired Bhaskar's thoughtfulness in handing over the house keys to the driver, he took a look at the street. It had changed so much. The door of a house that he had heard in his childhood was haunted was open. Somebody brave had decided to live there. The Japanese clock ad poster on the wall was missing.

He entered his house. As he crossed the threshold and stepped into the elongated living room hall they used to call the rezhi, in ten flat steps he found himself moving back ten years in time. There, right in front of him, there was a group photo of tenth standard students at The High School, Srirangam. He smiled as he spotted himself in a corner of the picture—big face, short crop of hair, half-pants. Who was it who had put a circle around his face and decided that this man was going to smile from photos across the country? In the left-hand corner of the photograph, there was Sundaram. He already had thick glasses then and a mature look on his face. Sampath Teacher, KVR, NSN...all of whom had specifically assigned nicknames: Thayir Vadai, Three-by-Two...

His father's glasses were still perched exactly where they used to be. The easy chair was empty. All of his mother's picture deities were intact. Did they die only two minutes ago? The house was spick and span. Bhaskar had made arrangements for it to be cleaned once a week.

He picked up a paper and wrote: 'Sundaram, I am here. May I come and see you?' and sent his driver across with the message, asking him to fetch a reply. He waited as he thought to himself of the lines he might speak to his old friend.

'*Sundaram, I have already acted a lot in my life. But what I say right now on the banks of Kollidam is totally true: All of my being, my body, my soul—everything loves your sister.*'

What he had said that day was true even now. After all, it was for Kalyani that he had embarked on this strange journey. *Bhaskar is a genius! He understood the state of my mind so well and packed me off here!* he thought.

What could possibly happen now? They both were now married to other people. He had embraced so many women in his life. Why this obsession with this very specific woman?

Question: Why do you climb the mountain?

Answer: Because it is there.

I got trapped in a quick-fix marriage. She was trapped in a traditional marriage. Both were sent away in different directions. Despite all that, even today, I just have to look her in the eye to revive all those happy moments of their childhood. A moment is all I need. We can stand ten feet away from each other and yet can hug and kiss and eat each other up. Amid all the formal meetings, a secret rendezvous is all I need.

The driver was back. 'He said he will be here in about ten minutes, sir.'

'Okay, you leave now. Take a coffee break.'

The first disappointment was that Sundaram did not invite him to his own home. *Let's see*, Arun thought. *How will she be now? Is there still a shade of red where she ties her long paavadai around her waist? Are her breasts still small? Does she still wear those jingling anklets? Does she still wear henna?*

'Viju is just like in his movies, really tall. His complexion shines like sandalwood. He seems so ill-matched with that Premalatha.' The lines from her piece in her handwritten magazine came back to him. *Sundaram! I am ready to erase all the things of the past and marry your sister afresh, Sundaram!*

Sundaram turned up to meet Arun after a while. He had trimmed his beard a little and seemed as if he had aged a few years within a few months. There was an unfathomable sadness in his eyes. 'There's no point in asking when you arrived because I did see you come.'

'Why did you go in when you saw me? Are you angry with me?'

'Yes, I am.'

'What did I do now?'

'You phoned Kalyani.'

'Is that wrong? Is it wrong to call once and ask how she is?'

'Is that all you did? Did you not ask her to meet you? Viju, in the social circles that you move in, such a thing may not be wrong. But…I am sorry I am attacking you like this right away. Let's have some coffee and talk. It's on the way. Kalyani said she would bring some over.'

Kalyani was going to bring him some coffee. He felt something flutter deep inside. 'Tell me, Sundaram. If I did something wrong by telephoning her, I am sorry.'

'You phoned her. For you that is a small thing, but in the process, you did something that has more or less ruined my sister's life.'

'What are you talking about?'

'Viju, you don't really know our wonderful son-in-law. He started this whole thing with a lie. He said he is a bank officer. Turned out to be a clerk, appearing in an exam to be an officer. Let that be. If he kept his wife happy, we could forgive anything. But no. He has tortured my sister in an elegant way. He did not hit her or bite her but made life hell for her in an indescribable way. He viewed every damn thing she did with suspicion.'

'What was he suspicious about?'

'That she had a secret liaison with Arun.'

'My God!'

'He found out about your telephoning her. She told me everything that happened to her like it was some story. Can you believe it? He even locked her up inside the room when he left for work.'

'The creep! I am so sorry, Sundaram.'

'He has now sent her off here.'

Arun stood shocked, at a loss for words for a while. 'Sundaram, I contacted her without a clue about all this. I am such a fool.'

'Such husbands exist in every town, every street of Tamil Nadu. I had sent my sister to him like she was a tender flower. I still remember the angel I saw off at the railway junction.'

Arun suddenly found some enthusiasm within. 'Sundaram, I want to make it clear. I still like your sister. In fact, I love her. It may come as a shock to you, but my marriage has also been a disaster. It turned out to be a big accident. We have no compatibility in any matter whatsoever. She is…well, why talk about her? Sundaram, I am ready to accept your sister as my wife. I can handle any opposition to it. You are an educated man, and my thoughts are progressive. If we both stay strong, we can make this revolution. What do you say?'

'It's too late, Viju.'

'No, it's never too late.'

Then Kalyani arrived.

'Come, Kalyani. Look, Viju is here.'

Arun looked up, butterflies fluttering in his heart. She had entered the room with a coffee tumbler. He saw her and was startled.

Kalyani was fully pregnant now. She had lost a good bit of hair. Her forehead looked big, and her breasts sagged. She looked blanched, apparently as a result of her anaemia. There were dark shadows under her eyes. The bangles slipped, eager to slide off of her wrist.

My God! This is not Kalyani!

'This is Kalyani,' Sundaram said. 'Look at the flower I sent and see the way it has returned home.'

'Kalyani, are you okay?'

'Mmmm.' She put the tumbler down. 'Please check if the sugar is okay.'

Kalyani suddenly looked up at him. 'Mr Arun, please don't phone me anymore now. He scolded me a lot.'

'Sorry, Kalyani. I heard about all that.'

'Anna,' She spoke to her brother now. 'Amma asked for the bullock cart. We have to go to Bichandaar Kovil and see the lady doctor.'

Kalyani turned away and walked off towards the door.

'He scolded her a lot. And yet he needed her every day. He has crushed her. Look how wounded she looks, clinging on to life.'

'Anna, are you coming?' she called out from outside.

'Tell me now, Arun. Are you ready to make a revolution?' Sundaram left.

Manonmani went to the bathroom, changed her sari and adjusted her hair. She adjusted the hooks at the back of her blouse. She opened the door and came into the room.

Plonked cross-legged in the middle of the bed, the man with sacred ash and kumkum smeared on his forehead looked tired. 'Here,' he said. As she took the wad of notes, he asked, 'What's your name?'

'Manonmani.'

'"*I will fear not the glance of a bangled woman*," goes a line in the *Thiruvachakam*. But I certainly fear your sideward glance. Sit down now.'

'No, sir. I have to be leaving now.'

'What is this? You are leaving so soon.'

'That's all. Are we not done?'

'How can that be? We have negotiated for the whole night.'

'No, sir. Nadarasu didn't say anything of that sort.'

'He did when he discussed the rates with me. What is this? He has said one thing to me and another to you?' He beckoned her with authority. 'Vaa di!'

'No, sir. Really, I have to go now, sir'

'Hey, I'll give you more. I'll double this—a good deal. Just sit here. You have to do nothing, really.'

'I have to go home, sir.'

'You will not get a taxi now. Let me drop you. I am not demanding much. A small thing. Look here, take this.'

He reached under the bed and yanked out a shining cane. He handed it to Manonmani. She worked like a machine and took off her blouse and loosened her bangles.

The man who spoke lines from the sacred *Thiruvachakam* now took off his vest, kneeled at the centre of his bed and showed his naked back. 'Hit me now, cane me like my teacher amma. Just once, di.'

Manonmani lifted her cane with both hands and raised her hands at the world: those men, the opportunities she missed, the lies they told her, her own body, the uncle who called her to teach some dancing, that Raja from Pondicherry, that Lakshmanan and that Pandurangan who said, 'This shirt is not good. Let's take it off,' and that Venugopal and those little Rajas who said, 'Shall we go by taxi, Mano?' and those Manikkams who spoke to her about 'Full shots on a black night' and those Kannada girls who stole roles waiting for her, and those directors who shut the door from inside and raped her with their eyes and their cameras…

She took out all the anger of her miserable life with that piece of cane. The pain went forth. *Spaaaaaaaaaaaaaaaaaaank!*

When Mano got home, her mother did not ask, 'Why did it take you so long?' Instead, she asked, 'Have you eaten?'

'I have, ma.' Manonmani looked at her face in the small mirror in the almirah.

'Here, take this money. Pay off the remaining rent and also the outstanding amount at Vanaja Stores.'

'Where are you off to?' Her mother counted the money.

'I am going to take a bath. The money is enough, no?'

'It is enough. You're bathing at this hour?'

'Yes.'

Mano, sweet Mano, went into the bathroom. She locked the door from inside. She stood for a while. Then she drenched all of her body and her sari. With kerosene.

30

Shadows of the tall coconut palms fell slanting on the sandy banks of Kollidam as Arun and Sundaram squatted opposite each other.

Arun grabbed fistfuls of the sand and let them slip through his fingers. 'I just don't feel like going to Madras, Sundaram.'

'Why? It's been eight days since you came here, right?'

'I don't like the truth waiting for me there. Sundaram, I am going to quit the film world.'

'But cinema is not going to leave you.'

'No! Cinema leaves us quite easily, in fact. Just have four flops in a row and no one will touch you after that. I am precisely in that place now. As if that was not enough, I am trapped in my own production. I don't think it could get any worse.'

'Has the film been released?'

'It may be released today or tomorrow. I have even forgotten the date. I don't think it is worth releasing. When I left that shoot, there were one or two shots still to be done. The re-recording had not been done either. Even after getting the dates from the censor board, the shooting was not over.

I dumped everything on my secretary like it was garbage and came running here. It's horrible!'

'What's the name of the film?'

'*Moondru Rojakkal.*'

'I think it has already been released. I recall seeing it in the papers.'

'Is that so? I have not seen the papers for a week now. I have just been reading the book you gave me. That means Bhaskar has somehow patched it all up and released the movie. My wife has also been working hard on this.'

'Did you read *The Fall*?'

'I did. Like that lawyer in the book, I feel there is hypocrisy in living now. Whatever I have done so far is a lie. My marriage is a lie. My films are a lie. The laughter, the acting, everything is a lie. That's why I thought I must do at least one true thing. I still have that ambition, Sundaram, and you have not given me an answer.'

Sundaram sat silently for a while. In the distance, people were walking on the river bank. There was a colourful marquee at the other end of the river. Whenever the winds obliged, the wafting sound of temple drums reached their ears.

'What's going on there?'

'The Lord of Srirangam is coming to the banks of Kollidam. The God of our town is going there to meet him. My mother and father would have gone there to pay obeisance and pray. Why don't you meet her discreetly and have a word with her?'

'Meet Kalyani?'

'Yes. Let her decide.'

'Great! Sundaram, come. Let's go.' He got up from the bank and walked fast. He recalled coming here a year or so ago. He had asked for Kalyani's hand then as well. Things had changed but not his deep desire for her. They reached Sundaram's home and waited for her.

Bangles jingled to herald her arrival. Kalyani came quietly and sat on a chair. She had plenty of bangles on her hands. There was red vermillion on her forehead, her neck and her gold maangalyam that hung on her thaali. Red stains of chewed betel leaves were around her lips. She had breasts that were ready for motherhood. She looked straight at him and then at her fingernails. 'Please sit,' she said, and looked at her brother. 'And you, Anna?'

'I am going out now. You keep talking.'

After he left, she looked straight at Arun for the first time and said, 'Anna has told me everything.'

'Yes, Kalyani. I am ready.'

'Are you taking pity on me?'

'No, Kalyani. This is desire. You are my only true love. I have been thinking of you since I was twenty. I remember everything: your going to school, drawing kolam outside your house, your playing Krishna during the Kolu at Navaratri... you have never been far from my mind.'

'Arun, I used to think about you in that way, too, before my marriage. But then, right at that juncture, I realized the greed in such a wish and stopped myself.'

'Look here, Kalyani, we have both been taken in different directions and separated by circumstances. I can change that. That's what I want, in fact.'

'Doesn't that include my wishes as well?'

'Certainly! That's exactly why I am here—to know what you want.'

She sat up now. 'Okay, let me say it clearly. Please go back to your city and your home. That's what I want.'

'Why do you say that, Kalyani?'

'If my parents hear about this crazy desire of yours, they'll give up their lives at once. They can't even begin to think like that. The husband I have is an ordinary man. He is not famous like you. And when you think about it, the doubts and suspicions he has had are those that come naturally to an ordinary man. I also did not like the way Anna scolded him. His world is a small one. It is uncomplicated, the world of office-goers, the world of those who write examinations and clear tests. Right or wrong, they have an image, a sketch, of what a wife should be. He could not bear the very thought of another man desiring his wife. He did all sorts of strange things with me because he could not swallow the burning embers of his suspicions. I could not take away his doubts with my words, but one thing is certain: if I do leave him, he will die for sure. Arun, the solution to my problems does not lie in leaving what I have in order to chase an elusive dream. At this time when I am ready to have a child, I have no desire to chart a new path and experiment with my life. Nor do I have the energy for it. I complained a lot about him to my brother, but I had a different intention. I thought Anna would speak to him and convince him about me. I felt outraged when I heard of this dangerous way to solve the problem. One marriage is enough for me. I will try to make it work or put up with it. The only way you can do me a big favour in this is to not chase me on the telephone or at my home. Will you please leave now?'

'Kalyani. I…'

'Please! Don't say another word. Will you leave now? Anna, please come in.'

He looked straight at her for a few moments.

Unable to withstand his gaze, she bent her head down and looked at her tummy and caressed it. 'He is kicking now. Just like his father.'

Sundaram came in. 'Have you finished speaking? Viju, these are not things that can be reversed. There are the rules of karma…'

'Nonsense! Go to hell! Spineless beings!' Arun rushed out of their house in a canter. He felt his blood boil. He walked some more.

What would he do now? Where would he go? Between the paddy and sugarcane fields there was a ribbon-like path that led somewhere. On a square patch of land carved out of lush green fields there was a tent cinema, the one they used to call touring talkies. *Vayasukku Vandha Ponnu* was running there.

Arun walked towards the makeshift movie theatre. It seemed that the 6 p.m. show would start only at 7.30 p.m. Two old women had spread out a jute gunny bag and were getting ready to sell boiled sweet potatoes, sugarcane pieces and peanuts. His own image was smiling down from a crumpled screen. There were two holes to sell tickets in the five-foot high cabins. An oil engine stood at a corner. In the slanted promotion cart stuck with movie posters, there was a clarinet and a kettle drum. A cow stood nearby, having chewed cud and salivating at its mouth. 'Fire, Fire, Fire', announced three red buckets filled with sand. What was he looking for? What was he searching here?

The owner of the cinema was washing clothes at a distance. He did not recognize Arun at first but later got excited. 'Is it really you, saar?' he asked. 'Aah, that's why they were talking about it at the Bichandaar Temple. What are you looking for, sir?'

What did he really want? *Too late, Arun. You have no place now in either of these worlds.*

'It is your film running here, sir. Would you like to see it? It will take half an hour or maybe three quarters of an hour. You see, those out for harvesting have to come as well.'

'Can you show me some of the reels—just for myself—for half an hour or so?'

'Why, sir?'

'I am going to quit films. I am going to leave everything.'

'Aah, stop joking, sir. Just wait, I will ask them to screen your stuff.'

'I'll pay you whatever it takes for this.'

'The fact that you have come for this is a big deal to us.'

In a remote village in the corner of the country, on a tin chair in an empty theatre, this, he thought, *is the perfect ending*. On the screen, the reel began its countdown. 7 flash. 6 flash. 5 flash. Then came the censor certificate and an image of a goddess with agarbatti fumes.

Arun. His name was sprawled across the screen.

Arun looked at Arun now. Here was the hero. He sang. He danced. He saved. He shed tears. He made love. He made sacrifices for his sister. So many lies to please the tired souls back from their harvests.

A line flashed in his mind: '*I progressed on the surface of life in the realm of words as it were, never in reality.*'

The film world is going to forget me now, he thought. *Go away! You are not required here. There are so many new faces. Vacate your slot. There is little room at the top. There are many lying in wait. You have stood long enough in the gentle yellow spotlight. Go away now! Go! Run to the edge!*

The only way you can do me a big favour in this is to not chase me on the telephone or at my home. Will you leave now?

Where do I go now? Run from this place? Here? How? In a car? He could always go where his thoughts took him. To some place far away. To a sudden turn.

Arun came out of the makeshift movie theatre.

'What, sir? Don't you want to see the rest of the film? The last scene is tops…'

'No, sir,' he said. 'Keep this. I'll see you later.'

He walked towards his house, towards his car. All of Uttamarkovil was away on the banks of Kollidam. Sannadhi Street was neatly awash with moonshine. In the house across his own, a light was glowing. Sister and brother were poring over some books. *Let them study. Let them go to hell.*

He got into the car, turned on the key and it roared. He saw Sundaram approach him with brisk steps. He was waving a piece of paper in his hand. 'A telegram arrived when you were away. I received it on your behalf.'

Arun took it and read the telegram in the light of the car, showing hardly any interest.

Moondru Rojakkal *is running housefull in all theatres in all centres. The early signs of an inevitable hit. Come back, Arun. – Bhaskar.*

Arun looked bewildered at the telegram for a while and then laughed out loud. He laughed till there were tears in his eyes. 'Absurd, it's just absurd! I just don't understand.'

31

'THE SHOPS WOULD HAVE CLOSED long ago. We have to buy five kilos of rice and coffee powder first thing in the morning. And some cotton cloth.'

Mano's mother counted the money carefully and kept it in the almirah and spoke in the general direction of her daughter. 'They have your photo in *Cine Express*. Did you see it?'

Mano took out a matchbox and lit a matchstick.

'What is this, di? You are not saying anything. Are you angry?'

As the sulphur tip of the matchstick caught fire, she waited till the early smoke left and the flame steadied.

'What happened to that film Manikkam was making? Why don't you ask him point blank if he is giving you a role or not?'

She touched the matchstick to the tip of her sari drenched with kerosene.

'What are you doing? Boiling some hot water or something? I can smell kerosene.'

There was still no reply. 'What is going on?' Mano's mother felt deep down that something was wrong. She went to the bathroom and called out. 'Mano!' She put her ear to the door, and she could hear some coughing inside. 'Amma, Amma di…' she heard some groans. Through the cracks under the door, some smoke escaped. 'Mano! Mano!'

Her mother banged on the door of the bathroom with both hands. The smoke now came in big, quick bursts. In the pit of her stomach, the mother felt a cramp, rolled up like a ball; she stood frozen in fear. She cried out loud now: 'Mano! Mano? What are you doing, di? Please open the door. Are you not my darling daughter? Open, di, open!' She screamed and banged her shoulders, hands and head on the door. The door shook with a thudding sound but did not open.

The groaning stopped now and there was an indescribable ugly sound from inside. As the voice said, 'It is burning, it is burning!' the mother went out and screamed: 'Somebody please come here. Somebody please rush here. Something has happened here.'

The mother screamed her guts out to wake all the neighbours. They came. They enquired. They got upset. They got together and crashed the door. The broke the door and opened it. Clouds of smoke escaped from the bathroom, as if they were liberated.

Mano was fully burnt by now.

As the cap opened with a popping sound, the golden-coloured Scotch poured into a clean whiskey glass. In went some soda. As the glasses clinked with each other, 'Cheers!' said Arun and swallowed half a glass in one go.

'Easy,' said Bhaskar, as he stood aside and sipped a glass of grape juice. Hundreds of telegrams lay in a pile on the table. One of them escaped in the swirling air of the ceiling fan. 'FIRST WEEK ALL SHOWS BOOKED CONGRATS FOR GREAT PIC,' it said.

Arun started laughing as the liquid entered his veins, drenching his being in some golden melody. 'I don't know what to make of this, Bhaskar,' he said.

'Don't try to understand it. It is a lottery.'

'No, it can't be. You have done something.'

'Arun! You know why this film clicked? First, it is a change from those village movies with a love story around the landlord and the way they run in slow motion. It is good that we cancelled the overseas shoots. They are all shooting abroad these days as if it was some neighbouring town. We have not seen any middle-of-the-road entertainment in recent times without either of these things. There are entire families committing suicide or a Muslim raises a Brahmin—that sort of stuff. We had a story with nothing of that kind. There was no need to rack your brains in the plot. There was a superhit song there, a dance here, and sex that is not too much in-your-face. It was Rao Gaaru's old-fashioned direction. That man crafts a delicious set-piece menu like an expert chef.'

'But how long will this last?'

'What? Our film? There's no doubt this will run for twenty-five weeks. There is no doubt about that.'

'What if we make another film like this?'

'It will bite the dust, but then you can't be sure of that either. Maybe the market will take one or two more like these. Anyway, we have to make one more just like this. Lots of demand for this hit formula. Lakshmanan has been after us for three days.'

'Lakshmanan? Don't talk to him now, Bhaskar.'

'No, Arun! After you left, he somehow raised a lakh and a half at the last moment. He is a master at raising funds.'

'So he has a currency printing press at home? A small one?'

'He is financing our next film. A.L. Combines. Arun-Lakshmanan. Enough, Arun—you have been drinking a lot now.'

As the phone rang away without a pause, Arun carelessly picked up the receiver. 'I am afraid he is not here, he is off to Mumbai for a shoot,' he said and started towards the first floor. 'Let me say a word of thanks to my darling wife. Don't go anywhere.'

'Arun, there is a small thing…'

'What?' He stopped.

'I don't know if I have the right to tell you this now, but I think you have not understood your wife well.'

'Oh, really? And you have?'

'I mean in the sense of being a husband.'

'So a bachelor is giving me marital advice now.'

As he entered the room, the smell of a cigarette assaulted his nostrils. Premalatha was reading a Tintin comic. 'Prem, have you been smoking?'

'Yes,' she said, without looking up. A little yelping sound came from somewhere. Under the bed were two poodles. 'What's this? Two dogs?'

'You have been living with me for so long now. Didn't you know I had two pet dogs?'

'Yes, I do now. One is Honey, thc other is Julie.'

'Then why do you ask?'

He went and sat behind her and rubbed himself over all of her back. Premalatha did not turn around.

'Why? Are you angry with me again?'

'No, not at all. How is Kalyani now?'

'What?' he said, startled.

'Arun, I know everything.'

'Who told you this? Bhaskar?'

'Bhaskar is on your side. It was the driver who told me.'

'The slimy rascal. I have to fire him now.'

'That's done. I have already sacked him. It's me who does the hiring and firing of the staff in this house now. How is Kalyani anyway? When is your wedding?'

'Don't be silly. She is pregnant now.'

'What?'

'Pregnant! Like a big cow or something…hmmm. It was Bhaskar who conspired to do this. It was him who decided to send me to Uttamarkovil. He sent me there lovingly to see her, only to give me a shock! When I saw her fully pregnant, all my lust for her dissolved in a second. He knew that. The crook! I have to sack him now after settling the accounts for *Moondru Rojakkal.*'

'There is no need for that,' Prem said. She kept her book down and looked Arun in the eye.

Arun went and sat near her. 'It seems like I am seeing you all afresh after a long time, Prem. Do you mind if I ask you something? Will you give me an honest answer?'

'I know what you will ask, Arun. So you want to know what happened that day in Hyderabad, in that room?'

'Yes.'

'Look here, Arun…you know why we are doubting each other and spying on each other like this?'

'What?'

'It means there is still some love and attraction left between us.'

'Is that so? Then where is that attraction? Here? He made an obscene gesture with his fingers.

'Chee!'

'We fight over so many things but in some things, we are on the same page.'

'For example…?'

'In bed.'

'And?'

'In our anger, in our stubbornness and our arguments, in not yielding any ground.'

As Arun spoke on, he steadily took off her clothes one by one. He gave her a hard, slow look.

'Arun, when we have so many intimate things and little secrets between us, how can you think I would be with another man?'

'Let's fight a lot now. Come.' He rubbed his nose on her face. 'You are smelling of some strange fruit,' he said. He then sprawled all over her body.

'Arun!' she said. 'Let's have a baby.'

She was wearing a pearl necklace now. That was the only thing she had on.

The flat was on the first floor of a house on Mahalakshmi Street, with a staircase on the side leading up to the door. The door carried the message 'Jesus Saves' and below that hung a blue plastic nameplate that announced: 'Arumairajan—Screen Lyricist.' A carpet was spread out in the living room. The almirahs had plenty of porcelain stuff. A TV set was playing Doordarshan, which abruptly ended its broadcast for the day with a man saying a late-night goodbye. The set was still on and showed black-and-white waves, while its speaker emitted a buzzing static sound. Mary stared vacantly at the screen for a while and then moved to switch it off. It would take at least one more hour for him to show up. Mary looked around. This was a house with all the comforts she could think of. The maid had made chapatis and was sleeping in the passage. There were photographs of her husband on the wall. And there was the first shield he had won. His books on the shelf spanned Siddhar songs, *Thiruvachakam*, Kambar's *Ramayanam*, Christian psalms and a compendium of film lyrics. Then there were his bottles full of pills. A clutch of fresh betel leaves awaited him in the fridge, neatly bundled in a wet piece of cloth. There were several pens and lots of paper in the flat. And lots of those shirts he wore.

But her husband was nowhere to be seen yet. Mary had come far from where she had been, and her simple mind could not figure out what she had gained in the journey. She felt a little dumbfounded by it all: what was all this for? She felt she would have been better off in a hand-to-mouth existence in Bangalore. At least their child would have survived. She must visit the Velankanni shrine once with a plaintive prayer. 'O our sacred Virgin Mary! Will you not give me a share of the joy you felt when you carried the Son of God in your holy womb in those nine months? O loving mother who blesses the miserable! Will you give me a small bit of joy? As I observe this penance will you give me a small gift? Will you give me back my Louis Dominic?'

She cried 'Hail Mary!' nine times. 'Divine Mother! I dedicate this prayer to you with the same devotion that the archangel Gabriel had for you! I seek no riches! I seek not glory! Just make myself and my husband come together again! That is enough for me! With much humility, I make this wish, with the kind heart of Jesus as my witness. Give me back my poverty again!'

With a thin film of tears in her eyes, she switched off the lights in the living room. She waited in the pale yellow light of the small bulb that glowed under the portrait of Virgin Mary.

It was 3 a.m. when Arumairajan returned home. 'Mary? You have not gone to sleep yet?'

'But you said you will be back home for dinner.'

'Oh, I ate in the room!'

'Which room?'

'Er, the composing room. We had to complete three songs. You carry on and go to bed. I told you not to stay awake for me.'

Mary watched silently as he took off his shirt and his trousers and got into his pyjamas.

'Let's go to our hometown,' she said.

'Why?'

'What do I get here, staring at the ceiling all day? Let's go home.'

'Where?'

'To Bangalore, where we came from. Where our folks are.'

'What folks? Who is there apart from your sister?'

'Let's go to where she is.'

'Why are you being so stupid? Look how many films I have been booked for. Look how many songs I have to write. Twenty-four hours a day are not enough for me. If you want, you carry on.'

'But why all this? Why all this?' Mary said.

Arumairajan said nothing and retired to his bedroom. 'It's the same bloody hassle every day, the same complaint every day when I come home. Tchae! I just don't feel like coming home on some days…'

'What do you have all this money for, these earnings? Why?' Mary said over and over again as she broke into tears.

Arumairajan shut the door and began to write a song. '*The evening flower shall bloom…the evening…*' As his imagination hit a wall, he threw his pen away.

32

Soon after dawn, Viswanathan got off at the Srirangam station and waited for the passenger train to Uttamarkovil. Without wasting the one hour he had, he studied a book on accountancy. When he got off at Uttamarkovil, it hurt that there was no one to receive him. It seemed that they were all angry. *Let them be angry!* he said to himself.

Should Sundaram not have come in his capacity as his brother-in-law? After reaching their place, without staying back for too long, he had to eat his tiffin and catch the next passenger train to Trichy and confirm his return ticket. He had to be in the office the next morning. He walked slowly. It had been three months since he had last seen Kalyani. How would she be now? The last time he saw her, her stomach was huge. It must have eased now.

'Vaanga Mappillai,' Sundaram welcomed him. 'I could not make it to the station. I had to go to the hospital to buy some medicines.'

Viswanathan went inside without saying anything. His mother-in-law jumped up, covering herself with her sari. 'Vaango,' she said. 'Are you well? Adee Kalyani! Mappillai has arrived!'

It was quite dark in the small room. Only a small chimney lamp was glowing. Viswanathan looked for the switch and turned on the electricity. Kalyani was squatting on the floor. Near her, in a huge pile of clothes there was an infant with its eyes and fingers tightly shut.

'Vaango,' Kalyani said.

Viswanathan sat on the floor. The little baby bearing three names already—Ramasubramanian, Suresh, Sivasankaran—opened its tiny eyes. To the call, 'Dei, look who has come,' he gurgled in reply.

'You have lost weight,' said Kalyani.

'Hotel food does not agree with me, Kalyani! And I have passed my exams. They are going to post me as an officer from May. They say my posting will be in the head office itself. But Madhavan Nair is also trying hard for that.'

'Is that so?'

'But I have a higher rank than his. I also have more seniority.'

'Look at him. Look! This fellow is already riding a bicycle. His fingers are just like yours. Look at those ears—they are stuck to is head. Just like yours.'

Viswanathan touched the child as if it would give him an electric shock.

'Look at his head. So much hair. Should have been born as a girl,' he said.

The baby paused for a moment as if to prepare and then broke out into a cry.

'He is crying,' Vishwanthan said, and the baby cried even more.

'Amma, he is crying,' Kalyani said.

'He must be hungry, di. Just offer it to him,' her mother's voice came from the other room. Kalyani picked up her bundle of joy and pressed the baby's face to her breasts. Viswanathan watched it keenly.

Kalyani smiled at Viswanathan. 'The demon! See how he suckles!'

'When are you coming home?' Viswanathan asked.

'Amma said I must stay at least another three months.'

'Why three months? Come in a month. I am getting a raise. I have fixed a new home on rent.'

'Please talk to my brother.'

'Why should I ask your brother about taking you back?' Viswanathan got up and came out of the room. He took the coffee his mother-in-law brought and downed it in a gulp.

Sundaram and his father were seated in the veranda. 'Mappillai, was your journey okay? I was at the orchard,' said his father-in-law.

'I am thinking of taking Kalyani back next month.'

'So soon?' asked his father-in-law and looked at Sundaram.

'The doctor says she has to be here for at least three more months,' said Sundaram.

'Why?'

'She is weak. And the child has to have vaccinations, triple antigen and polio drops.'

'But we have plenty of doctors in Madras.'

'Why don't we ask the doctor here to be on the safe side?'

'I am coming on the eighth of next month to fetch her.'

'What is this, Viswanathan!? I am saying one thing and you are again and again...'

'Look here, Sundaram. She is my wife. I know when to take her back home. Am I not concerned about her health?'

'Wife! *Humph*! Don't we know how she was treated?'

'What treated, man? What do you know about how she behaved with me?'

'What is this? Why are you fighting with him when he has just arrived?' an elderly voice intervened.

'Anna!' Kalyani's voice came from the passageway. 'Let us not have pointless arguments here. He says I have to return in a month. We can do that. Don't get into a war of words.'

Viswanathan got up with a start and went inside. 'I must take a bath,' he announced. After that, as he left for Trichy to check his return ticket's reservation status. His mother-in-law wailed.

'How unfair is this! The girl's body is barely finished with the pregnancy. She is going to have problems with an infant to care of. Why is this man so stubborn? We thought she could leave after two months when she's better...'

Sundaram looked at her nonchalantly. 'Don't worry at all, Amma,' he said. 'Kalyani will be back here soon. For her next baby.'

When you cross the reception area of Hotel Savera in Mylapore and go beyond the glass doors to your right, there is a small preview theatre. The special show for Manikkam's *Thiruppumunai* had just concluded. Film critics and actors streamed out as Manikkam courteously saw them off.

'Shake hands with me, Manikkam! Brilliant! You have killed it.'

'Congratulations,' said another man. 'Really a bold venture.'

'It's all your blessings, sir,' he said.

'There is no song in the movie. Do you think it will run?'

'Oh, don't we have a hummed tune? And there is the title song.'

'Whatever it is, you have shown a lot of courage in doing this. But why have they given an A certificate? I found the film pretty clean.'

'You know, the scene where the little boy is whipped with a lash? They wanted it cut, saying that it contained violence. But I argued that this was to justify his stubbornness later and it was important to show his psyche. I did not want to chop off the scene, and that's why the A.'

'True. That scene was very powerful.'

'I have been lashed like that as a child.'

'Good night.'

They all parted ways. Kittu came out of the theatre with a pompous stride. 'Manikkam!' he called out and gave the director a bear hug. 'You have done it. What a movie! What a movie! You have done it better than Polanski. So when is the release? Tomorrow?'

'Yes.'

'But won't it be bulldozed where *Moondru Roja* is running? There is no song or dance in this, pa.'

'This is a different kind of film.'

'Anyway, it would be safe for you to take a trip to the Mangadu Temple.'

As they talked, a young man who stood hesitantly at a distance approached Kittu. He was about nineteen, somewhat wheatish in complexion and had something that looked like a file in his hands. His eyes were sketched out as if they had been lined by kohl. The hair on his head was dense. His smile invited some sympathy. 'Vankkam, sir,' he said and stood near Kittu.

'So you turned up here? All right,' Kittu said. 'Manikkam, this is Ramgopal.'

'I am Ramkumar, sir.'

'Aah, Ramkumar! He is a good actor, has a diploma from Adarsh in Bangalore.'

'I have acted in many plays, sir. And in the *Pesum Padam* magazine...'

'We can cast him in our next movie,' Kittu said.

Manikkam took Kittu aside. 'Kittu, how much have you taken from him so far?'

'Just five hundred rupees, to make a portfolio.'

'Why don't you simply ask him to go back home?'

'That's also a good idea,' Kittu said.

'Manikkam, a pose for me, please,' a photographer beseeched the director.

'Wait,' Manikkam said. 'Let me call our technicians as well.'

'Manikkam, I wanted to tell you something,' Kittu said. 'You know Mano? This Mano…'

Manikkam had by then disappeared into the crowd.

'Come, Ramkumar,' Kittu said to the young man.

As Ramkumar approached him, Kittu said, 'I have discussed everything…he said we can take a screen test. He said this boy has a good future and a brilliant face. You know who Manikkam is, right? He is a top-level director today. *Thiruppumunai* has just been previewed.'

The young man's eyes glowed with hope. 'Okay,' said Kittu. 'Come and see me tomorrow at Vauhini. Bring along a thousand rupees in change. I have to prepare an album. I have told the photographer.'

'But I have an album already.'

'That won't do. This is not your play on Veerasimhan. You have to do it differently for the movies. Do you have the money now or are you going to bring it tomorrow? There is no hurry.'

'I don't have that much cash, sir.'

'How much do you have?'

'About two hundred rupees.'

'That won't be enough. Let's see later, then…'

The young man thought for a while. 'Sir, I have this watch and this ring…'

'I am not running a Marwari pawn shop here,' Kittu said with a chuckle. 'Go to China Bazaar.'

When Manikkam returned to his room, it was close to 1 a.m, and he could not sleep. The next day was judgment day. He would know tomorrow. In a week, *Thiruppumunai's* fate would be clear. He felt a pleasant kind of tiredness within. 'I have finished it. I have tried it. What next? First, I need to take a hot bath that feels like a massage. What I have done is an achievement. A grand achievement!'

On the table lay a pile of letters and envelopes he had not looked at for days. He opened them one by one. Screenwriters Guild. Kaushalya Weds Mukundan. Arun Pictures Combine Production Number 1. The last one, a glittering card, invited him to the poojai at AVM Studios…he must go there now. The grand success of *Moondru Rojakkal* pinched him a little. He had thought the days of such movies were over. Then, he finally looked at the letter. The address was written in large, slanted letters. He opened it.

Dear Manikkam,

I am writing my feelings after returning from Mandya. Just think about it—have you been fair? The loss I have suffered is not a big one. But in all the moments I spoke to you, I thought you were a well-wisher. I thought of you as a doorway to escape my miserable life. The disappointment I faced when I arrived with eagerness and excitement to your shoot was the biggest one of my life. What is left for me now?

Manonmani

'Oh Mano, how could I forget you like this? Let me come and meet you the first thing tomorrow. I am sure you will turn up at the launch of Lakshmanan's movie. If not, I will come looking for you at your home. Mano, I forgot you in the rush to complete the film. I have to tell you something important. I have to give you some happy news. Just you wait, Mano! I have a brilliant role ready for you in my next film. And then I want to say something special to you…here I come, Manonmani,' he said aloud, though no one was around nearby.

33

Outside the studio, a driver was reading an old copy of the *Dina Thanthi*. Peeking over his head was a freeloading reader. They scanned the headlines.

5 women dead.

Devotees visiting Tirupati shall get free meals.

Imposter writes exam for someone else.

Two young men rape teenage girl.

Junior film actress burnt to death.

They laughed.

'Who is this extra, anney? Let me check…'

'Wait, da. Let me read…

'Madras, 5 April. Manonmani, a small-time film actress living in Virugambakkam, was burned to death yesterday. She doused her body with kerosene at night and set herself on fire. It is said the reason for the suicide of the actress, who has played bit parts in many movies, was the pressure caused by debts.

'Who is this Manonmani?' the freeloader asked.

'Wonder who. Maybe some kind of a case,' the driver replied, insinuating that she was involved in some illegal racket.

The news item had left out many details. Such as the crackling force with which the flames spread over her body when she lit the match with determination and set herself aflame; and how the fire engulfed her and ate her up in a hurry, burning her eyebrows, hair, eyelashes and then her clothes. It did not explain the searing, agonising burning sensation as the fire scalded her skin.

If you touch a heated vessel or fire for a fleeting second by mistake, the burn you feel is called first degree. When burn wounds go deep and the skin gets burnt a little, it is second degree. Mano's body had eighty per cent third-degree burns. The fire crossed her beautiful body's skin, went inside, attacked her subcutaneous layers and touched her bones. Some parts that burned turned white. Some went black. The burnt skin spilled over like melted butter and revealed a splattering in red.

The news item did not bother to state all these details. It did not tell us how our dear Manonmani felt in just a minute or two the excruciating agony of an eternity.

'It was thoroughly finished, dear girl
Burnt across layers, dear girl
That fortress of stone, dear girl
Turned a fortress of coal, dear girl.'

But There was no Pattinathar around to sing those lines for her.

That news item did not say how her mother banged her head against the wall all night, crying, 'Why did you do it, di? Why did you do it, di?'

Two dark-skinned gentlemen drenched in sweat pulled a handcart with rubber tyres. On the cart was the upturned side of a huge banner. An urchin walked in a friendly gait by the cart moving from Nungambakkam to the Gemini Square and tried to read what was written in the colourful hoarding.

'What film is this, brother?' he asked.

'Poda, dei!' he was shooed away by a chiding voice.

The handcart entered Gemini Studios and rested awhile. There was a vacant space amid a slew of gigantic banners perched over the towering walls of the studio compound. Toiling workmen tied ropes, slapped on the pulleys and hoisted the banner slowly. Its letters now shone forth and announced the title: *Kanavu Thozhirsalai*. Dream Factory.

Slippers and sandals were discarded at the doors of the recording studio. Doors slammed shut gently on the cars that brought in prominent men who loyally waited for their silk-sari-clad wives so that they could enter the studio as well-matched couples.

'Vaanga! Vaanga!' Lakshmanan welcomed them all. Chimanlal Seth was eyeing a woman in a yellow silk sari at a distance without blinking. Bhaskar was busy preparing for the poojai.

Kittu got out the car and went straight to Lakshmanan, who welcomed him with much affection.

'Vaayya, Kittu. Where is our poet Arumairajan?'

'He is coming, he is coming. How can we carry on without him? There was a party last night. So Lakshmanan saar, what is this? A new project? What happened to your case?'

'What happened? Huh! I paid my fine. That's what happened!'

'You know, they were gossiping in the industry that you were finished.'

'Look here, Kittu, there is no end in this industry for you, me and this seth. Directors, actors, lyricists and composers will come and go. They will disappear without a trace. You cannot destroy Lakshmanan, Kittu and Seth. Look at him. He has been observing Manju for a while. What, Sethji?'

The financier's heart skipped a beat when the woman in question slowly adjusted her sari that slipped off her shoulder when she lit the auspicious lamp.

'Who is that?' Chimanlal Seth asked tersely.

'She is a new girl.'

'Are you involved in this film, Lakshmanan saar?'

'How is it possible without me? Arun and I are starting something called A.L. Combines. We plan to spend about fifty on this.'

'And the actors?'

'Who else but Arun and Premalatha! As of today, they are at the top, no? Look at that *Moondru Rojakkal.* Looks like it will eat up *Trishoolam.* The same gang. We're getting call sheets easily. The same Pasumarthi is directing it. He is a phenomenon! Can't speak a word in Tamil but what a splash he is making!'

There was a podium with pictures of a plethora of deities, and amid them sat a clapper board smeared with vermillion announcing the film *Kanavu Thozhirsalai.*

'Nice name. Isn't there a serialized novel by this name in some magazine?

'Oh, that one is over, but this title is something I had thought of earlier.'

'Is that so? You sure have a fine imagination.'

'Look, there comes Arun!'

There was a commotion. The car rolled to a stop and three people competed to open the doors. Arun got down and put a cigarette to his lips. Three more dashed to light it.

Lakshmanan went straight to him and held his hands. 'Vaanga! Vaanga! Where is Prem?'

'She will come a bit late. It seems that the Hyderabad flight is delayed. What, Lakshmanan? Will you give the funds this time? Don't leave me in the lurch like you did last time.'

'What, thambi! Why are you talking like this in front of everyone? Just ask Bhaskar.'

'Bhaskar!'

'Money is not a problem, Arun,' Bhaskar said. 'There is heavy demand from all areas. We are just not able to manage it.'

Kittu piped up. 'All we have to do is drop the name of *Moondru Rojakkal*.'

'This is absurd,' Arun said. 'I just don't understand what is in the movie, Bhaskar. I just don't get it. I am still amazed.'

'In this industry you should never try to make sense of things,' Bhaskar said.

'Is everybody here?'

'Arumairajan is yet to arrive.'

Arun now looked at Manikkam standing in a corner of the room. 'What, Manikkam? How come you're in these parts?'

'It was you who invited me here, Arun.'

'Oh, I am sorry.'

The priest arrived on a scooter, wearing a dhoti and a helmet.

'Did you see *Thiruppumunai*, Arun?'

'I did. It was fantastic.'

'*Vikatan* gave it 61 out of 100.'

'What's the point? It is just running a noon show at Ega. Will it recover the investment?'

'No, Arun. We are short.'

'That's what I was saying, Manikkam. Come and join our dream factory. Let's all get together and smear sugar on Eastman Color film rolls to show two-dimensional men and women.'

Kittu spoke up. 'Do you know that girl Manonmani, Arun? The slim one with dusky skin. It seems that she killed herself.'

'Ohhhhh. Are the musicians ready?'

Manikkam stood stunned. 'Kittu, what the hell are you saying?'

'You didn't know? The girl who was in *Ilanthalaivan*.'

'Of course.'

'She was burnt. By suicide.'

'When was this? When?' Manikkam was visibly upset.

'I don't remember the date, Manikkam. Here comes Arumairajan!'

Manikkam gripped the wall nearby. His world shook for a while. It swirled. He looked at his watch, left the studio and got into the taxi that brought in some background musicians. 'Go to Virugambakkam,' he ordered.

Arumairajan arrived in a brand-new chocolate coloured Ambassador. Kittu rushed to open the door. 'Vaanga Arumai. We are all waiting only for you. Where is sister Mary?'

'She has gone to her hometown.'

'What? Have you done something wrong?'

'Aah, you could say that.'

Arumairajan was sporting a silk jubba and Ray-Ban sunglasses. A brocade silk veshti was tied firm to hide his small paunch. A huge shawl hung loose over his shoulders. Gold rings glittered on his fingers. His sandals were from Singapore. He walked, his arms swinging in an air of confidence, and approached Arun. A young man walked behind him carrying a notebook, a betel leaf box and some bottles that contained some pills. 'Vanakkamn-ga,' he greeted Arun.

'Vaanga Arumairajan.'

Arumairajan looked at his watch. 'It is 9.32 a.m. We can finish by 10.30 a.m., right?'

'Certainly.'

'The song is ready. Are they all there?'

'They are ready! Raja has come up with a splendid tune.'

'It seems like I have seen you somewhere, Arumairajan,' Arun said.

'Is that so? Where could that be?' Arumairajan smiled.

They all trooped into the recording studio.

When Manikkam reached Virugambakkam, the rickshaw puller was asleep under a tree. Beyond that was a tea shop, International Steel Works and film box makers. A sign announced: 'Paper flowers, dresses, bullets and linoleum wigs available here at cheap rates and on rent. Affordable typing of story and dialogue also provided.'

He slowly approached Manonmani's room in the elongated single-storeyed building and stood at the door. It was locked and freshly painted. He looked up to see a signboard: 'Famous Palmist & Astrologer Who Made Dreamgirl Hema Malini's Dreams Come True. K. Nagaraju. Meet him to know your past, present and future. Visiting Hours…'

Manikkam squatted on the narrow doorstep and took off his sunglasses. Then he burst into tears and wept aloud.

They lit some camphor on top of a coconut and performed an aarti for the recording console. Beyond the glass partition, an array of musical instruments stood waiting. As they tuned up the instruments on the other side and matched the needles on the console, the composer turned the knobs gently to find the perfect mix. There were about twenty violins, a piano and about seven types of percussion instruments besides a wide range of other instruments, including a vibraphone and a synthesizer. The singers stood at the right-hand corner with headphones on. The chorus girls were at the other end, ready to sing.

In the control room, a wide spool of tape waited inside a recording machine. Behind the music director were a set of chairs on which sat Arun, Bhaskar, Lakshmanan, Arumairajan, Kittu, Chimanlal Seth, the woman in the yellow silk sari and a bunch of gentlemen who would finance the forthcoming film.

'A.L. Combines *Kanavu Thozhirsalai*: song number 1, take number 1.'

'Running.'

The tape moved in rotations.

A thumb clicked. *Tick. tick, tick, tick*, followed by silence. Then, as the assistant director waved his hand in the air, the violins came to life in a burst. The cello joined in. The flute played a soft melody. The double bass came on. The guitar jumped in. The synthesizer blended in. Without missing a key, the instruments played together in a splash of colourful tones. And as the opening music came to a pause, Arumairajan's lines rang out:

'The evening flower blooms in the magical garden's story,
The morning shall end the spell of this dream factory.'

THE END

STORY, DIALOGUES AND DIRECTION BY SUJATHA

Translator's Note

A Front Seat to *Dream Factory*

A DISCUSSION WITH SUJATHA

P.S.

Insights
Interviews &
More . . .

Translator's Note

THE IDEA OF TRANSLATING 'SUJATHA' Rangarajan, who became famous with his wife's name to avoid being confused with a writer who was well known when he took to writing, came on an evening when I was reading Nobel literature prize winner Orhan Pamuk. Passages from the Turkish writer reminded me of Sujatha's style of observation and humour, and I suddenly realized that Tamil's arguably most popular writer who straddled multiple genres was barely known outside of his province and deserved a wider audience.

Although a handful of his voluminous works have since been published in English translation, a lot more can be done. But the challenge is that Sujatha is a modern writer in an ancient language said to be the oldest classical language, with about five thousand years of recorded history. Sujatha's ability to play with and transform the language with Western influences, creativity and a keen sense of observation of everyday street phrases demands the translation of not a language, but a rich reading experience.

Translating a Tamil work set in Tamil Nadu and Bangalore at the turn of the 1980s nearly forty years later turned out to be quite challenging—although, while reading, the writer can be a delight to those familiar with his milieu.

Kanavu Thozhirsalai (Dream Factory) has elements of both deep literature and pulp novels. The plot, set mostly in what was then Madras and yet called Chennai locally, is a difficult terrain in terms of language, with a mish-mash of Kannada, Telugu, Urdu, Hindi, Malayalam and English criss-crossing slang words and archaic terms. The protagonist, Arun, in his novel about Kollywood, as Kodambakkam's Tamil film industry is called, inevitably bears the stamp of the writer in his psyche as he straddles the ancient temple town of Uttamarkovil, on the one hand, and an avant-garde global film culture, on the other.

I chose to translate *Kanavu Thozhirsalai* because it reflects Sujatha's rich mind, his creativity and the innards of a movie industry known worldwide for its colourful style and ability to produce political leaders.

Besides Arun, there are other familiar-sounding characters spewing their flavours in the language they speak, the religion they follow, the food they eat and the clothes they wear. The bonus in a delayed work of translation is a journey back into machines and technologies of the times in which the story is set, with their own amusing quirks and cultural insights.

To knit all of them together in English involved frequent bouts of doubt, but naturally. After the editor came back with queries and suggestions, this multiplied manifold. It turns out that the novel is not just about the film industry, but also marked Sujatha's baby steps as a screenplay writer that he became a decade after the work. Some of his sentences are fragments—as if they were written as bits of screenplay for a seasoned director filming his story. I have retained the flavour in some parts and not in others, so that there is not too much disruption in the expectations of the reader.

Also, the novel was serialized in the magazine *Ananda Vikatan*, and as was his style, Sujatha would supply his story in instalments on the go, juggling parallel developments in the lives of several characters. What this meant, in hindsight, is that some of the elements of time or flow needed to be adjusted, though that might have escaped the reader catching a weekly fix of a popular writer. It seems that the writer also expected his reader to be intelligent enough to grasp his love of French new wave cinema and its narrative adventurism. Strange gaps had to be filled carefully, much like the work of a movie editor in the story—fixing films shot to please thrifty producers and demanding censors.

There is also the issue of how one connects with an imagined reader in a work of translation. English is now almost like a native language in India and some Tamil words are better translated into more common Hindi words.

In bringing all these issues into a work of translation, I have kept in mind a desire to evoke the same feelings that the writer evoked in me when I read it in the original. This involved some risks in guessing the mindsets and cultural backgrounds of the readers while trying to be as faithful as possible to the writer's language in the translation. I may be forgiven my trespasses. Translation can be a trapeze art, with no safety net in sight below. I would also like to mention that the movies and publications mentioned in the book are a combination of the real and the fictional.

I wish to thank my agent Kanishka Gupta of Writer's Side, who worked with me on zeroing in on this novel and provided able support, and the editors at HarperCollins for their patience and competence.

Like many creative works, the task never looks quite finished. I can only hope readers find the translation good enough to kindle a wider interest in the writer and that the ghost of the writer does not mind anything lost in translation.

Madhavan Narayanan
December 2021

A Front Seat to *Dream Factory*

A DISCUSSION WITH SUJATHA

Dream Factory is set entirely against the backdrop of the film world. The following discussion with writer Sujatha was recorded after well-known actor Lakshmi and director Mahendran had read the first chapter before it was serialized in the magazine *Ananda Vikatan*, whose editor moderated the conversation. Sujatha and his film-world friends went beyond the story to talk about show business, in general, in an engaging conversation that the author acknowledges as having provided material to craft the novel that subsequently emerged in weekly instalments. This discussion also serves as an effective Preface to the novel and reveals some interesting aspects of a robust, successful and controversial Tamil cinema industry.

Lakshmi: I have just read the first chapter. Right at the outset, you say that this story is not about 'those who you know a lot, those who you know and those who you know less'. That reads like an excuse. What is that supposed to mean?

Sujatha: It is easy to write about those you know. The readers, too, can figure out who I am writing about. My purpose does not lie there. I want to speak about the idea of an Eternal Hero. You yourself know a lot about cinema. To understand that through my interactions with you and to bring that out in the shape of a novel is what I have in mind. I have even said that somewhere in the first chapter.

Lakshmi (Interrupting): It says Scene Number 67.

Sujatha: Yes, my hero knows that scene is absurd. He may be more interested in meditation or in reading a book. Or he may want to read a script by Godard. But then he is trapped in the Tamil film industry. He is somehow trying to get out of it.

Mahendran: I have, in fact, seen many an actor feeling frustrated like your hero. They would feel a sense of ennui in doing even simple scenes. Even I have a personal taste that is quite different (from the films I make). However, the audiences love simpler movies. You can't be making a dry sort of a movie with no sense of satisfaction on the grounds that you are trying to say something different. I don't want to make movies that way.

Sujatha: I do agree with that…

Lakshmi: I think we are only talking about the stars of the screen. Do you seriously think these stars think about a Stanislavski or a Godard? I don't think the stars think about such figures.

Sujatha: Is that so?

Lakshmi: If you do take a star, whether it is the Tamil industry or the rest of India, if you generally ask around about these names they will only say, 'Where can I buy them?'

Sujatha: Well, the way I have handled it is…he would say, 'I have read them', but in real he would not have done that. He would just say that as a bluster. Many directors do know about them. He gleans it from them.

Lakshmi: If you look at it that way, even many directors would not be knowing about these figures.

Sujatha: I have myself read a lot of Godard scripts. Not because I wanted to write movie scripts. There is a lot of surrealism in his writings. For instance, a guy will buy himself a copy of *The New York Times*…and just when you think he will open and read it, he will use that to polish his shoes. As far as he is concerned, he believes that the news is not important these days…and that only these things are. Similarly, he will show an egg being tossed up in the air, which falls on the ground only after the character has gone outside the room and returned after doing some talking outside.

Lakshmi: I do recall that. Godard's wife had acted in that film, in fact.

Sujatha: There's a lot of interesting stuff like that. I do know of many film-makers who are well-read. The stars who have talked to them do say that they have read the stuff and boast about it.

Mahendran: So, you say that there are indeed such artistes but they are not stars.

Sujatha: As a writer with a creative right, I do have the power to fuse the artiste and the star, I believe. Perhaps there is no such hero in our times. Who knows? There may be one such person in future.

Lakshmi: I have to ask you something. All the heroes in your stories are similar. Everybody is an intellectual sort of a person. Like that character in *Vanam Ennum Veethiyile*…and also Ganesh the lawyer. Why can't the hero in at least this novel be a common person?

Sujatha: I think you are saying that in haste. You should not be coming to a conclusion on the basis of a single chapter.

Lakshmi: Yes, that's true. I suppose this is like judging a full movie after having watched only one reel. Well, they only gave me the first chapter to read!

Sujatha: Even I have only one chapter now!

Lakshmi: But we do know right at the start as to what sort of a person he is. He can't be changing now. You have outlined clearly what kind of people Arun and Bhaskar are. That's why I had to ask that question. People with such intelligence cannot be successful in the current market. If he talks and behaves like that no one would really cast him.

Mahendran: So, you mean to say that there is no one in the market now who is intelligent?

Lakshmi: I didn't mean it that way. If I say that I would be confessing that I am a fool as well.

Sujatha: My characters are intelligent because I am also intelligent to some extent. However hard I try, there is a part of me in the kind of writing I do. It is like you. Whatever role you play, there would be a little bit of you in that.

Lakshmi: You are right. That is inevitable.

Sujatha: By the same yardstick, there would be a part of me in my writing…After all, I write for my own satisfaction… Suppose I make you the heroine of my story, I don't think I lose any realism by saying she is educated and intelligent.

Lakshmi: Thank you! At least you acknowledge that I am intelligent.

Sujatha: I am very surprised. You have read Godard and you have appreciated his cinema.

Mahendran: I think you have answered your own question. You know about such stuff even if you are a star (in Indian cinema).

Lakshmi: No…no. I did not ask this question as a film star but more as an average reader.

Mahendran: So, what kind of a character is the hero of the story you are writing? Or let me put it this way: What do you think of Tamil movie stars in general?

Sujatha: I do think what Bob Hope said (about movie stars) rings true: 'A guy with a swimming pool and the worried look.' That means a luxurious life with mental problems.

Mahendran: And that doesn't apply only to stars.

Sujatha: Indeed, it applies to all…to the director, yes, and the most worried person is the production manager. He faces a lot of pressure. He is the first one to get ulcers!

Lakshmi: Not just him! Everybody gets ulcers.

Sujatha: Most important, the film hero has no privacy at all. I think that is a big loss. Take yourself, for instance. Could you possibly go to the main street and buy yourself something?

Lakshmi: Don't you realize that is the price he pays for his influence and fame? You can't eat the cake and have it, too. They signed up for this when they entered the world of cinema. How could you call this a loss?

Sujatha: I do think you have a point. In fact, I had my own little experience…I was signing some autographs for a few people. Ten became hundred and then a thousand! A big crowd assembled. They were all well-behaved but there was a collective violence of sorts. Someone put his hand on me. Someone wanted a strand of hair. If I was careless they might have made me bald! If somebody who has much less popularity than a screen hero like me goes through this, I am amazed by what stars go through. I do think they yearn for a life like everybody else.

Mahendran: There is a new trend now…a crowd chases the star, ogles at him, mills around him…and directors feel deep down, 'I am the one who made him the star…if it were not for my script the industry would have tossed him away.' But then we are just around. The crowd is around the star. Isn't it natural for a director to get such a feeling? That is precisely why we say we are making a new sort of a movie and casting new actors in them.

Lakshmi: Excuse me! He is writing the story, and instead of asking him questions, you are giving him more raw material!

Sujatha: That is precisely what I want. I am very happy now. I am going to use all these dialogues in the story.

Mahendran: You know, there is a bunch of folks standing around the star telling him stuff like, 'Bro, you killed it in that one…or…after this film, the other star is finished!' He knows very well this is all just puff. To put up with all this is truly unbearable, if you ask me. He knows his glory is going to fade away one day. That is a worry haunting him.

Sujatha: You are absolutely right. There was a time when the singers in this field (a probable reference to *The Beatles*) used to earn an amount higher than Britain's defence budget. When they were asked what they thought of this, one of them said, 'We are preparing for the fall.' To withstand such a fall is a big deal. In the same vein, my hero, Arun, would be replaced by some Arumugam. This crowd would be chasing him now. Some people cannot easily accept such a decline. You know, when folks retire, the next day they wonder, 'What's this! How can my office run without me?' Some people even get heart attacks because of this. See, I am writing this now. Three years hence I may not be wanted. Someone else will come and take my place. If I don't prepare for this now, I would suffer a lot at that time.

Lakshmi: So, how did you get inspired to write a novel on a movie hero?

Sujatha: Well, I get a lot of opportunity to interact with the film world these days and I felt like writing about it. I was once travelling in a car with a film hero…and wherever we went, people surrounded the car. There were faces pressed against the windows. Can one remember even one such face? I have put that in one of my chapters: 'Saheb, saheb, sing a song, said a moustache…and a ten rupee note asked for a signature…Arun, Arun…you act so well…says a voice as a hand caresses his cheeks.' I get fascinated by all this.

Lakshmi: How many of your stories have been made into films?

Sujatha: There's *Gayathri*, *Priya*, *Ninaithale Inikkum*.

Lakshmi: Are you happy with the way they have been made?

Sujatha: No. Not at all! That's precisely why I started writing this novel.

Lakshmi: Have they adapted the story or simply ruined it?

Sujatha: They ruin it a lot.

Lakshmi: I have also acted in movie adaptations of novels and a couple of them have done well. In *Kaaval Deivam*, I had no major involvement in the role. Didn't know much about the film world either. I was more interested in the chocolates they gave at the shooting. I got interested when I learnt about cinema. When I was acting in *Sila Nerangalil Sila Manithargal*, I even had arguments with Jayakanthan (the writer). But then, as far as that story is concerned, this is how the character was supposed to be. Jayakanthan was firm on how the role should go. That's why he was happy with the way it went. Why could you not do that with your stories that were made into films?

Sujatha: I had no involvement in the making of the film. They didn't even show me the script or tell me anything about the treatment.

Mahendran: Don't you demand that you are shown the treatment of the story?

Sujatha: That is something I have learnt only now. I am going to ask for the treatment henceforth. However, the number of people who watch the movie based on a story far exceeds the number that reads the story. Panchu Arunachalam (the director) once said, 'If you had written the treatment for *Priya*, the film would have flopped in a week!'

Mahendran: And what did you tell him?

Sujatha: I was in a state of mind to agree with him, to some extent. In my story, the heroine disappears halfway through the story. But what kind of a film is made without a heroine? If I show the Scotland Yard or computers, what kind of a picture would that be? Producers have a measure in mind. If there is a movie hall in a semi-rural spot near Chengalpattu that sees the house full for three shows, they say that it will run for twenty-five days. When the fourth show goes full, they say that it will run for fifty! They know their audiences only too well. That's what I like most about them. There's no compulsion that they make a movie out of my story. If we don't like what they are doing, we have the choice to opt out. That is why after *Priya* was made into a movie, I wrote a few novels in an act of revenge. You can't make even one of them into a movie!

Lakshmi: Now! You can't talk like that. I am sure there are those who want to turn those into a movie. Why don't you give them a chance?

Sujatha: If I do, they will retain only the title. They will say that they have changed it a little and then change it paragraph by paragraph. I actually went through this. I wrote a story called *Jannal Malar* in *Ananda Vikatan*. A key point in the story is that a man gets married by deceit and goes to jail. While he is away, his wife falls into bad ways, goes astray. The guy who made it into a movie says:

> Sir, we have made it the way you wrote. We just had no issues turning into a movie script. You have written it just the way I needed for a movie. We have retained it frame by frame. Do come and see it. But there's a small thing. It won't be proper to show the wife going astray when he is in jail. Womenfolk in India won't like it. You see there's a big section of ladies in the audience. So, we changed it to how the woman struggles to bring up her child. Likewise, you show the guy going to jail again in the end. But you can't show a hero going to jail. So, we made the villain go to prison. That's all. Just two changes. The rest is all the same...

I don't know what kind of movies these guys make. They also changed the title. *Jannal Malar* (Window Flower) became

Yaarukku Yaar Kaval? (Who Guards Whom?). Why do they need my story for this?

Lakshmi: Actually, this *Jannal Malar* subject first came to me. I asked them if they would film the story as it was. I said no when I learnt they were going to change the main story. Why don't you resist such changes, anyway?

Sujatha: Well, they say that they have not changed a thing.

Lakshmi: But things have been changed!

Sujatha: Oh, well, they don't tell you anything until the censors give their certificate. And at that time, they say, 'We've only changed it a little.'

Mahendran: Don't you put down these things in your contracts?

Sujatha: By profession I am not a writer. I just started this out as a hobby. It is difficult enough for me to write a chapter every week for the serial stories...I did, for instance, want to write the script myself for *Karayellam Shenbagappu*...then I had my own doubts on whether I could write a movie script. In screenplays, more than the story, you have to imagine things visually. Not just that. A lot of people invest their money in the movie. Can you imagine the responsibility that comes with this? I just don't have the time. I don't have the confidence that I can do it either.

Mahendran: When you film a novel, it is not imperative that you have to follow it exactly. But we need to bear in mind why we chose to make a movie out of that novel in the first place...what kind of characters do you have...what is it that one likes about the story...we need to bear all this in mind and take the project forward to improve upon the story. We cannot be spoiling it.

Sujatha: A good director can show in a single shot what I strive hard to tell at length. I do recognize he has that liberty.

Lakshmi: You seem to know so much about screenplays. Why can't you write one yourself?

Sujatha: I have to learn a lot to get there.

Lakshmi: You say that you have interacted with a lot of people in the show business. Is *Kanavu Thozhirsalai* going to feature some important incidents that you have come across?

Sujatha: It will have many such incidents, in fact. But I won't duplicate something from an individual; I will collate what I have heard from many and also write about the censor board that no one seems to have written about before. They just ask film-makers to cut a line, but no one knows how much loss the maker bears for that.

Lakshmi: So, are you against the existence of a censor board or for it?

Mahendran: It should be there. But it matters a lot as to who sits on it. For instance, recently the censors saw my *Uthiri Pookkal*. It is a neat picture, yet they gave it an A (Adults Only) certificate. I asked them why and they said, 'This Vijayan character in the movie is too much of a sadist and kids will get spoilt if they see this.' I said, 'But then the bad guy gets punished in the end and why can't the kid learn that you should not be like that guy?' They still insisted. 'If I make a movie out of the Ramayana tomorrow, in which Ravana abducts another man's wife, would you give it an A certificate?', I asked. They wriggled their way out of that by mumbling something about sadists. What can I possibly do about them?

Sujatha: When I went abroad recently, I watched some blue films. There are no censors out there. But do you know what kind of crowd shows up for that? About ten people smoking away and not even watching it properly…the real crowds show up for Walt Disney movies! And here, the ones that escape the censors are the most vulgar…some dialogues and some songs.

Lakshmi: So, you think there should be no censors in India?

Sujatha: I think we don't need the kind of censorship we have now.

Lakshmi: There is a huge difference between audience sensibility in the West and here. I do think we need censorship here.

Mahendran: I think what Sujatha says here is right.

Lakshmi: You are saying that because you suffered at the hands of the censors, right?

Mahendran: It is not just me. Everybody is going to suffer in the coming days.

Sujatha: In the story I am writing, one guy is certainly going to get into trouble with the censors and is going to go mad and run away.

Mahendran: Write like that, sir. Good going.

Sujatha: You cannot legislate good behaviour and discipline. Look at what happened to prohibition. And then in some of our Tamil movies, the love scenes are more sexually provocative than films with nudity.

Lakshmi: I think you are right. In a film appreciation course held last year, one man stood up and asked a censor board officer as to why kissing scenes should not be allowed. The officer replied: 'When a woman is going out of town in Western countries, the man kisses his wife on the railway platform. Do you have such scenes here? That's why we can't show kissing scenes here.' And this guy shot back: 'We don't have song-and-dance duets in public parks here in India. They do show them, don't they?' But there is no end to such arguments. What the censor board man says seems right and so does Mahendran here.

Sujatha: I am not saying that there should be no censors at all. I am just saying that they have to be somewhat reasonable. This is even with respect to written stories. I wrote a story called *Paalam*, and to some extent, I justified even a murder in it. Someone then wrote me a fourteen-page letter on that and asked: 'I feel like murdering YOU now. Should I come by?' When I read that, I realized that my writings are read by a huge number of people and it affects them deeply. We have to impose some restrictions on ourselves. I believe film-makers also need to do that.

Lakshmi: I am also trying to say just that. We don't seem to have that kind of self-discipline. Somebody needs to keep on telling us not to do some things.

Mahendran: Me as well. I am not saying that we should totally do away with the censors. Those who are in it should be knowledgeable and understand the medium. How can we put up with someone who knows nothing about cinema and bosses around as if he was holding the bureaucratic job of a district collector?

Lakshmi: Well, if those who know all about cinema sit on the board, they may end up approving anything! Only if there is an outsider would they be able to say what they want and what they don't...and which scene bothers them.

Sujatha: What I am trying to say is that the scenes that they do allow are not decent either. There is a couple smooching nose to nose and then the camera pans to show two flowers... here's where imagination takes over. I think this is worse than a kissing scene. We need censorship mainly against graphic violence. In Charles Bronson's movies, he pounds someone, and we can hear bones break. I don't think we can bear that.

Mahendran: I loved the way you describe Arun's height in the opening chapter.

Lakshmi: Chee...So you accept all that...that his height is such that he can look at the parting of the heroine's hair and peep into the brassieres of the women who lean on his chest…Mr Mahendran, I think you are biased. You only seem to support Sujatha here. You appreciate certain things in a written work, but you call it obscene when that is shown in a movie…So you say that something is right if a Sujatha or a Venugopalan or Sivasankari (writers) write it, but when a Vaali or Kannadasan (lyricists) pen it, you call it vulgar.

Sujatha: Writing is an evocative medium. In this, it is essential to describe a man. I write some of that and leave the rest to the imagination of the readers.

Lakshmi: Well, when they show noses touching and focus on flowers and leave it to the imagination of the viewers, you call it dangerous. By the same token, isn't it dangerous to say something and leave the rest to the reader's imagination?

Vikatan Editor: I think there is a short answer to that question. A writer writes only for the literate. Their imagination does not run riot. But cinema is liked by even those who no more than see with their eyes and listen with their ears. One has to be a bit cautious there.

Mahendran: I think it is vital that you write one more thing—about the junior artistes. You know how they are treated? Like cattle! 'Hey, you there…'…that kind of stuff.

Lakshmi: Why do you have to go that far? It is enough to be a newbie actor. Poor girl will be standing on her legs all day…with make up on from morning to evening. Such things are there from A to Z, Mahendran…and if there is a hero who has ten years behind him in the industry, everybody has to stand up on the ready. If we don't, there's someone to tell you, 'Anna is coming, please get up.' Who has the guts to say, 'Get lost! I don't care about any Anna or Thambi!'

Mahendran: Don't say such things about new faces. You just have to see them after they have acted in two scenes and completed one schedule. Next she will turn up with a chair!

Lakshmi: You know why that is? There's no one to offer her a chair!

Mahendran: That is precisely why I say when I cast new faces, 'You have no role in my next film...because you will show up on the sets with a chair.'

Lakshmi: In what way does that disturb you? I am also a director. My heroine also sits on the sets with a chair of her own. My cameraman asked me, 'You are an artiste, why are you on your legs?' I replied, 'I stand behind the camera. I am no artiste. I am the director!'

Sujatha: So, is there this habit of drawing up chairs for the stars?

Lakshmi: In fact, there is much more bandobast for them. There is one person to pull up a chair, one to light the cigarette...a lot of things like that. By the way, sir, the heroine of your story...is she very intelligent?

Sujatha: Yes. My heroine is going to rise and overtake my hero.

Lakshmi: I like that. Because the moment they talk about a movie heroine, it has become a habit to say things like,

'She was in Guduvancheri (a remote rural town). She was just a rural girl making cakes out of dung in a farm and they dragged her into the movies and added a Sri or Priya to her name.' They only mock the women. In that sense, I have to thank you.

Sujatha: In my story, there are two women. Both are smart and use their opportunities to equal the hero. Certainly not the Guduvancheri type.

Lakshmi: It is satisfying to hear that. I don't know why but we all seem to be male chauvinists in some way. We describe a movie hero as 'anna', but if it is a 'she' we say that she doesn't know anything and that her mother eats food ordered by the production manager.

Sujatha: Agreed.

Lakshmi: I do enjoy Madan's (*Vikatan* cartoonist and humourist) jokes. But he has got into the habit of mocking heroines as people who know nothing. The folks coming into cinema now are not like that. They are somewhat educated. They know their stuff. And because they are educated, they also have some attitude. They do know a lot about what to say and how to behave.

Sujatha: I want to ask something here. When heroines achieve some fame, they seem to deliberately show extra childishness in the way they speak...why this faking? Seems like if you open their handbags you will find some Amul and Glaxo (baby food) tins.

Lakshmi: Do you say that they act like kids? Perhaps there are some...but what I think is that they depend a lot on the film industry. I have never been so dependent on this industry. I have always believed I can survive somehow. Maybe that is why I am not a big star. I have not earned that kind of money either. But not everyone who comes into the movies is like that. One may be the eldest child of her family...or the last. Maybe she has the responsibility of providing for her family. They do not have the courage to leave the film industry. When they get the jitters from the thought that they have to be around in this industry for 10–15 years more, they are not ready to grow or to accept that they have grown up. They want to be kids in their hearts. Even an aged heroine is addressed by her makeup man as 'paappa' or 'baby'. Of course, if I say that now I will get a stern letter from the makeup men's union... You know, those who surround this woman say stuff like, 'You are still young. That's how you will stay in this industry for another ten years.' And they end up changing the thoughts of these women. But...is that restricted to cinema? I have met so many women in my life. They speak affected Tamil like it was English.

Sujatha: I have also seen a lot of such fakes. Many of them even tell me, 'Sir, you really write well. You write very well. But my wife reads it. I don't read such things.' In fact, he would have read it himself. If you probe him deeply, he will recite it all.

Lakshmi: This is the type that says, 'I don't watch Tamil movies.'

Sujatha: There are still some more…'Saar, you really write well saar. That *Pon Vilangu*…you have written it really well. Beautiful, saar.' And when I say, 'I didn't write that…' they switch to, 'Oh you mean you wrote *Sivakamiyin Sabatham*' (adapted from a well-known novel by 'Kalki' Krishnamurthy). They praise me with such meaningless stuff that I have nothing to do with.

Lakshmi: Have you noticed the difficulties that technicians go through in the film world?

Mahendran: The most hassled lot in this are the production drivers. Even at 2 or 3 a.m. they would not have had their dinner.

Lakshmi: If you look at it that way, the most troubled person is the producer.

Sujatha: Well, he signs up for this. He may as well sit at home otherwise. What's the compulsion that he sells his wife's jewels to do this? He has to learn the hard way.

Lakshmi: By the way, are you even going to write even about the poojai ceremony (to inaugurate the shooting).

Sujatha: That's the first thing they do…they decorate the place with plantain trees and all that pomp.

Lakshmi: And about the distributors…?

Sujatha: Hm, yes, that, too. They introduced me to a distributor when my *Ninaithale Inikkum* was being filmed. He asked me which magazine had carried this particular story. I said that it was not from any magazine but was written specifically with a movie in mind. 'Then you please first serialize it as a novel in some magazine because movies run only if you say that it has been published as a story in some magazine', he said. These distributors are a superstitious lot. In general, I can say that the entire cine world is a bit extra superstitious. Sometimes I think the new moon happens every month purely for them.

Mahendran: But there's no one out there now who speaks arrogantly the way you have portrayed. Nor is there a jubba-veshti-clad PRO. They no longer exist. That's way too outdated.

Lakshmi: At the same time, you put that Gnanasekharan (journalist) on the verge of getting bashed up and then make the hero change colours when he learns the interview that he has scheduled is with women…I think that is authentic. By the way, are you going to base your writing only on Tamil cinema or are you going to bring in the Hindi industry as well?

Sujatha: I am not going to bring in films in other languages into this story. If I bring in Hindi and Malayalam, the readers of my novel will think this is not about the Tamil film industry.

Lakshmi: Well, one has lost sense of time talking to you.

Sujatha: As for me, I have got a lot of material to write about from this conversation. I am glad to have met the two of you.

Sujatha (3 May 1935–27 February 2008) was the pseudonym of Tamil writer S. Rangarajan, who started writing under the name of his wife to avoid being confused with a well-known writer sharing his name.

'Sujatha' Rangarajan was a senior manager at the state-run Bharat Electronics Ltd; he was a key figure in the team that invented the electronic voting machine. On the other hand, in the literary world, he was a cult figure of sorts. Rangarajan wrote pop novels in the detective and romance genres as well as serious literary explorations and science fiction. As a screenwriter, he helped script hits such as *Boys* and *Thiruda Thiruda*. He was a regular contributor to topical columns in Tamil periodicals such as *Ananda Vikatan* and *Kalki*. He also served briefly as the editor of *Kumudam* weekly.

Madhavan Narayanan is an editor, writer and columnist who has worked for well-known media organizations, including Reuters, *The Economic Times*, *Business Standard* and *Hindustan Times* after starting out in The Times of India group.

He has written on topics that include business, economics, public policy, politics, technology, diplomacy, entertainment, culture and social issues, and has covered events such as the Indian general elections, global G-20 summits and the Kargil War as a correspondent.